GOD MAKER

Eric Swan Thriller #3

DOM TESTA

Profound Impact Group

God Maker: Eric Swan thriller #3

By Dom Testa

This is a work of fiction, and a strange one at that. All organizations, events, and characters portrayed in this work are products of the author's imagination. Any similarity or resemblance to any person, living or dead — or reinvested — is not only purely coincidental, but downright remarkable.

Published by Profound Impact Group, LLC

PO Box 506

Alpharetta, GA 30009

Reach us at EricSwan.com

Library of Congress Control Number: 2020912785

ISBN: 978-1-942151-12-8

Cover art by Damonza

WAIT . . . IS THIS YOUR FIRST TIME?

Did you just discover this secret agent named Eric Swan?

Sure, you could start here - but there are two previous books in the series that you might want to check out first.

It all begins with Power Trip, followed by Swan's next adventure, Poison Control. Everything will be much more clear if you start at the beginning.

Regardless, welcome to the Swaniverse. Have fun!

Dom Testa

CONTENTS

CHAPTER ONE

One in ten people suffers from claustrophobia. For some it's tough getting into an elevator, others are bothered by small cars, and I once knew a woman who triggered a claustrophobic fit just by putting on a sweater that was too tight.

It had never bothered me before, but now that I'd been locked inside a small closet for hours, an uncomfortable sensation produced a quasi-claustrophobic reaction.

I had to pee.

Compounding the problem was a little matter of my hands being tied to a strong metal hook at shoulder height. That prevented me from unzipping my pants, which eliminated the option of just urinating in a dark corner and letting the building manager worry about it later.

I was already irked at having to wait in the closet for the gang of would-be terrorists to summon their fearless leader. But if I pissed my pants, so help me, I might shoot every one of them in the head out of infantile embarrassment. I imagined the upcoming confrontation and me duking it out with a giant wet spot spread over my crotch.

In movies spies may be portrayed as superhuman, but sometimes, no matter how tough you are, you've just gotta go. I've trained for years, learned every form of battle with hands, feet, and weapons, and never had a single class covering this particular problem.

I decided to distract myself. I recalled an assignment that had wrapped up in the Mojave Desert in Southern California. There I'd suffered serious dehydration and sunburn, nearly costing me one of the best bodies I'd ever used.

But that memory only led to the follow-up image of finally flagging down a car on Route 66 not far from the town of Amboy, then guzzling the greatest chilled bottle of water in history before a shocked and speechless family of four.

Now the memory of that life-saving drink caused my bladder to swell another inch. I bit down hard on the bandana serving as my gag.

I decided that soggy pants or no, the time had come. But just as I reached that decision I heard footsteps and voices. This delivered a shot of adrenaline that temporarily drove the piss pain from my brain.

At least two men exchanged muffled words right outside my closet door. They were likely deciding who would get the honor of putting a bullet into me. Boy, were they in for a big surprise. If there were three of them it might be challenging to pull off an impressive win, but certainly not impossible.

If there were only two, it wasn't even fair.

When they'd cornered me several hours earlier, while I'd prepared to break into a storage room in the building's basement, there'd been four of them, each armed and itching to shoot. I'd played dumb and acted scared, knowing that could pay off later. That led to a discussion about what to do with my sorry ass, which led to my imprisonment, which now led to my abdominal discomfort.

As the lock turned in the door handle, I went into my frightened act again. By the time the door swung open, I was sniffling like a lost 4-year-old.

A hand reached up and removed the gag from my mouth, then dropped it to the floor. In a pretty nice stammer, if I do say so myself, I said, "Wh-wh-who are you guys? Wh-wh-what are you—"

"Shut it," said the biggest of the three. Yes, three; two from the first group that had collared me, and a new guy, who I took to be either the one in charge or at least one rank up from these two pawns.

"But I wasn't doing anything," I said in a whine. "I'm supposed to do random checks of our buildings. You-you-you can ask my boss."

The leader stepped up to me, squinting, as if I was some strange bug.

"You do all of your *random checks* with a Glock?" he asked. His voice, slightly European, perhaps a touch of French, carried a scratchy sound, like Rod Stewart when he sang.

"I hate that thing," I said, raising the pitch of my voice. "They make me carry it."

He continued to squint at me, but didn't respond to this. Then he turned and nodded to the second underling, who stepped forward with a knife and sliced through the rope connecting my hands to the metal hook. With my arms now relaxed at my sides, it relieved some pressure from my bladder, thankfully.

But that gave me an idea and I chose to go with it, as disgusting as it was.

Carrying on with my sniveling act, I let the pent-up pee run free.

All three of them saw it at the same time and took an involuntary step backward. Which was funny to me, because it's not like it was going to splatter on them. My pants just suddenly bloomed with a coarse, dark stain in the groin, and then some excess dripped out of my pants legs into a small puddle on the floor.

I struggled to keep from laughing. Not just at the fact that I'd intentionally pissed my pants, but that it had accomplished exactly what I'd wanted: taken these idiots off high alert. I'd sold at least the two soldiers on the fact I was a, well, a pissant, and nobody to be feared.

But my hands were now free, there was no one else in the room, and only two of the three had a weapon visible. One held his handgun, the other his knife, in a nonchalant fashion, as if merely brandishing these was enough to keep me in line.

The leader had made a decision, and I had a pretty good idea what it was. He jerked his head toward the door. The plan, I surmised, was to dispose of me outside, quickly and quietly. One soldier shoved his gun into the back of his waistband and grabbed my upper arm. The other goon, still holding the knife he'd used to free my hands, gave me a shove forward, which was juvenile, but probably meant to show his boss he was tough, too.

I let out a long, drawn out cry, and performed the best reluctant, terrified walk I could.

Right up until five feet from the door.

Let me slow down the action sequence, like a *Matrix* scene. With a slight twist to the side I landed a boot into the throat of the knife-wielder behind me. Continuing the spin I brought my right hand down hard along the neck of the one grasping my arm. He gave a grunt, and, as he crumpled, I grabbed the gun from his waistband and used the butt on the back of his head.

The knife was on the ground, the larger goon behind me on his knees, and I put him to sleep with another vicious kick, this time to the jaw. As he fell sideways I raised the gun into the face of the leader, who was in the process of drawing something from a jacket pocket. He froze, staring at the barrel of the gun.

Everything, from first twist to gun-in-nose, took three seconds.

With his underlings unconscious, he stared at me, but it was no longer a squint. I had his full, undivided attention.

"Knees," I said. "Now. Fingers laced on top of your head."

He hesitated just a moment, then followed directions.

"So far, so good," I said. "Now, sit back on your butt. Keep your fingers laced."

Another hesitation, but he eventually dropped into position.

I scooped up the knife and stuck it in my belt, then walked behind my new captive and reached around into his jacket pockets. This turned up the suspected gun, a wallet, and a Mercedes car fob. I flipped open the wallet to his ID, and read *Tony Johnson*. It was so obviously a forgery — cleverly made, but bullshit — and I tossed it aside. I pocketed his gun and the fob.

Now I knelt on his right side and stuck the barrel of the first gun into his ear.

"We have places to go," I said, "so let me lay out the plan. First, we're going to retrieve my Glock, because I lied. I really don't hate it. In fact, it's so much better than the pieces of shit you guys are carrying.

"Next, we're going to go back to that storage room where I

met these sleeping friends, and this time we're going to open the door together. Are we clear so far?"

He chose now to play it cool and not say anything. Instead I saw a small smile creep across his face.

I gave a low chuckle, then, with a quick motion, raised the gun up over his head and brought it down hard on the laced fingers. I'm pretty sure at least one broke, maybe two. It couldn't have felt good on his head, either. He let out a shriek.

"Look, Tony, or Antoine, or whoever the hell you are. You may have a fractured finger or two, but I just pissed my pants on this job, so I'm not in the greatest mood either, you understand? Let me ask again: Are we clear on the itinerary? Or do I need to take out some of your teeth, too?"

He clinched his eyes in pain, then blinked a few times and managed to say, "Yes. Clear."

"Now we're making progress," I said, standing and stepping back. "Up you go. Good boy. Now, walk over there and pick up the bandana." When he had it in hand I told him to wad it up and stuff it into his own mouth. With broken fingers it took him a moment. The whole time his eyes watered.

I shoved the gun under his chin, pushing his head up an inch. "And now your final instructions, Tony. Your little buddies here got lucky. One's gonna sound like Steven Tyler when he talks, and they might both have a concussion, but they're breathing. You will not get that same deal. I kill people for a living, tough guy, and fairly often, so it will mean nothing to me to leave your brains dripping down a wall. You don't want to test me on this. Again, are we clear?"

He nodded, with the blue bandana bulging his cheeks.

Now I jammed the gun into his kidneys and pushed him ahead of me to the door. A quick glance into the corridor turned up nothing.

"Which way?" I said into Tony's ear.

Without answering, he led us down the hall to the left. Around a corner we approached an open office door. It was quiet.

Nudging him forward, we entered the empty office. My Glock and cell phone rested on a desktop, along with my small backpack. I forced my new pal into a chair and did a quick appraisal. The gun was in good condition, with a full magazine, so I flipped the safety on the confiscated gun and stuffed it into my waistband. If things heated up again I had a Rambo-ish arsenal of weapons at my disposal.

The backpack contained three spare magazines; I hoped that would be enough.

The phone showed two percent power, and my extra charge pen was nowhere to be found. Pocketed by one of these shit-heads, no doubt. I'd have to use the phone while I could.

I called Poole at Q2 headquarters in Washington.

"Have you found it?" she asked.

"Not yet. But I found the caretakers, so I'm sure it's here. Phone's about to die. Send the cavalry to this address. Do you have it?"

She paused a moment, dialing up my GPS coordinates. Then she said, "I—"

The phone died.

"Shit," I muttered. Had she found me or not?

Regardless, I had to move. Sundown meant reinforcements on the wrong side.

Our limited intel had told us there'd be no more than five or six assholes in the building before nightfall. Two were napping where I'd left them on the floor, Tony made three, the others could be anywhere; I hoped they wouldn't be in the storage room.

At dusk the entire stash of weapons in that locked room was slated for shipment, and we estimated another six helpers would join the party. I wanted to wrap up Q2's business by the time these extra hands arrived, and to have a nice welcoming committee in place. Finding a working phone would help my cause if Poole had been unable to lock in.

We made our way down another hallway, down one flight of stairs, and soon found ourselves outside the same door where I'd been cornered earlier.

"How many are in there?" I asked Tony, keeping my voice low.

With the gag in his mouth he simply shook his head, trying to indicate the room was empty. Which meant it wasn't.

"Well, that's good news for you," I said. "Because you're going to be my shield."

I noted the quick widening of his eyes but didn't wait around. Although the shots would alert the room's occupants, the lock on the handle and the door's deadbolt required some surgical work. Holding my captive to the side, I raised the Glock and fired multiple shots into both locks. They splintered away and the door shook.

With the speed acquired from incessant training, I grabbed Tony's collar and, taking a deep breath, launched a solid kick to the door. As it exploded inward, I pushed Tony inside and followed behind him, as low as I could get, firing rounds across the room.

His muffled shouts to his companions were almost comical. I felt him straining to force the words through the bandana.

It was fruitless. The first three incoming shots cut into him, one of which clipped my left arm as it passed through his body. Several other rounds slammed into the wall behind us.

Tony was useless to me now, literally dead weight — or

soon to be. I pushed off as he collapsed, found a stack of crates and dove behind them. Another dozen shots landed all around me. A real shit show was underway in the storage room, and I was the featured act on center stage. And a bleeding act, to boot. The pain in my arm was just enough to really piss me off. I gave the wound a cursory inspection, jammed a fresh magazine into the Glock, then looked around the storage room.

It was larger than I'd expected, about the size of a Walgreens. Crates were everywhere, scattered haphazardly. Fortunately, many of them were clustered near me. If I had to move, at least I had cover.

With the amount of firepower raining down, it had to be three people. I ventured a quick glance over the top, just fast enough to see one of the shooters leaning against a different crate. The idiot wasn't even taking cover; just so confident he'd nail me that he'd assumed the stance you see cops take in the movies, not bothering to conceal himself.

Poor fool. I ducked back down as another volley began, whipped around to my left, leaned out from the side of the long crate and put two quick kill shots into Dirty Harry.

One down. But the rapid demise of their brother-in-arms was enough to temporarily silence the other two. Experience taught me that they'd take a minute to assess this change of fortune. I always used those minutes to tilt every bit of fortune my way.

I scrambled across an open patch and dropped behind another large stack. There was no incoming fire during this sprint, and I wondered if they were so busy with their own maneuvers that they hadn't seen me. I was just about to test that theory with another dash when I glanced at the crate behind me.

It was open, so I peered inside. Unlike most of the crates in this arsenal, it didn't contain handguns and assault rifles. It had other military gear: compasses, canteens, food rations, binoculars, spotting scopes.

And night-vision goggles.

I chuckled as I pulled out a set. They were designed to clip to a helmet, which I didn't have. But I could hold them up. Now I just needed to tilt that fortune a bit more.

There was a scrape of boot against concrete from across the room, so at least one of the gunmen was on the move, hoping to triangulate with his buddy and mow me down. I took a moment to assess the lighting in my current hunting ground.

Three large overhead fluorescents, an exit sign above the door, and an oddly-placed wall light directly opposite. I'd start with that.

Leaning to my right, I fired toward the space where I'd heard the commotion. That would get their heads down for a moment. Then I straightened, took out the wall light with two quick shots, pivoted, shattered the exit sign, and ducked back down as my targets opened up again.

I let them expend two dozen rounds, then rolled across to my left and blew up two of the fluorescents in the ceiling. The room immediately took on a dusk-type feel, with only the one remaining light plus the faint glow bleeding in from the battered door to the hall.

This would have my assailants on their heels and confused as hell. I had to risk that they hadn't stumbled across the same gear I now had. There were more sounds of scrambling, which was helpful.

I replaced the magazine, leaving a single spare. With the new-found goggles, I wouldn't need it.

Grasping the expended magazine, I hurled it high and far, arcing across the room to land with a crash somewhere to the right of the gunmen. Then I raised my gun and finished off the room's lighting.

Now the dim light spilling in from the door covered no more than a few feet, and the rest of the room had plunged into darkness.

I held up the night-vision goggles and, as quietly as I could, crept across a large open space to the far corner of the room. A little help from the inexperienced goons would come in handy, and, as expected, they obliged. I heard a shuffling sound, then one of them stood and began firing toward the area I'd just vacated. What he hoped to accomplish, I had no idea.

I put him down with a single shot.

A few seconds later his companion, obviously now spooked, called out.

"Hey! Whoever you are. Hold on. Listen."

His voice helped me to begin tracking him.

"I'm going to put down my gun," he yelled. "Don't shoot."

I inched closer. Although he was hidden somewhere ahead, I estimated about twenty-five feet separated us.

"Hey!" he cried again. "Did you hear what I said? I won't shoot if you won't."

I closed the distance to about fifteen feet. Then I saw his head, just above one of the crates, trying to peer through the gloom. I edged beside a large stack that provided me with cover so I could talk to him.

"All right," I said, and was about to lay out the terms when he rose, turned toward the sound of my voice and let loose with an explosion of rounds.

"Son of a bitch," I muttered, then lifted the Glock and blew out the side of his head.

The air was filled with the acrid odor of firearm propellant as I cautiously made my way around the stacks of crates on this side of the room. It was possible a fourth asshole was hiding somewhere, but after a few minutes I was confident the battle was over.

Walking back toward the exit I grabbed Tony's collar and dragged his body over to prop open the fractured door. This allowed a little more light inside, enough for me to find a crate with other supplies, including lanterns and flashlights. In the meantime I discovered a lot more than that.

Dozens of crates filled with assault rifles, handguns, an insane amount of rounds, and various other naughty tools. It was one of the largest stashes I'd ever encountered, all bound for some of the most wicked characters you'd ever meet.

But this arms cache was officially closed down.

I wandered back out to the hall just as I heard approaching sirens. Bless Poole's heart, she'd found me.

When the SWAT team entered the building I was leaning against the wall, my hands held high. The officer in charge approached me, his weapon raised. I identified myself, offered the code word Poole would've provided, and lowered my arms as he did the same with the weapon.

He looked at the blood covering most of my left arm and called for medical help. Then, as he walked up to me, he laughed.

"What's so funny," I asked.

He nodded toward my soaked crotch. "I take it that's not blood."

CHAPTER TWO

Traffic out of Dulles had been snarled by a grisly accident between a tanker truck and two cars, but had grown exponentially worse because of several other accidents in the backup. I summoned all the patience I could and shuffled through one of my favorite playlists. I'd get to Quanta's house when fate allowed. For the time being a song from Beck kept my blood pressure stable.

The text message from my boss had been unlike any I'd ever received. Not a peep about the mission I'd just pissed my way through, nor any comment regarding my request for the weekend off to spend at home with my newly-pregnant wife.

Instead Quanta, the head of Q2's field agents, had been terse, even more so than her usual blunt communication.

Come at once, the minute you land. Highest priority.

That last part — *highest priority* — was a phrase I'd never seen her use before. Generally one assumed all of her requests were of supreme importance, but this indicated I shouldn't even stop for gas.

If I'd learned one thing over the years about the diminutive-but-tough woman who ran our clandestine agency, it was that she wasted neither time nor words. *Come at once* yanked me out of the chill mode I'd been in during the flight and threw me back into heightened alert status.

Now I stared at the glow of brake lights ahead of me, a line of red stretching into infinity as dusk descended. I sighed, tapping a finger on the steering wheel to the beat of the song.

Ordinarily I'd make either a routine stop at headquarters or a quick dash home to see Christina. That is, unless I'd been killed in the line of duty and was being brought back to life in the basement laboratories deep below Q2's drab building just outside Washington, D.C. Eventually I'd wind up at Quanta's suburban home office for a grueling martial arts workout followed by new marching orders.

It was no use wondering about it now. Something had erupted and I'd find out soon enough.

Assuming they cleared the highway before midnight.

There was no use updating Quanta on my progress; when she got into this mode she knew every detail, and that included traffic conditions. I could call Christina to pass the time, but for the next few hours she'd be knee-deep in the kitchen at the four-star restaurant where she produced award-winning dishes. It was just me and the music.

It took another hour, but finally things broke free and I drove up to the sprawling ranch-style home just before eight o'clock. Another car, an Audi S5 coupe, sat in the circular drive.

This, too, was unusual. Meetings with Quanta at her residence were always private. The intrigue ratcheted up another notch.

The door was unlocked. I slipped inside and made my way to the kitchen. I heard voices as I approached, both women, and both sounded familiar. I paused in the hallway and tried to identify the one talking with Quanta. I couldn't quite place it.

Quanta raised her voice. "Swan. Join us."

I walked around the corner and stopped short. Sitting with the head of Q2 at the round table in the kitchen nook was a short-haired woman with a remarkably athletic build. She glanced at me over Quanta's shoulder and said in a crisp, British accent, "Hello. I wondered what you might look like now."

After a moment's hesitation, I moved to the table and sat down.

"Holy shit," I said. "Parnell."

She nodded at me, but offered no smile.

I turned to Quanta. "Okay. I knew it was something big. But not this."

This, for the record, never happened. The organization ran under a particular set of operating rules, and one of those was simple: Q2 agents did not associate with other Q2 agents. We didn't work together. We didn't communicate. Hell, we didn't even know each other's identity. We weren't told the reasons for this isolation, but I had my theories.

That was assuming Parnell was now one of ours. I'd last seen her on a private island in the Caribbean, where I'd tracked down a pair of wicked twins bent on destroying America's power grid. I'd been in a different body at the time, bleeding profusely from a bullet wound. And Parnell, during that mission, had been on the wrong side of the law.

While recuperating in a Miami hospital room I'd suggested to Quanta that she recruit the former British intelligence agent to *our* team. It appeared she had. But why were we here together?

I started to ask Quanta, but she dove in. "Now that you're

here, I can brief you both. We have an unprecedented emergency on our hands. One that borders on catastrophe."

Parnell may not have been familiar with the spy master's style or history, but these two sentences shook me. Quanta was never one for hyperbole. In my years as an agent I'd never heard her say anything even remotely like this. I sat quietly and let her continue.

She laced her fingers on the table, on top of a manila folder. "This morning, around two a.m., two incidents took place, both of a profound nature. First, there was an incursion at the home of a scientist in Rhode Island. She was abducted, along with her 14-year-old granddaughter. The kidnappers broke through very intricate security, and killed two people.

"We've not heard from her abductors, which is also troubling. If the crime had been motivated by the possibility of ransom money, we expect we would've heard something by now. The silence is . . . disturbing."

I stared at her for a moment, then asked, "Who's the scientist?"

Quanta took a deep breath. "Devya Nayar."

I felt Parnell shift her gaze back and forth between us, wanting to ask questions, but respectfully waiting. She no doubt understood the significance of the name purely by the intensity of our lengthy silence.

Finally I sat back. "Devya Nayar. And we've heard nothing? No clue about who did this?"

"At the time we had no idea," Quanta said. "Now we know."

"I'm sorry," Parnell said. "Who is this Nayar woman?"

I looked from her back to Quanta. "How much does Parnell know about us?"

"She's going through the initiation process. But she's been briefed about what we do."

I looked back to the former British agent. "So you know how it works. Have you freaked out yet?"

"Certainly startled," she said. "But I suppose with the way technology expands I shouldn't have been surprised. Seeing you now, in this new body, is my first exposure to the realities."

"Have you uploaded?"

"No."

"No?" I turned back to Quanta. "If she's being inducted, why hasn't she uploaded?"

"Because she's spent the past month passing all the requirements."

"Did she clear with Miller yet?"

"He said I won't crack, if that's what you mean," Parnell said, an edge to her voice.

This was actually a critical stage of training. To be accepted into Q2's small cadre of field agents you had to make it through the rigorous mental and emotional studies of Miller, the organization's psychiatrist and full-time therapist. And it wasn't a one-and-done proposition; every agent met regularly with him, no matter how experienced. I saw him about once a month.

"It's not a lifetime pass," I said to Parnell. "You could qualify now and wash out in six months."

"I won't *wash out*," she said.

Quanta raised a hand. "She hasn't uploaded yet, Swan, but consider her a fellow agent. I'll expect you to help bring her along as quickly as possible."

"So now I'm a tutor?" I asked.

Ignoring this, Quanta addressed Parnell. "You know about

the uploading and downloading process that we call invest-ment. Devya Nayar is the woman who developed the process. She's the mother, if you will, of Q2."

"Oh," Parnell said. She chewed her lip and fell silent again.

"The important question," I said, "is whether this was some random kidnapping, just someone trying to profit by abducting a wealthy, prestigious scientist, or . . ."

"Or someone who understands the significance of Nayar's most important work," Quanta said. "Honestly, at first I hoped it was the former, someone who thought they could score a big payday by holding her and her granddaughter for ransom."

"But we haven't heard from the kidnappers," I said. "So you're leaning toward option two."

"It's no longer just an option," Quanta said. She paused, clearly distressed, which made me anxious.

"I told you there were two incidents this morning," she continued. "At the same time Nayar was being taken from her home in Newport, there was another incursion. This one took place at Q2 headquarters."

"That's impossible," I said. "How could anyone get past security?"

"There's really only one way, which I'll get to in a moment. The point is, they did."

My brain may have atrophied over the years through all of the uploading and downloading, or maybe it was simply all of the experience I'd accumulated during my tenure. But just as I was about to ask which part of the building the criminals had targeted, it hit me. Hard.

If they'd taken Devya Nayar, they weren't interested in anything on the upper floors of our grungy home base.

"They broke into the basement labs," I said. It was a statement rather than a question. Quanta stared at me. That was answer enough.

The rooms deep below Q2 headquarters aren't listed in any public files or recorded on any county blueprints. They were built as part of the most secret project in Washington's history. The number of people who knew *anything* about Q2 was already small, fewer than 100; the number who knew about the basement labs was smaller still.

There, far below the surface of the streets, the actual investment procedures took place. It's where donor bodies were brought, unconscious, to have their own minds uploaded to a special storage device. Then, field agents for Q2 were downloaded, taking up residence inside the body of a person who, hours before, had been serving a life sentence at a federal penitentiary.

The basement labs also contained all of the storage devices, complex machines holding the essence of real people. That meant every former convict, and the stored consciousness of each Q2 agent. Including my own.

While we acclimated to our new body we were put through basic medical testing and evaluation. It took a few hours before we got on an elevator, exiting the Q2 dungeons, leaving behind rows of blinking lights emanating from the highest-high-tech equipment ever developed.

Developed by Devya Nayar from the Massachusetts Institute of Technology.

I swallowed hard. "How bad is it?"

"The worst."

Parnell continued to listen, but her eyes had grown steely and sharp. She was back in her element, the world of high-stakes espionage. It was clear that, while she probably didn't understand everything being exchanged, she certainly recognized the gravity.

Quanta straightened in her chair. "There were three of them, all masked. They accessed the labs and spent only 17 minutes inside. Fortunately no one was there, so we didn't suffer any loss of human life. At least not traditionally."

"Oh, shit," I said.

She nodded. "Yes. They had portable power supplies that they used to hook up a dozen of the stored minds. They also took much of the vital equipment we use for the actual exchanges. And they destroyed several other pieces. It was all very direct and targeted. They knew exactly what they were looking for. And they took it."

I didn't want to ask, but had to. "Do we know *whose* storage units they took?"

My boss let out a long, slow breath. "Eleven of the twelve were convicts. One was a Q2 agent." She paused, then looked at me. "Yours."

My stomach dropped. Someone now possessed the electrical equivalent of me, the ones and zeroes that made up Eric Swan.

"Just *happened* to be mine?" I asked Quanta. "Or was this intentional?"

"I don't think we'll know that for a while," she said. "With so little evidence, we can't know if they simply grabbed random hard drives or if they had a shopping list."

This didn't satisfy me at all. If someone snatches your consciousness, you don't want to be left wondering if you were just part of an overall smash-and-grab, or if you were on someone's Christmas list. This case had instantly become personal.

"And they have Devya," I said out loud, but mostly to myself.

"And *that*," Quanta said, "is why we haven't heard any ransom demands. They have no intention of giving her back. They took her, and some of the equipment, in order to use the technology for themselves."

I tapped on the table, a nervous tic when I was deep in thought, a habit I carried along from body to body.

"Can they do it?" Parnell asked. "I mean, do they have everything they need?"

"I don't know for sure," Quanta said. "We're still processing everything. Their breach of the building's security was so first-rate that we didn't know about the break-in until almost seven a.m. when our technicians arrived. That gave them more than four hours to get away and meet up with the team that took Nayar."

She turned to me. "This is why I've brought you in. All of our agents, now including Parnell, will begin working on this immediately. All other assignments are on hold until we recover Nayar and the stored minds. There can be no failure."

There was silence in the room for a full minute. Then Quanta, her voice low, spoke to me.

"Between the equipment stolen and destroyed, you're unable to upload now."

"How long until that can be repaired or replaced?" I asked.

"I don't know. But you understand what that means?"

I nodded. "If I'm killed, I'm dead. For real this time."

Again, she didn't need to respond.

"Well," I said, "do we have *anything* to go on? Tell me we know something about the people who did this."

"Oh, I can tell you exactly who did it."

This was the last thing I'd expected her to say. "What? You said they wore masks. You've identified them already?"

She shook her head. "We haven't identified the others, but

the one in charge couldn't resist. As they were leaving, he positioned himself directly in front of one of the cameras and lifted his mask. Grinned, even. Proud of what he'd done."

"And you know him?"

In response, she finally opened the folder on the table and removed a photo. She slid it over to me. "This was the last picture we had of him before the break-in. It was taken six years ago."

I spent a long time studying it. He was rugged looking, hard, cold. His hair was cut very short, his nose crooked, obviously from more than one break. A tattoo crossed above his left eye and dropped vertically down his cheek. It was a symbol I didn't recognize, but it exuded hostility. Just one look and you knew he was a dangerous man.

"Who is he?" I asked.

"His name is Butler."

"All right. But who *is* he?"

Quanta pushed the rest of the folder over to me. "You can read all about him. Butler . . ." A pause. "Butler was the first Q2 agent. The one who, six years ago, disappeared without a trace."

CHAPTER THREE

I t was late, I was tired, and I'd just had more than one bombshell dropped right onto my head. In my years as a Q2 agent I'd seen my share of bizarre cases, and I was used to the intrinsically secret nature of the job. Often I was sent into battle knowing just enough to get a job done without filling my mind with the sort of details that could either inhibit my progress or cause me unnecessary thought static.

That happened a lot more than you might think. When they finally figure out robot spies and assassins they'll be able to complete missions without mucking about with those most-untidy human emotions clouding the picture.

Through all of those secretive operations I'd never worried much about the parts left out of my briefings. Mostly I just didn't care; if Villain A needed to be stymied and put down, I could do it without having to know his hopes and dreams, deep-seated motivations, or what his childhood had been like. In the espionage world there's a *need-to-know* basis and a *don't-give-a-shit* basis. I generally hovered in the latter. Made the work so much easier. Take them out and move on to the next problem child.

But remember I said *mostly* I didn't care.

There was one piece of Q2's history and management that, from the beginning, had tormented me from the shadows. As the second person indoctrinated into a clandestine organization designed to protect citizens from the wicked schemes of domestic terrorism, I naturally was curious about the first.

Until tonight, here was the sum total of my knowledge:

It was a man.

Things "didn't end well with him."

He was nowhere to be found.

And that's it. Any attempt at squeezing additional details from Quanta were not only squashed, the discussions themselves were abruptly terminated.

Well, my momma might've raised a hellion who rebelled against authority and occasionally drank his beer with ice in it, but she didn't raise a fool. That level of suppression meant the disappearance of Agent One—which is the only way I knew to refer to him—was a major issue for Q2. I got the feeling it still kept Quanta up at night, regardless of how many hours she spent in quiet meditation.

Every unspoken word spoke loudly to me: This guy was considered a critical problem, one that would someday land right on our doorstep.

Someday had arrived, and quite literally at our door.

I chewed on this during my drive home from Quanta's house. Because I'd just come off a grueling case and had barely caught my breath, I'd been granted a whopping nine hours to go home, get some rest, and pack a fresh bag. I'd fly to Rhode Island with Parnell at 7 a.m.

That quick respite at home meant I could spend at least a

few hours with Christina. Q2 agents were forbidden to have close personal relationships, which is why I'd done my best to keep my common-law marriage a secret. But I'd underestimated Quanta's own abilities as an intelligence officer. She'd known about Christina the entire time. The teacher was, as usual, way ahead of the student.

The Stadler Building was a high-end collection of condominiums filled with people who appreciated their privacy and didn't need collective holiday parties or weekend socials. People minded their own business in a courteous, professional way. Christina and I kept two units on the 7th floor, connected by a private, sliding panel that allowed access to each other without venturing into the hallway.

She'd only been home from the restaurant for a few minutes, and from the tone of my text I expected her to be waiting on my side of the panel.

She was. With a bourbon poured and waiting.

"What flew off the menu tonight?" I asked when we'd settled onto the couch, my hand on her leg.

"Well, we ran out of the scallops and crab cakes, so there was a definite seafood vibe going around for whatever reason. In my opinion they should've ordered the chicken and sausage cacciatore. It was the best thing coming out of the kitchen tonight."

I loved the way she graded each night's output, and it was never just a flippant observation. Christina was one of the best chefs on the East Coast, and I think her palate could distinguish if a dish had four extra grains of salt in it. I never tired of asking her about the nightly culinary experiences.

She was more judicious when it came to *my* line of work. I was open about much, if not all, of what I did, but I think Christina preferred to maintain a thin shield between our very-different worlds. For me, hearing about her normal day provided a lifeline for me, keeping me in touch and somewhat grounded. That equation, however, didn't work the other direction. If anything, knowing too much about my day might completely depress her.

Especially in her current physical condition.

"How are you feeling?" I asked, glancing down at her belly. A child percolated in there. But it wasn't mine.

She gave an indifferent shrug. "I know some women go through monstrous bouts of morning sickness. I guess I'm one of the lucky ones. A little bit of discomfort now and then, but nothing that keeps me off my feet."

I took a sip from my drink. "And I imagine Antonio and Marissa are jubilant?"

"You have no idea. She calls me at least every other day, asking how I'm doing, if I need anything." She laughed. "I think in a roundabout way she's checking to see if I'm being good. You know, eating right, exercising, no alcohol. Antonio even stopped me tonight and apologized in case they were going overboard."

I smiled. "That's cute. Can't blame her, I guess. You're carrying the baby they've always wanted. I think it's damned beautiful."

She nodded, then scrunched up her face. "Get a load of this. Antonio told me some of his family members are pissed off they're using a surrogate. Said it's *unnatural*. He said his aunt has practically disowned him."

I took another drink. "Screw them. There will always be small-minded and selfish assholes out there. I hope he ignores them."

"Yeah," she said, then grew quiet for a moment before

adding: "One thing I do know is that the biggest change in me isn't physical."

"No?"

"No. Rationally, I know this child isn't mine, but . . . for a while it is, you know? For a few months I'm responsible for another life until I hand it off to someone else to care for. It's really made me think. Mostly about how I *do* want to do all the right things, not just for the child, but for Antonio and Marissa. Sometimes I want to tell them, *Hey, you don't have to worry. I've got this.*"

She lowered her head onto my shoulder and we sat quietly for a couple of minutes. I knew she was thinking about the baby, but she'd made me think about the bodies *I* temporarily cared for. I was given a similar responsibility.

I just never gave mine back.

She pulled away and looked up at me. "Enough ignoring the obvious. What's going on up there? I know when something's bothering you."

I filled her in on the rough details. Christina knew enough about the program to understand this was easily the most critical assignment I'd ever been dealt. She finally let out a long breath and looked out the window at the twinkling lights of the city.

"Why would he surface now? If he's known how to bust into Q2 for all these years, why now?"

"I've been wondering that, too. The only thing that makes sense is that he either had to really plan everything down to the tiniest detail, or he was waiting for the right help."

"The right help? Like who?"

"I don't know. Just something that occurred to me. No evidence for it whatsoever." I finished the bourbon. "It's also possible his anger, or whatever's been driving him, finally reached the breaking point."

Christina absorbed this for a moment. "And he hasn't left any kind of note? Nothing? Strikes me as unusual."

I looked at her. "It does, doesn't it? This is the kind of grandiose crime that always seems to include a speech of some sort, or at least a phone call to vomit out psychobabble. Of course . . ."

She waited patiently.

"Of course," I continued, "Butler might also be so crazy that he's going off script for everything. That's one of my biggest fears about all this. That we'll never hear a word until he does something catastrophic."

I felt her shiver next to me. She said in a soft voice, "Babe, he has your mind in his possession. That has to terrify you."

"I told you I had more than one fear about all of it."

"Could he . . ." She searched for the right words. "Could he somehow download your mind into another body? I mean— there couldn't be two of you, could there?"

"Supposedly there are safeguards. It's part of the signal that's installed in our heads when we invest into a new body. The same signal that lets Q2 know if we've been, you know—"

"Killed," she said.

This couldn't be easy for her. It wasn't exactly thrilling for me to discuss, either.

"Look," I told her. "I don't think that's anything to worry about for the time being. He has several of the hard drives, but he doesn't have all the equipment."

"But he has this scientist who invented it all."

Yeah. He did. He also held Devya's granddaughter, and I had a pretty good idea what *her* role in all this was. Pure leverage. Butler was probably already threatening to murder the young girl if Devya didn't cooperate.

But cooperate with what? What was Butler's ultimate intention? Why steal Devya, some of the equipment, and a dozen stored minds, most of which belonged to the original felons who'd occupied bodies used by Q2 agents, including me?

And why take *mine*? Why bother with the mind of someone who would be coming after you? He could destroy it, sure, but all I'd have to do is stay safe long enough to upload again. None of it made sense.

There were too many questions and absolutely no answers. When Parnell and I arrived at the Rhode Island crime scene we'd be operating blind, hoping to find something. Anything. Hope was a powerful motivator, but a horrible strategy.

I put an arm around Christina and pulled her close. After a moment I heard a subdued question from her.

"What else has you afraid, Swan? I know there's more."

I didn't want to answer. But this was one of the many reasons I loved being with Christina. It gave me a chance to talk about this with someone other than Miller at Q2.

My voice was low, matching hers. "If all of this works out the way we need it to, then it means I'll come face-to-face with Agent One. And that means I'll be able to explore what he's . . . what he's become."

Her hand was on my leg now, and she gave it a tight squeeze. "Babe. You're nothing like him."

"How can you say that? Nobody knows anything about him."

"We know he broke into Q2 and destroyed important equipment. And you said his other team killed two people before kidnapping Devya. That's not you."

"No, it's not me." I paused. "Not yet."

Now Christina pulled away from me and stared hard into my face. "Just because Butler went insane doesn't mean the same thing will happen to you. You have no idea what his mental state was when he *started* with Q2."

"Listen—"

"No, you listen," she said. "I know damned well this scares you. It's scared you for years. You hide it, Swan, behind this silly mask. A mask of humor and bravado, or some bullshit like that. Acting like it doesn't really bother you if you laugh your way through it. Why don't you just face it instead of ignoring it?"

"And just how exactly do you want me to face it, Christina? How do I face the fact that I might be turning into the same goddamned monster I'm now supposed to hunt down? How do I face the idea that my mind is no longer really my own? At least not the one I started with years ago? What's your prescription for facing that?"

I hadn't meant to raise my voice. As my rant continued, though, the decibels increased. When I realized it, I shut up. To break the tension I grabbed my drink, but the glass was empty. I set it back down and rubbed a hand through my hair.

"God, I'm sorry. I'm so sorry. I didn't mean to go off like that."

She let a few moments pass, then she shook her head. "You're such a dumbass, Swan."

I almost laughed. "What?"

"You're a dumbass. You should've gone off like that a long time ago. Instead of acting so tough all the time."

She took my hand. "You think I don't know how this affects you? And don't you think if I saw any change like the one you're describing that I'd say something?"

"I don't know."

"See?" She shook her head again. "God, for being one of the smartest people I know, you can be so dense sometimes."

She snuggled back up against me. "The fact that you're even worried about becoming this monster means you *aren't* becoming a monster."

"Jesus, now you sound like Miller." I sniffed at her hair. "But you smell so much better than he does."

She gave a soft laugh. I held her for a few more minutes before we shut off the lights and went to bed.

I'd let the matter drop. But Christina's passionate argument hadn't swayed me a bit.

If I was slowly devolving into a Butler-ish beast, just analyzing it wouldn't prevent the transformation. In fact, it might even produce a more formidable beast than Agent One.

One who used the knowledge to protect himself from capture.

CHAPTER FOUR

A flight from D.C. to Providence takes about an hour in the air. Quanta had arranged for a private jet, so Parnell and I climbed aboard, not saying much. It felt strange to sit next to this woman who'd once worked for British intelligence before an *incident*—the lone description I'd heard so far— forced her out.

There were things I wanted to discuss with her. I was curious to find out about her work in England, about the circumstances surrounding her exit, and why she'd agreed to work for the killer twins.

And maybe we could finally have a meaningful talk about the fact that she'd blatantly come on to me, and how later I'd shot and killed her husband.

He'd had it coming. But still.

I'd done my best to scan the copious notes on Butler before leaving Quanta's house. Then her assistant, Poole, had trans- ferred all of it to me digitally, and I had access through an encrypted file in my phone and tablet. But even what I'd gleaned the night before was enough to tell me the man we sought was a special kind of evil.

Parnell hadn't been privy to the information, but if we were going to work together she'd have to know a lot more than she did now. And, like any good agent, she'd waited just long enough to be proper before she began exploring. We were alone in the plane's luxurious cabin. She pulled down the shade of the window next to her and fixed me with a long gaze.

"How many times have you invested?" she asked.

"Oh, hell. I don't know the exact number. Plenty."

She nodded. "Does it scare you?"

"Not any more." Then it dawned on me what she was hinting around about. "Look, I could tell you not to worry about it, not to be afraid, but that's pointless. It's like skydiving. Telling you to not be nervous before your first time is a waste of breath. Be nervous. Be terrified. Doesn't matter. Once it happens you'll adapt to it soon enough."

"I'll get used to it?"

"Used to it? No. Let's just say it won't be as freaky the tenth time as it is the first."

We spent another five minutes talking about the various bodies I'd inhabited. I could tell it bothered her. Why wouldn't it?

"Are you worried about what your new body will look like?" I asked, a slight smile on my face. "After all the work you've obviously put into this one?"

"I'm not vain, if that's what you mean."

"Sure you are. But so what? That's part of what keeps an agent on top of their game." Before she could object, I kept going. "Look, the investment process is a leap in science that our limited brains aren't designed to handle. Even if the technology was released to the general public—and I don't see that happening for a long time, if ever—it would take at least a generation or two before we acclimated to it. Maybe longer than that. So what I'm saying is, don't worry about worrying. It'll be weird for you, but you'll have your intellect to pull you through. Fair enough?"

When she didn't respond I added, "And it's better than the alternative."

Now she spoke. "Is it, though? We're playing God. I accept the science; I'm not sure I accept the morality of it yet."

She was actually speaking my language, but I wouldn't wish all of my second-guessing on anyone. The best thing I could do was subtly nudge her out of this thinking.

"I think it's playing God if you use the science irresponsibly. But what *we're* doing? Using it to serve and protect? I don't have a problem with that. It's a tool."

Going by her face, she wasn't buying it, which was fine. I didn't feel like discussing it. With all of the new data I'd received, a chat with Miller may have been helpful for me, but it would have to wait.

"We'll have time later to dive into all that," I said. "For now, let's focus on Butler."

"You didn't know anything about him until last night?"

"All I knew was that I was the second agent invested. The first one was a guy who disappeared, and I wasn't told any of the details. *Nobody* was. In fact, we were never even allowed to ask about it without getting our hands slapped. It's the first I've heard a name attached to Agent One."

Parnell leaned back in her chair, waiting for me to continue. Without consulting my tablet's file, I shared what I remembered from my brief scan the night before.

"Butler was only an agent for Q2 for a little over a year. In that time he became increasingly hostile toward not only the program, but to Quanta personally. His last assignment was a complete failure, mostly due to incompetence on his part. Which was very unlike him; he was apparently a first-rate agent when he began. Now he exhibited sloppy field work. Very little communication. Missed exchanges with other field personnel, mostly FBI agents. Quanta called him in for one of those meetings at her house."

"And?"

"And he pulled out his weapon and shot at her."

Parnell's eyes narrowed. "He shot *at* her. Does that mean he missed?"

"Not by much. Splintered the door next to her head. Which seems suspicious."

"In what way?"

I let out a long breath. "Butler was trained as well as you and I were. He wouldn't have missed unless it was deliberate. I'm guessing it was simply a final '*piss off.*' Quanta's reflexes are good, so she scrambled to safety before he could re-think his strategy. When she checked a minute later, he was gone. And that was the last anyone ever heard from him."

"I'm sure there was an exhaustive search."

"Which turned up nothing. Butler may have flown off the rails and had a complete breakdown mentally, but that part of his training didn't fail him. You and I both know that if an agent wants to disappear, they can. Nobody's better schooled than we are in the ways of stealth."

Parnell gave a slow nod. "Do we know what might've caused this mental breakdown? Could it just have been the stress of the job?"

"The file doesn't contain Miller's notes, sadly. Those are apparently still classified. But I have to believe Agent One was eventually considered a mulligan. Which explains why you and I—and the other three agents—were vetted much more vigorously. Nobody wants another Butler."

"Why do you think he's shown up now?"

I pulled the shade open slightly to peer at the landscape gliding past us, 31,000 feet below. "He's had a few years to let his anger simmer, and to dream up some ultimate revenge plan."

Looking back at Parnell I added, "And based on the initial steps of his plan, it can only be monstrous."

POOLE HAD ARRANGED an SUV for us, a Jaguar F-Pace. Parnell drove, pulling out of T.F. Green Airport toward Newport. It would take us 35 minutes to reach the crime scene at Devya Nayar's home. I used the time in the passenger seat to look over the notes of Nayar's abduction and read the salient points aloud for both of us.

"The security system was taken down at 1:55 a.m., but the way it was done made it appear to be a system reboot after an update. No one got suspicious for the first minute until it failed to come back on. By that time the kidnappers were inside. One security guard from the grounds was found dead, his throat slashed from behind, exactly the way a professional would do it.

"The woman in the security command room was knocked unconscious, says she never knew who or what hit her from behind. She was trussed up and left in a closet, very lucky to be alive."

I flipped a page on the screen. "The guard inside the home wasn't as lucky. Like the outdoor security man, he was found murdered. In this case, though, it looked like he put up a fight.

There was some damage in the home, just outside the room where the granddaughter was staying."

"So they took her first."

"Yeah, looks like it. Probably grabbed the 14-year-old and used a threat of killing her to force Nayar to come along quietly." I sighed. "That's the best guess, anyway. All security footage was deleted, and, again, professionally. Three different tech people have been unable to retrieve anything. But one other person on the premises was alerted by phone when the security system had been down for five minutes. He got from the guest house to Devya's room three minutes later and it was over."

"In and out in less than eight minutes?"

"Looks like it."

She pondered that for a moment, then glanced at me. "Either Butler took the time to exquisitely train his help, or he's hired people who were already pros."

"He doesn't strike me as the training type. That takes a lot of patience."

"You think he's working with someone else as a partner?"

I looked up from the tablet and checked out the Rhode Island scenery. I didn't answer the question.

But yes, I was pretty sure this was something bigger than anything Butler could pull off alone.

It had been a long time since I'd been a passenger in a car during an assignment. It was a nice change. Parnell deftly steered the powerful Jag south then east, and soon we sailed over the Jamestown Bridge. Then, a couple of minutes later, we crossed the final stretch of Narragansett Bay on the Newport Bridge. Once on Aquidneck Island it only took a few minutes to reach the estate.

It was impressive, and brought back memories of a similar

compound I'd recently visited in Telluride, Colorado. This, too, was in one of the pricier zip codes in the country, but, unlike the mountain chalet, this one came with waterfront property. Four vehicles with official government plates sat outside the front gate, and, once we were waved in, another five came into view, a mixture of local police and feds. It had been 31 hours since the abduction.

No one outside our organization even knew the name Q2, so we introduced ourselves using cover identities designed to get us in the door without drawing many questions. My badge identified me as a U.S. Marshall, pursuing an investigation about a fugitive with possible ties to an international ring. That, in turn, provided a nice cover for Parnell and her British accent, who posed as a visiting agent from Europol.

We got the initial report from an impeccably-dressed police detective named O'Mallon.

"It's a real bitch," he said. "No video recovered, no prints, no eyewitnesses. We've started a search of neighbor video to see if we can capture vehicle plates just before or after."

"That's fine," I said, "but it won't matter. You'd find the plates were either stolen or phony, and that car has likely been destroyed. Maybe sunk into the bay."

O'Mallon gave a resigned nod. "Unfortunately we don't have much else to work with. We've got some of the estate staff here now, trying to see if anything's missing."

Before I could respond, an FBI agent came striding up. She introduced herself as Agent De Luca. The agency could officially get involved since the two crimes were deemed connected, and the abduction of Nayar was considered a national security breach. De Luca sized up Parnell and me in a quick glance.

"I can take you through the three specific rooms they

targeted," she said. We thanked the police detective and followed De Luca into a small building just outside the massive home. This was the security command room. It was in shambles, but not in a haphazard way. It was obvious the perps had known exactly what to destroy and what to not waste time on.

"The security guard stationed here was found in that storage closet," De Luca said, pointing behind us. "The best we can figure, this could've easily been managed by one person. As soon as the system was down, two, perhaps three, other people were ready to bust into the house."

"Why didn't they kill her?" Parnell asked, indicating the closet. "Why kill the other guards but not her?"

"They might've realized she hadn't seen anyone and wouldn't be able to make any kind of identification," De Luca said. "Or because she was a woman, perhaps. The two dead guards were both male."

"I don't think we're dealing with chivalrous criminals," I said. "It could be that this perp just didn't have the stomach for murder, while the one who took out the two men is an animal. My guess is this one is more of a tech wizard than a hired killer with a taste for blood."

I gave another glance around the mess. "There's nothing here, just mayhem. Let's see where Nayar and the girl were grabbed."

As we followed the FBI agent across a graveled drive toward the entrance to the home, Parnell spoke to me under her breath. "Are you looking for anything specific?"

I chewed a lip and looked up at the looming facade of Devya Nayar's mansion, a well-earned sanctuary after years of developing technology that had served the country's defense well.

"Just a feeling about something," I said. "Let's see."

There was a hush inside the home. Police and FBI were talking with a couple of staff members who looked to be in complete shock. Who could blame them? This was stuff out of one of those *Mission: Impossible* movies, certainly not something they'd expected when they took a job looking out for a semi-retired MIT professor.

Walking down a hallway I studied photographs on the walls and tables. Many included the 14-year-old granddaughter, Tisha. I immediately saw the relationship with Devya. The only real difference was Tisha's sunburst smile; her grandmother's shy demeanor meant she abhorred smiling for pictures.

Just outside Tisha's room an overturned table and the shattered picture frame that once hung behind it made a pile of debris. There was blood, a lot of it, including a sizable swath streaked across the wall. The security guard's death here had been violent. There was a trail of bloody footprints from the killer leading into the room. Size 11, according to the crime unit. A popular running shoe. These were likely at the bottom of the bay by now, too. Or burned somewhere.

Inside, the girl's room held nothing of significance for the search. She'd been snatched from her bed and likely carted away without so much as a change out of pajamas.

"And the staff says nothing is out of place here?" I asked Agent De Luca. "Nothing that seems unusual?"

"Not a thing."

I began to wonder if the feeling I'd mentioned to Parnell was complete crap. The kidnappers had been ultimate pros, and it looked like they'd left nothing behind, other than some faint bloody tracks.

Until we got to Devya's room.

Detective O'Mallon was talking with a member of the household staff. He nodded a greeting as we walked in, and held up a finger, indicating he had something to share.

Here there was no sign of a struggle whatsoever. The bed was still in its rumpled, unmade condition; Devya had likely jumped out at the sound of her granddaughter being brought into the room. Again, with the speed of the operation, no change of clothes was likely. They were up and out within a minute.

This was the only opportunity I'd ever had to get an intimate portrait of the woman responsible for my multiple lives. Framed photos and awards took up a small section of one wall. I stood before it all, gazing at images of this slight woman, an immigrant from India during her awkward teenage years, who'd gone on to one of the most remarkable academic careers in history.

From there, and in the highest demand imaginable, she'd agreed to work directly with the U.S. government on the project that became Q2's edge: A form of immortality.

But was it immortality with a nasty flaw? Was Butler evidence of the dark, malignant side of the investment program? Or was he, as both Quanta and Miller insisted, an aberrant one-time miscalculation?

Before I could think more about it, De Luca and O'Mallon walked over to me.

"We have something," the detective said. He nodded toward the staff member, a woman, who stood by the door, terrified. "The only thing that Ms. Nayar's housekeeper can find out of the ordinary."

I exchanged a look with Parnell. Her face registered a *How did you know?* look.

"All right," I said. "Show us."

They escorted me to a dresser. Upon it were scattered the usual trappings of a woman's bedroom, things normally tucked out of sight if she expected visitors, but otherwise left handy for daily use.

"What's unusual here?" I asked.

"Ms. Jackson says this was definitely not here when she cleaned the room two days ago, and Ms. Nayar hadn't left the house since then." De Luca pointed to a small jewelry box in the center. Sitting atop it, standing out from everything else, was a smooth, porcelain figurine, about four inches tall. It was delicately crafted, and was quite striking in a simplistic, yet classical way.

I knelt down and looked at it from eye level.

"Is that . . .?" Parnell didn't finish.

"Yeah," I said, inspecting the figurine closer. "It's a swan."

CHAPTER FIVE

"All right."

They were not the words I'd expected Quanta to say. In fact, my initial reaction was a flush of anger at her calm, understated reply.

I sat in the passenger seat of the Jag, the porcelain swan propped on my thigh. Parnell hadn't bothered to join me when I told her I needed to contact Q2; she was a pro, and she knew when to quietly withdraw.

"*All right?*" I said, staring at Quanta's face on my tablet. "That's it? Butler had his lackeys leave a porcelain swan for me to find, and you respond with *All right?*"

Her expression didn't alter a bit. "What reaction would you have preferred? There isn't time for us to lose our cool over the evidence."

"I haven't lost my cool, Quanta. I'm expressing concern that a rogue Q2 agent has obviously targeted me as part of his Vengeance Tour. And for reasons that nobody seems to understand. Or, at the moment, seems to give a damn about."

"On the contrary," she said, still showing no sign of

emotion. "I'm thrilled that he's so interested in you."

I almost laughed. "Well, then please clue me in."

She looked off to the side for a moment, then returned her gaze to the camera.

"Think about it, Swan. Our biggest fear with the operation he's staging is that he'd do everything completely off the grid. He could do it, too. He could dive deep underground, complete his task, whatever that is, and never once leave a single clue regarding his motives or his location.

"If he's truly interested in *you* specifically, and he's bothering to let us know that he's interested in you, it means we'll hear from him. Otherwise, there's no reason whatsoever for these games. So, yes, I'm happy that he's involved you."

It made perfect sense, and if I hadn't been so surprised by the attention I might've seen it for myself. Probably would've eventually, anyway.

It's just startling when you're on the receiving end of a monster's preoccupation.

She studied me across the electronic connection and added, "Besides, were you really shocked to find *something*?"

I sighed. "No."

Glancing out the passenger window of the car I watched Parnell talking with de Luca. "It's the reason I wanted to check out the crime scene. But I thought we'd find more of a vague message for Q2."

I returned my gaze to the screen. "Or for you. Isn't Butler's beef with you?"

She raised an eyebrow. "Butler's *beef*, as you call it, is with the world. It's not as simple as an individual grudge."

"But you're the focal point."

"Maybe." Her voice mellowed. "But at this point, given everything he's done since yesterday morning, I can't worry about that. Butler's grievances may explain his actions, but they don't help us locate him. His fascination with you, however, might."

She changed her tone back to all-business. "I've had a chance to study the images of the porcelain figurine. How do you interpret the numbers on the bottom?"

I picked up the swan and turned it over. On the flat base a small, plain white sticker contained a string of numbers, printed in red.

04051915

"I don't think it's as complicated as a code," I said. "Probably just a simple message, one he wants us to figure out relatively quickly. It's not a phone number; not enough digits. And it's not an address, or map coordinates."

Quanta was silent as I worked through this. I think she was glad to see I'd recalibrated after my mini-outburst.

Then it hit me. "Oh. It's today's date and a time."

"Very good," she said, nodding. "Seven-fifteen tonight. So he counted on you showing up at Devya's estate sometime today and finding this."

"And he knew I'd be the one assigned to the case."

"No," she said. "He made *sure* you were assigned to the case. That partly explains why he took your hard drive."

I squinted at the sticker. "It gives me a date and time. But so what? What am I supposed to do tonight at 7:15?"

"It's safe to assume Butler will take care of that."

We ended the video call and I sat still for a few moments, rolling the porcelain swan around in my hand. At the same time a light mist began to scatter across the windshield, a cold rain that would likely turn to snow in a few hours.

It really had become a game for Agent One, and a deadly one at that, with me as the game piece, to be moved around whatever board he'd created. I didn't like it. As an experienced field agent, I wanted to control each situation. Being at the whim of a madman was not the optimal way to navigate a case. It led to *re*action rather than action, and reactions were, by their nature, spontaneous. And often dead wrong.

Emphasis on *dead*, in my line of work.

I made eye contact with Parnell and indicated that she should get out of the rain and join me.

"What's the plan?" she asked once behind the wheel.

I showed her the numbers on the swan and explained what I thought they meant.

"This Butler character is bloody nuts," she said. "Why bother with all this? Why not just hide out and get what he wants from Nayar?"

"I just had the same conversation with Quanta. Whatever his grudge is with her, and with the organization, it looks like he's finally ready to tell everybody all about it. Just needed the right platform, I suppose." I shrugged. "Maybe we'll get some answers tonight."

We both watched the drizzle, deep in thought.

Finally, Parnell chuckled. "Agent de Luca seems quite good at her job, but she's very curious about us. Or suspicious, rather. Lots of subtle references to our *departments*, and a stray question or two about where we're based."

I grunted. "Par for the course. We're an oddity on this case, and they want it explained. She must be relatively new."

"Why?"

"Because veteran agents don't ask a damned thing. They've learned it doesn't do a bit of good and just makes them look green or incompetent."

"You mean veterans like your friend, Fife."

Fife. An oddity himself. Former Q2, now a plant within the

FBI, although Parnell didn't know about his former life. Few did. I'd met him on the same mission where I'd crossed paths with her. In fact, it was Fife who'd arrested Parnell at the conclusion of our case. He was someone I'd happily work with again.

"He's a good agent," I said, and dropped the subject. I looked again at the porcelain taunt from Butler and wondered what his next move would be.

WE GRABBED a meal and spent the late afternoon at a nearby cafe before returning to the crime scene. Parnell certainly had questions, but, to her credit, picked up on the fact that I was occupied by the strange turn to the case and mostly kept herself busy on her own tablet. I felt bad that I wasn't coaching her the way Quanta had expected, but for the moment that would have to wait.

When seven o'clock rolled around I made another call to the boss.

"We're back at Devya's estate," I said. "Whatever's going to happen tonight, if this is ground zero we have plenty of support."

Indeed, there was a buzz of activity around us. Four local police detectives and half a dozen FBI agents quietly milled about inside, with several more patrolling the grounds. I knew, without seeing them, that at least another dozen law enforcement types were in the vicinity, laying low.

Parnell, who desperately wanted to be of more assistance, quietly sat at a kitchen table, studying background information on Nayar. I wanted to tell her she'd be busy enough before too long. As a fellow agent, though, I appreciated her professional impatience. I'd feel exactly the same way.

"We have a full house here, as well," Quanta said. "We have recording traps on everything. But I've been thinking this afternoon about Butler's fascination with you. If he's indeed going to reach out in just a few minutes, I don't think it will have anything to do with the house."

"Oh?"

"He left the date and time of contact specifically for you. So I think you're the one who will receive it, regardless of where you are."

"How could he do that?"

"Let's wait and see," was all she said before hanging up.

The rain had, as predicted, changed over to a light snow. It was one of those soft, early spring dustings, the kind that muffles every other sound until your simple footfalls seem impossibly loud crushing the powder. Zipping up my light jacket, I walked out the back door and stood on a covered deck, admiring the lush landscaping now turning white. Tendrils of steam rose from a hot tub, and behind that lay a tarp-covered pool.

The estate's lighting, substantial while still subdued, faded to darkness at the point where the property spilled into the ocean. A solitary ship's light managed to cut through the light snow.

It was a remarkable home, in many ways projecting the style and personality of its reserved owner. Devya Nayar's work had paid off handsomely, and rightly so.

For a moment I speculated on how much more money she'd left on the table by opting for a government contract rather than private enterprise. But she'd recognized the potential nightmare her technology would create on the open market. The MIT genius had birthed an idea featuring wildly contrasting possibilities: It could either help to prevent national disasters, or could spark a global riot in a lustful race to achieve immortality.

In the end there'd been only one path her conscience allowed her to take.

A door opened and closed behind me, and a moment later Parnell stood at my side. She followed my gaze across the sprawling grounds and said, in a hushed voice to match the snowy serenity, "It's almost 7:15."

I nodded. After a few moments of silence, I said, "You must be second-guessing your decision to take Quanta's job offer. Maybe cursing me for suggesting it to her in the first place."

"Why would you think that?"

"First, you have your mind completely blown by our, um, unique twist on spy methods. Then your first case involves a rogue former agent, and you discover his parting shot was an actual shot. At the boss, even." I turned to look at her. "You're probably wondering if it's too late to get out of everything."

"Oh, I don't know," she said. "It's all quite thrilling, really. And better than sitting in a jail cell."

I laughed. True, that *had* been her only alternative.

Before either of us could say anything else, my phone vibrated, then, a moment later, did it again. Then again.

It was exactly 7:15.

The screen reported three text messages from an unknown number. I glanced at Parnell, but her eyes were locked on my phone, every ounce of emotion drained from her expression. Some would refer to it as a game face, but trained agents recognized it as the exact opposite of a game. It was all business. Parnell was indeed a pro.

"Well, he has my number," I said, trying to sound as relaxed as possible, even though my heartbeat had accelerated.

"Unless this is delivery confirmation for the couch I ordered last week."

I swiped open the texts. I'd expected plain, ordinary words, or maybe a set of map coordinates. Hell, it would've been funny if it was just some ridiculous meme, trying to goad me. That would be my style, too, and at least I could appreciate my new nemesis.

But instead it was a long string of code. I scrolled for a moment, wondering if something more concrete would appear toward the bottom. But the message was the same from top to bottom, something the geniuses on the second floor at Q2 would need to decipher.

I switched to the second text, with the same outcome. More mysterious code. A strange feeling of disappointment bubbled up within me. I hadn't known what to expect, no idea what method of contact he'd choose, and certainly no clue what his message would say. This, in an odd way, was a giant letdown. If his warped plot was going to require the department's computer nerds to untangle it, why bother to include me at all? Was I simply meant to be a conduit, some sort of messenger boy between Quanta and her failed first experiment?

"Should I even bother with the last one?" I asked, more to myself than to Parnell. Then I clicked open the third message.

It was a photo, taken at a crooked angle, but with the image clear as day. It showed a small plaque, embossed with three large numbers.

700.

It was an address plaque affixed to a wall, the kind you see in hotels and condominiums.

It was the address plaque outside the front door of *my* condo, in the Stadler building.

CHAPTER SIX

I didn't even hear Parnell's confused questions as I hurried back into the house. I'd dialed Christina's number and cursed quietly as it rang and rang before going to voicemail. *She's at the restaurant* I kept telling myself. Of course she's at the restaurant. It's her busiest time. She's working.

I tried two more times, just on the odd chance she'd pick up, but with the same luck.

By the time I disconnected the third call I was out the front door and approaching the car. Parnell had given up her pursuit, clearly exasperated at my emergency exit and the fact I was ignoring her. I was ten paces from the Jag when it dawned on me: Parnell had the keys.

I stood there, snow gently gathering on my shoulders and hair. Then my phone vibrated. It was Quanta.

"He sent a photo from my home," I said without bothering with a greeting. "The son of a bitch took a picture from my home."

Her voice carried exactly the same tone I'd grown accustomed to: total calm and control. "I just got a call from Parnell. Forward everything to me, right now."

"Did you hear what I said?" I yelled. "He—"

"Yes," she said. "I heard you. I'll have a team at your home in minutes."

"And at the restaurant," I said. I couldn't ever remember ordering Quanta around, but my adrenaline was driving this train at the moment.

"Yes, as we speak," she said. "But Christina is safe. Believe me, if Butler was going to do anything he wouldn't send you a warning. He would've simply done it and then crowed about it later. It's just the way he operates. He's a master manipulator. He gets a rise out of getting his adversaries worked up, just like he's doing with you. Do you understand?"

I managed a few more deep breaths and paced around the parked cars. "Yes," I finally said, my voice returning to normal. "All right. But please send someone over to check on her anyway."

"I told you I'd take care of it. And we'll have a small team watch her."

"Without worrying her," I added.

"Of course. She won't know they're there."

At the far end of the parking area I turned and saw a silhouette against the light spilling from the front door of the house. It was likely Parnell, confused and probably angry. At the moment I didn't care.

"Okay, I'll forward the texts to you right now," I said to Quanta. I hung up and sent all three messages, including the image. Then, after one last calming breath, I trudged back to the house.

Parnell moved aside, but as I walked past she took a vice-like grip on my upper arm.

"We're going to have a talk, Swan. Now."

I slowly looked down at her fingers digging into my bicep, then back to her face, which was set into a hard stare. I matched her intensity. "We'll talk when I'm ready. Take your goddamned hand off me."

She leaned in to within inches of my face. "You can't intimidate me. Remember, I've already kicked the shit out of you, Yank. I can do it again, any time. Clear?"

I pried her fingers away. "And you better be prepared to kill me, limey, because I'll keep coming until I land a punch to put you down for good. Or just put a bullet in your brain. Are *you* clear?"

We kept up the stare for another five seconds before I broke off and walked into the living area and headed straight for the bar. I took a glass from the counter, found a bottle of Knob Creek, and poured a healthy sample. Who gave a rat's ass if it was unprofessional?

A couple of the FBI agents looked over, perplexed to see what they assumed was a fellow law enforcement agent downing a shot of whiskey at a crime scene, but they went back to their own conversations. Parnell sauntered up and leaned against the wall beside me.

After a moment she said, "Did you just call me *limey*?"

I glanced over and saw the faint trace of a smile on her lips. It was enough to break the ice.

"Yeah," I said with a small grunt of laughter. "It was all I could come up with to answer *Yank*."

"What is this, 1944?"

I laughed again. "I don't even know if the word is offensive to Brits. Is it?"

"No, it's not offensive," she said. "It's antiquated and stupid."

"Fair enough. I'll try to come up with something better next time." I held up the glass, my offer of a peace token, but she shook her head. I set the glass in the sink and looked around to make sure no one was within ear shot.

"The photo that Butler sent was taken outside my home."

She let that sink in for a moment, then said, "That was quite a reaction on your part, though. Have you got a girl stashed in there or something?"

Well, this was interesting. No one besides Quanta knew about Christina. During my initial meeting with Parnell months earlier I'd casually mentioned "my wife," but at the time—and given the circumstances—I was sure the British agent hadn't bought it. To her it had been a convenient lie to get out of an awkward situation.

But she was right; my emotional response to the photo had been over the top and demanded some sort of explanation. The only thing to do was to put her off and deflect.

"Maybe I don't like strangers in my place," I said. "Had a bad experience one time with a real creeper going through my underwear drawer." When she just stood there, silent, I added, "Look, I have some sensitive things lying around from the department. Things Butler could use against me."

None of this made sense, which is actually the way I wanted it.

"Are you saying you have things you're not supposed to have?" Parnell asked.

"Maybe."

It was better, I decided, for her to think I was breaking some sort of Q2 rules than to know the truth. Besides, she'd been a bit of an organizational outlaw herself, so perhaps it would act as a bonding moment between us. I let the subject drop, even though Parnell looked far from convinced.

"Quanta has the two strings of code," I said. "Her data monkeys are probably already tearing them apart. My guess is the messages won't be tough to figure out."

"Why not?"

I looked out the large picture window at the snowfall, which had grown in intensity. "Because Butler's not trying to make us solve a puzzle. That's not his M.O., and definitely not his goal here. He's just screwing with us, like he did with the crystal swan and the easy code on the bottom. For now he just wants to throw us off our game. Which he's already done," I added.

"And maybe stall for time?" she threw in.

"And that, yeah. Even if Devya spilled her guts right away in order to protect her granddaughter, it would take time to fill in the missing pieces."

"So what do we do now?"

I shook my head. "No sense heading back to Washington yet. Depending on the translation of those codes we'd probably be right back on the road. I doubt seriously if his base is anywhere near D.C."

A minute ticked by as I sifted through all the facts. A lot had happened in 36 hours.

"There were two coded messages," I said. "Does that sound like two different trails to you?"

Parnell studied my face. "Well, there *were* two separate crimes committed by Butler and his cronies. So yeah, maybe the messages are meant to send us off on two separate chases."

"One of which could be totally meaningless, just a blind alley to keep us wasting our time."

"Or both?"

"Or both. An easy way to divide our forces and dilute our resources." For a moment I considered a second shot of the Knob Creek, but no. One was understandable, two was cliched Hollywood bravado.

"Let's go for a ride," I said, stepping out from behind the bar. "How are limeys when it comes to driving in snow?"

WE SPENT close to an hour carefully making our way around the island, looking at the impressive estates and occasionally crossing the primary bridges to break up the drive. The spring snow storm made for mostly-deserted roads. An occasional snow plow passed going the other direction, and twice we pulled to the side for an emergency vehicle to get by. Each of these threw up thick, sloppy bucketfuls of wet snow onto the windshield. It wasn't really a night meant for driving, which is partly why I enjoyed it.

I'd sent Christina a couple of text messages, not wanting to alarm her, but just to make sure she was able to respond. After 45 minutes she did. She was hard at work and would call me later. That took a huge load off my mind.

Parnell and I didn't speak much, contemplating the bizarre start to the case and wondering what Butler's coded text messages would turn out to be. She attempted once or twice to pry into my reaction to the *700* photo, but I played it off as unimportant.

In a somewhat juvenile game of tag, I asked about her disgraced exit from British intelligence. That elicited roughly the same bullshit answers she got from me. Neither of us, apparently, was ready to reveal our secrets.

From her guarded manner I gathered Parnell had about as much experience with a partner as I had. In my case it was part of the job description—Q2 frowned on it, for reasons I didn't fully understand—but I got the impression Parnell was simply a lone wolf by temperament.

Which made her marriage to the animal known as Richter even more baffling. It hadn't made sense when I first discovered their relationship, and it made even less sense now. Knowing that particular backstory wouldn't help with the Butler case; it was my own pure, base curiosity. I decided this evening would be as good a time as any to pry and find out.

We stopped at one of the few food joints still open and took seats at the corner of the bar, always the best seats in any establishment. It allowed for better eye contact than sitting side by side. We passed on alcohol and instead ordered tea, much to the amusement of the bartender.

"Now that we're friends again, I want to talk with you about what happened earlier," she said, stirring a touch of milk into her glass mug.

"We don't have to do that," I said, only half-joking.

"Sure we do." She took a sip of her tea and grimaced. I mean, was she expecting gourmet tea at a roadside greasy spoon?

"You seem to think that I want to know everything," she said. "I don't. I want to know enough to be more than just some worthless sidekick."

"I get it," I said.

"No, you don't get it. This isn't the type of mentoring arrangement I signed up for. I may not know shit about the investment process and what that experience is like, but I don't need hand-holding when it comes to field work. I'm quite sure I've had just as many cases as you, Swan, and put down more than my share of bad people. So let's cut out the master-and-grasshopper crap, all right?"

"Did you just make a *Kung Fu* reference? They had that show in England?"

She ignored me. "If you wanna keep personal things personal, that's fine, as long as it doesn't tie my hands later on with this case. But if it's relevant to the shit we're dealing with, enough with the quiet act. You're gonna have to trust me eventually. No sense making me work twice as hard for no good reason."

Parnell's words made sense, and I knew she was right: I *would* have to trust her at some point. Butler had made this case personal, which meant my partner—if Parnell was indeed a full-fledged partner—would need to be let inside. It was all still so new. And overwhelming.

I sipped at my own tea, which, to my tongue, tasted pretty good. An old-fashioned sounded better, but this would do on a snowy night.

"Speaking of keeping personal things personal," I said, leaving it hanging there in the air.

She raised an eyebrow. "You're going to share something?"

"No. I'm hoping you will."

"Sorry, I'm not comfortable talking about what happened back in London."

I shook my head. "Not that."

It took her a moment, and then she got it. "Oh. Richter." Then she squinted at me. "Are you seriously snooping into that part of my life? Not the MI5 mystery, but *him*?"

"When we're working I'll probably be in the mood to hear you talk about work shit. But this is after hours, and I'm a big fan of rag magazines. I love me some dirt."

She rolled her eyes, then shrugged. "All right. What do you want to know?"

"Are you shitting me? All of it."

"Well, you won't get all of it. You're being kind of a pervert right now."

I laughed. "I don't mean the sexcapades, Parnell. I have to know how a former British agent marries a hitman."

For the longest time she just sat there, looking down at her glass. I figured I'd come this far, I wasn't going to give her an easy out.

Finally she said, "Richter was on a team of suspects we cornered on a case in Manchester. I have no idea what a Yank was doing there, but I guess he was helping out some old friend. The truth is, he had no idea of the scope of the operation; he was just muscle."

"How long ago was this?" I asked.

"Oh, three years ago? Four? Yeah. Anyway, I'd followed a lead to an office building. It was late, after midnight, and the place was pretty much deserted. I caught Richter alone in a room, had him raise his hands, and was about to cuff him. And the whole time he's flirting with me. I thought it was an act, and told him to shut up and turn around. And he kept coming on to me. I mean, it's the oddest situation: you're busting a guy, about to send him up for hard time, and he's asking my name, wants to know my number. He made some quip about the best cop's arse he'd ever seen. I'm almost laughing, but not quite.

"Anyway, I didn't notice the other one coming up behind until he clubbed me, knocking me down."

"So Richter was bullshitting, distracting you so the other guy could move in."

"That's what I thought. At first. But when the other guy pulls out a knife and is about to finish me off, Richter . . ."

I stopped with my glass of tea halfway to my mouth. "Oh, you've gotta be shitting me. Richter saved you?"

"He knocked this guy out. One punch. I just looked up at him like he was crazy."

"Okay. Then you married him?"

Parnell laughed and took her own sip. "No, there was a lag. He took my weapon, kind of tied me up loosely. Then picked up the other guy and was about to walk out. But he stopped, and he said, 'You never told me your name.' Well, he'd just saved my life. So I told him. He smiled and said he'd call me some time."

I narrowed my gaze at her. "You're making every bit of this up."

"I swear it's all true. He called me a month later, just as I was, well, having a difficult time at the office. I told him to meet me somewhere so I could arrest him, maybe leave my job on a high note."

"Instead you married him."

She finished her tea. "By the time I finally did meet up with him I'd left the organization. Looking for anything to shake up my life, really." I didn't respond, so she added: "Of course, it was all stupid. He didn't turn out to be a savior. Turns out he really just liked my arse."

IT WAS ALMOST nine o'clock when the boss reached out with a video call. Parnell and I had just returned from our tea party and were again parked outside the Nayar estate. I was behind the wheel this time.

"The team on the second floor finished going through the two coded messages," Quanta said. "The first one is complete garbage. Just a bunch of sentences lifted from random web sites and blog posts, we think. Enough to fill up a large binder, maybe 150 pages. Obviously meant to keep us distracted and busy."

"And the second message?" I asked.

Quanta looked pained. "I guess you could call it a manifesto."

CHAPTER SEVEN

I had to stifle a laugh. Which, given the circumstances, was the best course of action. Laughing at anything when you're investigating kidnapping and murder is generally frowned upon.

But come on. A manifesto? What makes every psychopath convinced the world is dying to hear their rambling, disjointed rants about anything? Did they learn nothing from the Unabomber and his abuse of quotation marks?

Personally, I've got a few things to say on just about every subject, too, but you won't find me publicly pontificating on them, and certainly not without a few more shots of rye in me. Even then my brilliance would be limited to people within a six-foot radius at the bar and would never make it into a Word document.

Manifesto authors were the people in your college Rhetoric and Composition class who never got to read their papers aloud to the other students. They were robbed of an audience back then, and, by God, they'd have an audience *now*.

I once proposed to an FBI agent that every manifesto

should be graded with a red pen and mailed back. She did not take my suggestion seriously.

And now, lo and behold, I discovered that Q2's Agent One, the guy I'd wondered about—and worried about—for so long, the first agent to really experience the miracle of investment, was a goddamned manifesto writer. It was enough to make you sick.

Instead of laughing, I just sighed. "You'll share the entire text, I'm sure," I said to Quanta. "But for now can you give us the bullet points?"

"The most succinct way to put it? Butler feels that Q2 and other law enforcement agencies tasked with protecting the security of the country are gutless. He believes he could do a better job of hunting down knaves and shutting down their operations."

I pondered this. "Wait. You're saying he and his team broke into two different high-security compounds, killed two people, kidnapped one of the country's greatest scientists and her granddaughter . . . all so he could do a better job of *law enforcement*?"

Now it was Parnell's turn to hold back a laugh. She put a hand over her mouth and turned toward the car window so she'd be out of camera view.

"Swan, we're dealing with an unstable mind," Quanta said, in what I recognized as her patient voice. "Whether or not his ultimate motive aligns with this rambling text is something we can unravel later. For the time being we'll assume he means what he says. Butler may have disappointed me in the long run, but generally he spoke the truth."

"And yet the truth from *an unstable mind* could be drastically different a week from now."

She gave one nod of her head. "I'll say this: The position

he's taking in his manifesto is congruent with the attitude he displayed during his tenure as a Q2 agent. At least during the last few months of his service."

I raised an eyebrow. At last I was being shown more than just the black-and-white dossier on Agent One. Was I getting a glimpse into the secret behind his departure? A government agent who believed he was destined to strike out on his own to defend national security?

If so, he wouldn't have been the first. History was littered with people and organizations frustrated by a civilized society's rules of law and order. A vigilante mindset was nothing new, especially in a country that, in many ways, still embraced a wild west mentality. Why wait around for the marshall when we could handle these outlaws ourselves?

The real danger was not in an individual's actions, but how those actions inspired others to do the same. Hive minds were bad enough; *bloodthirsty* hive minds were frightening.

Quanta closed out the video chat after saying, "Read through the file. We'll talk tomorrow morning at seven to discuss our next moves."

I grunted when the screen went blank. "Right. *Our* moves." I turned to my new British partner. "Thoughts?"

Parnell didn't answer at first, and just stared at the large snowflakes making silent, sloppy impacts against the windshield. I waited her out, watching the concentration on her face, the slight narrowing of her eyes. Like most good field agents, she'd learned to spend the bulk of her time digesting the facts of a case. Movie spies strolled onto the screen already knowing everything and simply flashed a gun, a dazzling smile, and killer abs; in the real world of espionage you invested hours inside your own head, working through hazy details and tenuous facts before ever getting a chance to flash a smile, an ab, or anything.

As I studied her in the faint light, I recalled one of our earliest meetings. On a ship in the Caribbean, a ship laden with island supplies and despicable characters, Parnell had wandered into my room. Within minutes it was obvious the lady had intentions, and talking shop wasn't at the top of the list. I'd turned down her sexual advances, which had surprised the hell out of her.

Look, Parnell was tough and could be downright vicious. I mean, the closest I'd come to actually fighting her was an entirely one-sided affair, and my ass was the one solidly whupped. But that hard attitude nestled inside a hard body that oozed sensuality, and I was likely the only straight man ever to tell her no.

From the moment she walked out of my cabin shaking her head, throughout our misadventures on the island, to her unexpectedly switching sides and saving my life—well, I don't think either one of us really knew how to behave around the other. The last 24 hours had, if anything, made it even more awkward. We were two hard-headed agents from very different backgrounds, with a strange history together and a foggy future, now answering to the same boss.

She finally tore her gaze from the snow and leaned against the passenger door to look at me. "If this Butler wanker is taking the time to leave trinkets and send messages, he has more on his agenda than just antagonizing Quanta. Although it seems he enjoys that, too."

Now it was her turn to study *my* face. "Are you sure the two of you have never interacted in some way?"

I shook my head. "Not that I know of."

"Nothing? No communication of any kind?"

"Oh, you mean besides spending every Christmas together and the trip we took to Greece? Do those count?"

She broke eye contact, obviously irritated, and went back to watching the snow. "All right, shithead. I had to ask."

"You only need to ask once."

This was our second edgy exchange in the last few hours. Maybe our limited experience working with partners was finally showing. I didn't like having to continually explain things and Parnell obviously wasn't too thrilled with having to pry for information. This was already going to be a long, difficult case without constantly sparring with someone who was on my side.

I decided to extend an olive branch, even if it was just in the form of a gentler tone of voice.

"Look, it's been a long stretch for me without a break, plus some major-league douchebag is running around with the hard drive containing my . . . my whatever you call it. My essence; my self. Anyway, no, I've never had any connection with Butler—that I know of, anyway—and I have no idea why he's infatuated with me. Maybe it's nothing more than the fact that I was the next Q2 agent hired after him."

Parnell looked skeptical. But so was I.

Putting the car in gear, I nodded to the phone resting on her leg. "Mind checking in with Poole? She'll have accommodations set up for us somewhere nearby. I need sleep, badly."

THE MID-RANGE HOTEL was set a half-mile off the highway. Parnell was tucked into her room on the 2nd floor, I was at the far end of the 3rd.

This is normally when I would upload my recent experiences. The process would take about 90 minutes, a stretch of time when I couldn't be asleep, and yet couldn't be active, either. For me it usually meant stretched out on a bed, reading one of my trashy celeb magazines, my guilty pleasure.

The equipment we used for this process was camouflaged in boring, everyday toiletry items, sure to be overlooked by snooping eyes. My experiences, including memories, feelings, everything, would be uploaded to the hard drive unit in the basement of Q2 headquarters. If and when I lost my life in the performance of my duty, that file would then be downloaded into a new body, one acquired in a deal with a felon serving a life sentence without possibility of parole. His family got a tax-free check for $2 million, and the felon got out of his cell.

He'd have no idea of the particulars; all they were ever told was that they were donating their body to the pursuit of science. Which, in a way, was true. They were also told they'd be serving their country.

I don't think that mattered one bit to most of the volunteers. They simply wanted to escape their lifelong confinement, and to find peace in the knowledge that they'd set up their families for life.

The problem this time around, however, lay in the fact that Butler had made off with the equipment I needed to upload my day's work. Obtaining a new hard drive wasn't an issue, but it might be a few days until I was able to actually use the system again.

Which meant I had to stay alive while, at the same time, pursuing a ruthless, deadly knave.

I'd left a text for Christina to call me when she got home, so when the phone vibrated I was immediately on it.

"How's my little chef?"

She scoffed. "I don't feel so little anymore." When I snickered she added, "It's not funny."

"Babe, of course it's funny. You're not even showing yet. Well, not much."

That elicited another scoff.

"Look," I said. "Down the road I may very well have fun at the expense of your girth and your pride, but at the moment you have to let me console you. Those are the unwritten rules of pregnancy. It's basically a husband's inalienable right and you have to take it, whether you think it's bullshit or not."

"All right," she said. "It's just that Antonio walked into my office this evening at the exact moment I was taking a bite from a Reese's."

"Yum."

"Hey, I've been so good," she said. "All week I haven't touched one shitty thing, and tonight, the *one time* I allow myself a piece of chocolate, he has to walk in. He looked at me like I was murdering his child."

I laughed, and it felt good. "Oh, tell Antonio to back off. You can have all the damned Reese's you want. I'll bring you home a bag or three."

"Well, from now on I won't have them at work. Those will be rewards when I get home and get off my feet." She took a drink of something, probably her trusty hot tea. "Where are you? Still in Rhode Island?"

"Uh-huh. Probably leaving tomorrow."

"And?"

I exhaled, long and loud. "Quanta's on edge like I've never seen before, I'm already fighting with my new partner, and I'm now officially on the trail of a lunatic. A deadly lunatic."

"Partner?"

"What?"

"You said partner. Since when?"

"Oh," I said. "Since this morning. A new recruit."

"Wow. So he's, what, shadowing you or something? Like an intern?"

"No, not an intern. Pretty much a certified badass. And she, not he. Former British intelligence, now on our team."

"The British badass," Christina said. "Well, stop pissing her off."

"How do you know she didn't piss *me* off?"

"Please."

I pretended to sulk for a moment. "I don't want to talk about the case anymore tonight. Like you don't want to talk about your belly."

"Shut up about my belly."

After a pause we both laughed, softly, with a collective relief that the day was over.

At least I *acted* like it was over. No sense dumping my sense of dread onto Christina. She had her own work stress to deal with, not to mention another couple's child she was toting around.

When we finally broke the connection I settled in with my tablet and opened Butler's manifesto.

CHAPTER EIGHT

I 'm sure they're wonderful people. They're probably charming, well-read, and generous, and I'll bet they call their moms on Mother's Day.

But I don't know their names, not one of them. I'll never join them at the bar for cocktails, nor will I ever pin a heart on one of their social media posts.

To me they've always been "the smarty-pants on the second floor," or something similarly dismissive.

There's nothing intentionally hostile in my attitude. Like I said, I wouldn't know any of them if they came up and goosed me on the ass.

But there *is* a sort of simmering resentment on my part that's perfectly natural. At least its natural according to our shrink, Miller.

During one of our sessions I'd made a random derogatory comment about Q2's personnel on the second floor and Miller actually nodded while smiling.

"Did I say something funny?" I asked at the time.

"No," Miller had said. "Well, yes, it was funny. But I'm

smiling because you're always so worried about losing touch with your humanity and yet you demonstrate plenty of all-too-human emotions."

"They're total strangers and I called them turd-lickers. I would've thought you'd scold me for being immature, not start nodding in agreement."

He wrote in his notebook while he answered. "Oh, it was completely immature, Swan, but channeling your inner fifth-grade-boy is pretty much your baseline. No, you're reacting normally to a certain threat level."

I remember chewing on that statement for a moment before asking him to explain.

He set down his notebook. "It's pretty simple if you look at it from above. Quanta might issue your actual marching orders and send you off on a mission where you could be killed. But Quanta doesn't make those decisions in a vacuum. The department on the second floor sifts through mounds of data, examines hours and hours of audio and video, after which they compile their reports and send them off to your boss.

"So, really," he added, "*they're* the ones responsible for the cases you're assigned. If you're killed, it's because of the information they discovered and passed along to Quanta."

"So I'm, what? Subconsciously lashing out at them for putting me in harm's way? But I knew what the job entailed when I signed up."

"Sure you did," Miller said. "But it's human instinct to resent anyone who contributes to your harm, and especially to your death. They become your boogeyman. Your, um, turd-lickers, to use your creative vocabulary."

"Do me a favor," I'd said to Miller before leaving his office that day. "Please don't ever use that expression again. It sounds perfect when I say it, but coming out of *your* mouth it makes me cringe."

Now, more than a year after that conversation in an office at Q2 headquarters, I sat propped up on a bed in a Rhode Island hotel and looked at the data translation supplied by the worker-bees on the second floor.

Butler's manifesto sprawled for nearly 4,000 words, and he got off to a rollicking start in his opening sentence:

"THERE'S nothing sadder or more disheartening to the evolved human species than talent and advantage that are neglected and wasted."

ALL RIGHT, so far I couldn't disagree with him.

He followed his thesis statement with a rambling litany of examples, some from world history, some from the business world, some from sports. If you ever wondered what ancient Rome had in common with the New York Yankees, all you had to do was ask Butler and he'd spell it out.

After a bloated 900-word sidebar on the back-and-forth dance between criminal masterminds and law enforcement, he began to steer the argument toward his views on protecting the masses from nefarious types. He referenced Q2 only obliquely at first, casually using phrases like *secretive government agencies* and *shadow operatives*.

It began to coalesce with this:

FINALLY, through the development of a technology unappreciated by its creator and misapplied by its overseer, we come to the ultimate case of bungled advantage. Government, whose primary responsibility is the protection of its citizens, was gifted an opportunity to infiltrate and eliminate the worst of mankind. Instead, it weakly stood by and did only enough to justify a few jobs, too timid to hurl a veritable thunderbolt into the dark underbelly of human behavior, lest the government officials be accused of playing God.

Fools! It was a naive God Maker who bestowed the tools in the first place! And now a chance to dominate the battle against devils has been squandered. Which, in itself, is a crime since the time will come when this same thunderbolt falls into the hands of those far less likely to tremble before its magnificent power.

FORGIVING his occasional lapse into comic book prose, like *tremble before its magnificent power*, Butler did have a way with words. The guy could've been a first-rate speech writer for numbskull politicians, turning dog shit into a Boston cream pie that the public would eat up.

What I couldn't get past was the break in logic. He obviously was a big fan of the science behind the investment program, and in its application, even though, in his mind, the program behind it was too timid. Or, rather, its leaders were.

And yet how could a rational mind justify the most heinous of crimes in the pursuit of justice? To kill in order to stop murder?

I let the tablet drop onto my lap and stared at the wall across from me.

I killed people in order to stop murder. I had for years. And, with only a few exceptions, I lost not one moment of sleep after putting the bad guys down. They deserved it. They were the devils in Butler's manifesto.

In other words . . . I still agreed with him.

Suddenly I dredged up the old argument over whose life was expendable for the sake of a civilized society, who *deserved* to die in order that others could live. If a homicidal freak threatened the lives of innocent people, I had no qualms about taking them out.

On top of that, I had no qualms about having no qualms.

Were Butler and I *that* different?

I got up, went to the minibar, pulled out a diet soda, then put it back and grabbed the full-sugar variety. I wanted every bit of kick I could get. I was disgusted with myself, disgusted that I could let a maniac like Butler seep into my brain and start working on me before I'd even had the chance to come face-to-face with the bastard.

What I did in my line of work was necessary. It was the dirty job nobody wanted to know about, let alone *talk* about. The cleanup crew, the sanitation department for human garbage, the guy who pumped out the septic system of life's miscreants so that John and Joanne Public could listen to their cozy mystery audiobooks on the way home from work and then sit on their back deck, drink a cold beer, and plan the usual summer trip to Lake Powell or Bar Harbor.

I drank half of the soda in two gulps, let out a wall-shaking belch, then paced back and forth between the window and the bathroom. As much as I hated to admit it, I could use a good chat with Miller right now. It pissed me off when I began to question my duties, which was a roundabout way of questioning my own soul. Or lack thereof. How many times would I need to defend my actions to myself? And what impact did these doubts have on the performance of my duties?

Still holding the soda can, I sat back on the edge of the bed and flipped the tablet around to read some more. Butler cited a few of his Q2 assignments where things turned exceptionally ugly. Well, we all had those stories. But he suggested that the problems could've been better handled with a larger team of agents. Why, he wondered, did Q2 refuse to expand the program beyond the single soldier they used? What kept the brain trust—a phrase he obviously used in a pejorative manner —from inserting an army of *immortal*—his word—killers into the field? Why just one? What were they afraid of?

As he said at one point: "*If you're going to commit, commit!*"

This is where I began to separate from Butler's argument. There was no way in hell I'd advocate for a large, unruly army of invested agents. I sometimes wondered how Q2 managed four, and now, with Parnell, five.

I'd often worried over whether I showed enough appreciation for life, given my ability to start over again. But it dawned on me that Agent One showed practically *no* value for life. The way he went on and on about sending in waves of investment agents to clear out undesirables smacked of someone who treated life like video game characters who could just level up and start the battle again.

And once you fell into that trap you *did* lose your last connection with humanity. It reminded me of the historic battles where soldiers would line up abreast, then marched together into a slaughter side-by-side, mowed down by enemy fire as they advanced. Butler would do the same, if given a chance. He'd stock Q2 with dozens, if not hundreds, of disposable soldiers, all in the name of law and order.

Toward the end of his rant, Butler got down to real business:

FOR THE LAST few years I've kept an eye on the operations coming out of Q2, hoping that my wish for a more-determined approach to the investment program would take shape. Alas, no.

Q2, and by extension the whole of the federal government's law enforcement divisions, won't do what's not only practical, but necessary.

Therefore, given my experience and my determination, it's fallen to me to make substantive changes to the way good confronts evil. I've taken steps to introduce a private, underground team of agents working for a just cause.

And not just for the United States. Evil surely isn't limited to one nation or one continent. Through an accelerated program of agent acquisition, I will lead a global revolution against crime. My agents won't struggle against the shackles of Q2's insipid management.

It begins with acquisition of the investment technology along with a starter set of suitably-aggressive champions.

Besides the services of the mother of investment, Devya Nayar, I'll require an audience with my successor at Q2. On the afternoon of the 7th Eric Swan is to report to me.

Details and location forthcoming.

This will be your only chance. Don't screw it up.

WHO WERE those last two sentences directed to? Was he speaking to Quanta, as in the organization's only chance at rescue and recovery? Or to me, as in my only chance to confront the shadowy myth whose legacy loomed large?

What struck me at the moment was the time lag. It was

nearly midnight on the 5th; Butler was making an appointment two full days out.

nearly midnight on the 5th; Butler was making an appointment two full days out.

There were methods to his madness that I saw right away. For one thing it gave him more time with Devya while we sat around with our thumbs up our asses, awaiting his final instructions. That was bad enough, and probably chafed Quanta more than anything.

But what I couldn't help but notice was that Agent One, the supposed-maniac Butler, had planted seeds in me and was giving them two full days to germinate.

He might be crazy, but he was still brilliant. And he had to know I'd be aware of what he was doing—which, in some respects, made it even more bold and impressive.

As an agent you understand some cases will be almost entirely action-oriented. You show up, you shoot-em-up, you wipe your hands and walk away.

But then there are cases that are much more thought-intensive. Oh, there will still be action and violence, but much of your time will be spent getting inside the head of your prey. Sort of John McClane meets Sherlock Holmes.

Butler was going all Sherlock on me right now, and probably loving every second of it. I know I would.

I set the tablet on the nightstand and stretched out sideways across the bed. Part of me felt like reading through the entire manifesto again, but I rejected the idea for now. I knew where the bastard stood on things, and clearly he'd selected me to pick on. Not Quanta, the primary target of his anger. Me.

Why would he do that? What could he gain from roping me into the affair?

Apparently I'd find out in 48 hours.

CHAPTER NINE

The coffee from the hotel's cheap breakfast buffet was surprisingly good, one of those small, unexplainable joys that can brighten a day. The rest of the fare was bland and borderline inedible, so I pocketed two of the pre-packaged blueberry muffins into my hoodie and, with coffee in both hands, took the stairs to the second floor and kicked on the bottom of Parnell's door.

She opened it but didn't wait for me to enter, making her way in a scratchy hotel robe back to her steamed-up bathroom.

"I brought you coffee," I said, walking past her and setting the cups down on the room's dresser.

"Not a coffee drinker, thanks," she called out from the bathroom. "Although it can't be worse than the tea at this inn."

"That bad?"

"Abominable."

I chuckled. "Oh-for-two, counting the bar last night." Walking to the window, I opened the curtains and gazed at the rear parking lot. A single set of car tracks cut through the small deposit of snow.

"Usually travel with a small packet of my own for just this occasion," Parnell said, her voice echoing. Then, after a pause: "For a nation that takes itself so seriously, you're unable to make a tolerable cup of tea. Don't know how you can claim to be the world's superpower when you're clearly uncivilized."

"What?" I said, feigning offense. "You don't care for the wide assortment of fabulous fruity choices in that little woven basket by the coffee maker?"

She leaned her head out of the bathroom long enough to fix me with a flat look that said everything without the need for words.

I removed the jeans slung across the corner chair and sat down, tossing the jeans onto the bed. I reached over and picked up one of the coffee cups and tried to ignore the scattered undergarments near my feet.

A minute later Parnell came out of the bathroom with her short hair brushed back and just a slight touch of makeup on her face. The robe came off, leaving her in another set of underclothes. She put the jeans on and, with no sign whatsoever of unease, fumbled through the small bag next to me until latching onto a clean shirt.

I sipped my coffee and realized there wasn't the slightest bit of sexual suggestiveness in her movements. The British spy wasn't trying to turn me on; she was simply reminding me how cut she was, how my new partner could more than handle anything dangerous tossed into our path. After venting her frustrations the night before, this was the punctuation mark. I got the message loud and clear.

"What did you think of your homework assignment last night?" I asked.

Parnell began picking up items from around the room and stuffing them into her bag. "Mostly boring."

I waited a moment before saying, "That's it? Boring?"

"Well, yeah. The usual posturing. Butler's much more verbose than the usual criminal asshole, but cut through all the puffery and it's the same message: *'I'm smarter than everyone else so I'll win.'* Boring."

I managed a "Huh," and took another sip of coffee.

She paused in her packing. "Are you asking specifically about his request to meet with you? At least that part's not boring. But it's also not surprising. Seems like he's wanted to connect with you from the beginning."

She went back to work, striding to the bathroom and returning with a handful of things that disappeared into the bag. She sat on the edge of the bed, glanced around to see if she'd missed anything, then leaned forward with her elbows on her knees. "Those are my thoughts," she said. "Now your turn."

I set the coffee back onto the dresser. "I, for one, didn't find it boring. I thought a lot of what he said made sense."

"Are you joking?"

"I know it's out of character but this time I'm not. Hey, I don't agree with his solution, but he does lay out the problem accurately. Crime is still crime, but criminal *behavior* has evolved. I know for certain that social media and all its viral bullshit makes a lot of people try to raise the bar on outrageous behavior. Anything to get noticed, anything to be in the spotlight, get people talking about you. *Just be famous*, isn't that the motto of an entire generation? Only stands to reason the same mentality would apply to bad guys. And especially to the *worst* guys."

"What does that have to do with you agreeing with Butler?" Parnell asked.

"It's a matter of countermeasures. The dark side keeps

upping the ante on malicious activity, so if law enforcement remains static—using the same techniques and tactics we've used for decades—our efforts will end up woefully inadequate. It'll get harder and harder to keep up with people whose only goal is to be more outrageous than the last shithead. Look, in Butler's file it mentions a brief connection to organized crime, some incident from his younger days. He knows exactly the kind of people who have made careers out of raising the bar. The investment program is one of the tools that tips the scales to our side." I paused, then added: "For now."

She stared at me. "But this lunatic isn't interested in using the technology for defense. He wants to go on offense with it."

"And that's where I *dis*agree with him," I said. "I'm just not sure exactly where the line is drawn."

Parnell's steady gaze didn't waver. "I assume you won't be sharing these thoughts with Quanta."

"Oh, hell no. I'm still not even sure what it all means. I'm just working through it and you're my sounding board. Quanta sucks as a sounding board, but that's not her job." I stood up. "And don't spend too much time analyzing what I just told you. It'll just distract you. Besides, my position is bound to change over the next 24 to 48 hours."

I picked up the first coffee cup and drained it, then swapped it for the second. "You're packing as if we're leaving. I haven't heard anything from the boss yet. Besides, we're meeting with her in just a few minutes."

"*You're* meeting with her," Parnell said. "She's called me back."

It was my turn to stare. "Why?"

She shook her head, then stood and grabbed her bag. "I don't know. Called me at five this morning and told me to get back."

Walking toward the door she paused and gave one last glance around the room, then looked back at me. "I'm taking the car. Someone will drop off another for you later. Goodbye. I'm sure we'll be in touch."

And just like that she was gone.

It took a full minute for me to realize I was just standing there, dumbfounded, holding a quickly-cooling cup of coffee, watching the hotel room door.

The coffee no longer appealed to me. I walked to the bathroom, dumped it down the sink, and went back to my own room for the seven o'clock video chat with Quanta.

SHE LOOKED HAGGARD, which didn't surprise me. Her recall of Parnell, however, did.

"I'm surprised you ordered her back. Did something pop up between midnight and five?" I asked.

"Butler and his partner have divided their forces. His accomplice took the granddaughter to some other remote location while Butler keeps Devya Nayar."

"How do you know this?"

"You do realize you're not the only person he's taunting, right?"

"He reached out to you? For someone who made it a point to stay silent for a few years he sure is chirpy now. Any details?"

"Only that he intends to meet with you. Alone."

"And that irks the shit out of you, doesn't it?" I said. Before she could answer I added, "How do you know for sure he separated them? Why would you believe anything he says?"

"Because that's exactly what I'd do if I were him."

It *did* make sense. Butler would know we were devoting all

our resources to this case, so naturally he'd want to divide them. "What are you going to have Parnell do?"

"She'll come back here to Washington until we get a lead. I want her free to act on her own when the time comes to move."

A thought occurred to me. "What about the other Q2 agents? What the hell are *they* doing during all this?"

Even on the small screen I made out Quanta's pissed-off look, but her voice remained composed. "Let me worry about the duty assignments. You take care of your own chores and everyone else can take care of theirs."

I started to grumble that I wasn't seeing anyone else doing squat, but there were plenty of things that Quanta kept from me. She'd once mentioned there were three other agents in the investment program, but for all I knew there were a dozen by now. The organization kept us in the dark about each other, for reasons I might never be privy to. The entire operation was so deep into the shadows that you couldn't even count the players.

She changed the subject. "Let's talk about this meeting that Butler wants with you."

"He's going to want to do more than just talk," I said. "The plan is for me to become the third hostage, right?"

"Undoubtedly. And you'll go with him, with no theatrics."

We were on the same page. Trying to take out Butler without knowing where Devya was being held could mean a quick death to both her and her granddaughter.

"You can't download today," she told me. "But you're going to have a visitor in a few minutes. He's dropping off a car for you, and bringing an STC. The new sleeper model."

I grinned. "You still refuse to call it the zombie model."

She waved a hand at the screen. "Call it whatever you like.

Leave your weapon with the agent. From here on out you go unarmed."

Although to the untrained this might sound foolish, it was pretty standard for us if we knew in advance that we'd be voluntarily walking into the lion's den. No sense handing over more weapons to them.

"Until I need to borrow one from the other team," I said.

Ignoring this, Quanta said we'd talk as soon as Butler made his move.

As PROMISED, the coded tap on the door arrived minutes after we'd disconnected. A severe-looking man of about forty strode into the room with what looked like a typical computer bag.

"Nice to know house calls haven't gone the way of the VCR," I said, rolling up my sleeve.

He wasted no time or energy whatsoever with small talk. Glancing at what I was doing, he gave a cold shake of his head. "Not there. We're putting it under your scalp."

It was my least favorite spot for the subcutaneous tracking chip—what we called an STC—but I'd get nowhere arguing with this machine of a man. Some people were completely humorless, which, at least to me, didn't fit with this particular job. If I was going to be shoving an electronic device under the skin of a total stranger, I'd try to make them laugh, or at least attempt to make them feel comfortable.

With a sigh I sat down on the chair and expressed my dismay as he put on latex gloves and probed around the back of my head.

"What do you guys have against arms?" I asked.

Without breaking his rhythm he said, "Another possibility

is within the lining of your rectum. I'm guessing you wouldn't prefer that."

I pushed his arm away and craned my head around to look up at him. "You're kidding, right?"

All he did was raise an eyebrow. I let him go back to work.

But something in my personality made it impossible for me to not badger the humorless. "Zombie model, right, Doc? What's it set for?"

"Yes, the sleeper unit," he said, apparently finding a spot he liked. He extracted a small scalpel. "Five every fifteen, rotating pattern."

The STC was a digital tracking device, incredibly small and flat, so it slipped just below the surface of the skin without standing out. The incision was small enough that it didn't leave a noticeable wound, but even so Q2 often insisted that agents wear them under the hair on their head to elude discovery from a cursory inspection.

But tracking devices can also be found with other electronic gadgets, often with a sweeping device over the body. The sleeper unit, or zombie model as I liked to call it, was dead most of the time. It put out no signal because it was completely inert, just a tiny wafer with impossibly small electronics inside, hardly enough to set off any kind of alarm. You could walk through airport security with one. But each could be programmed to briefly come alive at various times in order to pulse a few seconds of signal before going dead again.

In this case, based on what the technicians had told me, the zombie would wake for all of five seconds every fifteen minutes, with a signal that rotated its frequency. If you were searched with any kind of electronic device, the odds of a bad guy scanning you during those five seconds in a quarter-hour space of time were approximately 180 to 1, and that was for just *one* frequency. It was up to Q2's wizards to wait for the beep, coordinate its location, and then pounce when the time was right.

I felt the sting of the blade about where my spine met my skull, still below the hair. The rest of the process took almost no time at all: slip the wafer in, smooth the flap of skin, and dab it with super glue. Damned near impossible to see or to feel.

And much better, I had to admit, than dropping my drawers and bending over the table. That sounded preposterous to me and I told him so.

"Yes, it *is* preposterous," he said, closing his satchel. "I wasn't serious." Then he held up a set of rental car keys. "It's a BMW. Turn right out the hotel's front door. Good luck." Ten seconds later, after taking possession of my Glock, he was gone.

It took me a moment to realize the dour-faced bastard had totally punked me.

CHAPTER TEN

There are certain occupations where sitting around is just part of the job. During a professional baseball season, players might have entire days to kill. I'd heard a lot of them played golf or went fishing.

Despite the fact that heroics become necessary at crunch time, firefighters often fill the space between calls by cleaning the equipment and vehicles, cooking for the rest of the crew, mixing in fitness training, or just watching TV. And sleeping.

I know a guy who worked overnights at a hotel's front desk and used the peace and quiet to write his first novel.

Secret agents have way more down time than movies would lead you to believe. But can you imagine a James Bond film where 007 sits on his ass all day waiting to hear from one of the Spectre goons?

And yet that would be way more accurate than the frenetic pace we see on the screen. In reality, spies move in spurts, and while at times those spurts can roll out at breakneck speed, more often we're bored beyond belief. I only complained about this to Christina one time; her deadpan reply was succinct: "Why don't you use the time to listen to self-help audiobooks?"

A world-class chef in a Michelin-rated restaurant is on her feet and scrambling for hours on end each night. That made Christina the last person who'd dish up sympathy to a bored spy.

I had a full day until Butler came forth with info. It was another reason I was slightly pissed about Parnell's recall to Washington. Sure, I'd worked solo my entire career, but what was the use of getting a new partner if she wasn't around to help pass the down time? The weather wasn't horrendous but it also wasn't conducive to walking around outside. And a movie was out because my brain was too busy clicking through the details of my real-life case to concentrate on fictional drama.

Ultimately I wound up reading through Butler's rambling manifesto again. There was a portion which now captured my full attention.

SHACKLES COME IN MANY FORMS. The most debilitating is the fear of death, which, even in normal everyday life, can be a subconscious anchor, dragging against the bottom and preventing us from cresting at peak performance. How much has that prevented the average person from achieving anything beyond the safe and the mundane? How much has even the smallest threat of death pulled in the reins on those who otherwise would burst forth, out of the pack, and past the barriers we—simply through instinct—dread to approach? Daredevil performers aren't applauded because they have special physical skills; we admire them because they cast off the oppressive cloak of fear, and they rise!

AGAIN, it made sense. Lunatics may be nuts, but it doesn't mean *everything* they say is unworthy of consideration. It's that fuzzy border between insanity and brilliance. If crazy geniuses had their own club, Isaac Newton might be its president but he'd have to fend off a shit-ton of challengers.

Butler's point was evident: Purge the grim reaper from the unconscious mind and our inner drive would keep the pedal to the metal with no fear of consequence. When it came to cleaning up the most wicked individuals walking the Earth, a stable of pseudo-immortals would almost be better than the Avengers.

While I concurred with him on some of the advantages, there was an element to the investment process that prevented me from buying in completely: Why fight for the good of humanity if the method used to wage that war eroded the basic foundation of what made us human in the first place?

Cheating death bypassed perhaps the most important failsafe in our mental programming. Ask yourself: How differently would you behave if there was no *game-over*? And I don't mean just for yourself; how differently would you behave toward *others* when you factored that same element into the equation?

Sure, you could argue that it's only Q2 agents who—for now—hold this god-like ability in their hands. But after time, does that distinction become less and less relevant to a being who adopts a calloused view of the sanctity of life? After you've been killed and revived numerous times, you lose the awe you once held, the appreciation for life. How long could it take until *nobody's* life inspired reverence?

A popular trope from life coaches and social media memes is to "live like you're dying." But what if that's no longer an option?

As the first active participant in the program, surely Butler had considered these same questions, the ones that gnawed at me whenever I allowed them access to my conscious thoughts. How many of the other Q2 agents struggled with the same dilemma? If we'd all been subjected to the same vesting procedures, and each been required to pass through identical personality filters, wouldn't every agent carry the same doubts?

Or perhaps we did *now*. Maybe Agent One had lacked this particular ingredient in his chemical makeup, which led him to wash out. Or, rather, led to him being expunged.

For me these thought patterns were on an endless loop. Each question I raised only uncovered a dozen others, and all of it explained why I had no problem visiting with Miller, the Q2 shrink. At least he could be an outlet for my intellectual turmoil.

At the moment he was 400 miles away, and I was alone with my existential demons.

I decided to go for a drive in the light snow, and later ended up at a movie after all. The romantic comedy was exceptionally bad, but the popcorn—the theater's first batch of the day—was divine.

By the time I got outside, the skies had cleared and the still-impotent sun managed to reflect off the thin layer of snow without imparting much heat. A used book store across the street offered another 30 minutes of distraction and I walked out with a dog-eared paperback of Agatha Christie short stories.

The book was sprawled open across my chest when I woke up from a late-afternoon nap. I hadn't figured out whodunnit when I'd nodded off, but confidence was high that Hercule Poirot would soon save the day.

I checked my phone. No calls, no messages. It was almost seven o'clock.

THREE HOURS later the phone vibrated. The message was simple enough: *Instructions at 9a tomorrow.*

This was a gift from Agent One. It meant I could grab a late-night snack, catch some sleep, and be fully refreshed for the circus that was sure to be pulling into town in the morning.

By eleven I was sound asleep.

I rose at six, devoted some time to the hotel treadmill, ordered a light breakfast of mostly protein, and drank only water.

This particular body held up nicely. The convict who'd once occupied it had done a good job of keeping it toned and taut, although I could tell there'd been damage to the left knee at some point in the past. Sherilyn, my favorite tech in Q2's basement lab, recommended one of those flexible knee braces, which helped a little. But after wrapping up my last case—the one where I'd intentionally pissed myself—I'd washed the brace in a hotel bathroom sink and accidentally left it behind.

As long as I limited my run to five miles, and at a sensible pace, a few ibuprofen kept the ache under control.

The convict also either had great ocular genes or consumed mass quantities of carrots, because I appreciated the hawk-like vision. Other than that it was about the most average body I'd had in a long time.

Getting acquainted with a different body is like dating: you almost don't want to know everything right away because it can be overwhelming. Little sips, that's how I explained it to Parnell during one of our drives. Just take little sips, sampling it slowly until you feel reasonably comfortable. I even tended to avoid mirrors as much as possible, because until you live inside the skin for a while you're apt to fixate on something you see, which, in turn, might influence your otherwise-natural, reflexive ability to adapt.

So I noticed the knee issue the moment I stood up for the first time, appreciated the superior vision the next day during a walk near my condo, but only after three days did I pick up on just how much of a receding hairline I now had. A shitty follicle gene was the price I paid for the vision, I suppose.

Some of that mattered, much did not. The container might be reasonably important, but the contents poured into it are what counted. As long as my essence hadn't corrupted from overuse, the convict's body would function well enough to chase down bad guys.

And, if all went as planned, the entire package—skin, bones, and essence—would be put to the test within the next 24 hours.

PROMPT AS EVER, Butler texted at exactly nine. No wasted characters, just an address, a deadline, and the words *White Civic*. I had 30 minutes to make the appointment. That wouldn't be a problem. I was packed and ready to go.

His choice of meeting point told me a lot: A big box store in Fall River, just over the border in Massachusetts. It was clear Butler intended to dial up a pretty standard carousel of meetings. That meant I'd hurry to the first stop for additional instructions, rush to *that* location, then continue the hop, skip, and jump routine at least four or five times. Nobody trusted anyone, so it would've been a waste of time to add *Make sure you come alone*. We all knew someone would try tailing me at first, but wouldn't persist if things became intricate.

Thus the STC in the back of my head.

The runaround was also a subtle power play, just enough mindless dashing around to create a sense of status. Butler no doubt was anxious to establish the hierarchy in our relationship, and to make sure I knew our respective places in it. Fine, whatever got him off.

The brief respite from the snow had ended and I drove through a fresh layer of light powder. I got to the parking lot of the store and made a cursory pass up and down the rows. The only Honda Civic I saw was silver and it was driven by a tired-looking mother with a car full of three boisterous kids.

Then I saw it. Parked in the store's overflow lot, the one that generally didn't fill up until the holiday season, sat a somewhat-battered white Civic with very dark tinted windows. And, to make sure I found it, someone had tied a large white helium-filled balloon to a windshield wiper. I parked, then studied the car for a moment. It was empty.

Killing the engine and climbing out of my BMW I glanced around the lot, which was pointless. There would be someone watching, but *they* wouldn't have a gaudy balloon flying above them. Strolling to the Civic I spotted an envelope tucked under the wiper where the balloon string was tied. I pulled it out, opened it, and found a small piece of paper with two words:

Get in.

Not surprising. Piece by piece Butler would transition me from Q2's world to his, and it began with ditching my vehicle. There were other ways to track me, of course, but he was eliminating the easiest.

I locked the BMW, then bent over and set the fob on top of the right rear tire, out of sight beneath the fender. It was a fairly standard hiding spot when we needed to leave one of our expensive rides behind for the agency to pick up.

Before getting in the grubby Civic I yanked the balloon from the wiper and let it float away. Once behind the wheel I grimaced at the condition of my new transportation. At least fifteen years old and showing every minute of it. Someone had squeezed the final drops of dignity from the poor little car. I imagined the owner of the other Civic I'd seen in the lot would be experiencing the same conditions after her kids had their way with it for another few years.

Now all I needed was a destination. Right on cue, my phone trembled and I had a new address, this time in Worcester. I was given 63 minutes to reach a Dairy Queen there, which would be cutting it close. There was a key in the ignition, and the Civic started right up, because that's what Civics do. I cracked the windows in hope that a cross-breeze, even a cold one, would help to mitigate the awful smell inside the car.

I chalked it up to more of Butler's need to subjugate me. Whatever.

With a sigh, I said goodbye to the perfectly good luxury vehicle I was leaving behind and pulled onto the main road, heading toward Worcester.

CHAPTER ELEVEN

The car could have used some TLC, but otherwise ran okay. The only obvious need was an alignment; it was a battle to keep it from veering off the road to the right. I glanced at the directions on my phone, then settled in.

But not for long. Once I reached the Providence area a new text arrived, cancelling the drive to Worcester and plugging in a new address, this time in New London, Connecticut.

So this was how it would play out. Butler planned on me sharing my itinerary, and no doubt expected a squad of agents hightailing it to my next stop. I'm sure he got a kick out of orchestrating the mad rush to one spot, then cancelling it and sending the convoy scurrying off in another direction.

At some point, though, the game would have to end.

Ten minutes out from New London I was diverted toward Hartford. Before arriving there the detour flipped me south again toward New Haven. I'd discovered that the cruise control didn't work, which was annoying. Probably intentionally so. The Civic had a full tank, so that wasn't an issue. At some point, though, my bladder *would* be. And apparently

Butler planned on that, too. On the outskirts of New Haven I was directed to a fast food joint and told to grab a quick lunch to eat in the car, and to use the facilities. It looked like this might take hours. I did my best to keep my irritation in check.

And to keep quiet. I had to assume the beater was bugged.

By two o'clock I was parked, as instructed, in a vast, empty parking lot of an abandoned warehouse site on the outskirts of Danbury, Connecticut. I'd been behind the wheel for five hours and was pretty much sick of the whole thing. Road trips are fun unless some asshat is calling all the shots. With no further message awaiting, I got out of the car and stretched my legs. I thought about calling Quanta, but if I was under surveillance—which was a fair bet—I didn't want to give them the satisfaction of seeing me phone home. So I paced back and forth, occasionally picking up a small rock to chuck across the lot.

After five minutes that felt like 50, the next message arrived. Back to Providence. Another three hours on the road.

Besides his childish need to knock me down a few pegs, there were two legitimate reasons for Butler leading me on a tour of New England. One, he and his flunkies would have ample opportunities to spot any Q2 tails on me, and two, a day spent in a cramped car would dull anyone's physical and mental abilities, regardless of their conditioning. I grew up loving road trips, but after eight hours in a car all I wanted was a cocktail and bed.

The delay in Danbury made me think the end was near. It had the feel of a two-minute warning, where the action stopped and the coaches huddled to plan the last series of plays for a big finish.

Entering Providence a new text came in, directing me to a particular exit. After that came step-by-step directions as I made my way into the city. Turn left here. Turn right there. No advance warning of a final destination. Keeping the tension ratcheted up. This was definitely going to be the final stop.

As soon as a light turned green I was directed around a corner to a parking garage at a shopping area. I flexed my fingers along the steering wheel, trying to limber up. Without cruise control my legs also felt the burn, even after my brief stroll.

I rolled down my window, punched the button at the garage entrance, and took my ticket. A new text said: *Level four*.

Behind me a car stopped at the same ticket dispenser. And just sat there. Blocking traffic.

On level four a car pulled out of a space and the driver waved at me, indicating I should pull into the vacated spot.

"Here we go," I muttered beneath my breath.

The moment I put the car in park the side doors of the van next to me flew open and two men wearing ski masks pointed very menacing weapons at my face.

"Out. Fast," was all one of them said.

When I climbed out a dark hood was thrown over my head and I was shoved onto the back floor of the van. One man planted a knee in my back and zip-tied my hands behind me, all the while pressing down on me with all the strength he had.

Through the thick hood I said, "Jesus, take it easy." For my trouble I received a kidney punch and gasped.

I've test-driven lots of bodies through the years, and I'm here to tell you that very few could take that particular shot, especially with no warning, without uttering that gasp. You can pump iron all day, tough guy, but unless you've got one of those flak jackets you see quarterbacks wearing, well, you feel that punch all the way up to your throat and back down into your balls. If I started pissing blood some dickhead was going to get an ass-whooping.

The van started, and I heard the Civic fire up, too. Which meant someone would drive it right out of the garage and, with those ridiculously-dark windows, it would appear I was simply continuing my run-around.

I wasn't too concerned. The STC in my head was all Quanta needed to find me.

While I tried to recuperate from the sucker punch it occurred to me: Butler would have to suspect I was wired somehow. And, sure enough, I was flipped over onto my back and my babysitter proceeded to rip open my shirt. In the next minute I was thoroughly frisked, not just for weapons but for gadgets. At one point the search became intimate, but I was a good boy and kept quiet.

I heard the Civic pull out of its parking spot and speed away. Minutes later the van we were in did the same. I had the impression of three people in the vehicle with me, including the bastard who'd hit me and then ripped my shirt apart. Nobody spoke. In fact, during the entire abduction I'd heard a total of two syllables.

Now, as we rolled down a ramp toward the garage exit a radio came on. The music was bloody awful, as Parnell might say, but it wasn't for my enjoyment. They'd blinded me with the hood, and now they were covering any external sounds that might offer any clues. Probably covering their own muted conversations up front, as well.

I settled in for the ride, trying to clear my mind and get centered. To not let the violent punch or manhandling throw me off my game. Not let the fact that getting myself killed on this assignment would be the *actual* end, since the hard drive holding my stored essence was gone. And not let the sounds of 80s synth-pop push me into suicidal thoughts.

It's hard to gauge time when your head's cocooned, but after what seemed an hour we turned onto a road that couldn't have been paved. The van bounced through serious ruts, which, when you're prone on a hard surface, is not too different from getting beat up. Despite my efforts to remain stoic, I grunted more than once.

Then we came to a full stop. I was thankful the bumping and banging was over, but slightly happier that the music was killed. I could take a few more miles of physical torture, but only if they'd drive toward the 21st century.

The sliding side door was thrown back and a cold wind shot through the inside of the van. Two sets of strong arms dragged me out and lifted me to my feet. Still reluctant to use their words, they led me up a slight grade on a gravel path. I stumbled, because walking quickly up a rough surface, blindfolded, with your hands tied behind your back, is not easy. My companions had no sympathy; each time I came close to falling they'd clamp onto my biceps and haul me back up. A tree branch snapped across my covered face, startling me, but the march continued. Then, after painfully tripping over a step and being momentarily held aloft, I was pitched forward onto wooden planks, my head slamming hard on the surface. Somebody in our group enjoyed all of this just a little too much. Your standard asshole. Every small gang like this had at least one.

Breathing heavily, I ignored the small gash above my left foot and concentrated on trying to absorb as much information as I could from the sounds and the smells. There wasn't much to go on. There were no traffic sounds, so we'd strayed far from the main road. A solitary bird shared a territorial call.

Trees, still mostly bare from a long New England winter, nevertheless whispered as they swayed in the wind. It was almost impossible to pick up any scent with my head wrapped in the heavy cloth.

One thing I knew for sure was that I was getting very cold. My jacket had left with the Civic, and after getting practically strip-searched there was little to protect me from the elements. I started to bring this up with my captors—along with the fact that the time was rapidly approaching when I'd need another bathroom break and some water—but decided to hang tight a little longer. If they could take a vow of silence, so could I. Lying on my side, zip-tied like an idiot, my only option was to wait. Wait and do nothing to incur another punch.

Through the wind I made out a faint sound of conversation, one-sided. Someone on a phone. Gathering instructions, perhaps? It was difficult to make out the actual words.

Another man climbed the same wooden stairs I'd stumbled up. He stepped over me and I heard a door open. Suddenly I pictured a rustic cabin somewhere in the woods. It would make sense. No curious neighbors to wonder why you're bringing a friend home with their head wrapped in a sack.

And no one to witness that same head getting a bullet put in it.

But that wasn't really a concern right now. Butler wouldn't go to this much trouble just to get me alone and immediately whack me. And besides, nothing about this setting screamed *final destination*. This had the feel of a pit stop. Waiting. For what, I had no idea.

The phone call must've ended because things grew silent again. The next sounds I heard were additional sets of shoes on the steps. I was hauled to my feet, then taken inside.

Pushed down onto an uncomfortable chair, I didn't have to

guess about my surroundings for long. The hood was finally lifted. As I'd suspected, three men were in the one-room cabin. A small electric lantern provided a smidge of light. They'd put their masks back on, which seemed melodramatic to me by this point. Nobody spoke.

As if reading my earlier thoughts, the smallest of the group approached and held up a bottled water for me to see. I nodded and tilted my head back. He carefully poured a mouthful, let me swallow, then did it again. He set the bottle on the floor beside me and walked back to sit near a window.

We sat like that for another half hour, nobody talking. Now there was no doubt the three stooges were waiting for something, or somebody. Maybe FBI, or possibly one of those Q2 agents I hadn't met. Everything had the feel of a trap, luring any tail I might have to a remote location, dealing with the problem, before moving on to the next stop. Butler had been in my shoes, he knew the playbook, which made him one of the most dangerous adversaries we could face.

I finally spoke up. "I'm going to need a pee break."

The one by the window didn't look back, but the other two exchanged a glance that said, *Do you wanna do it?*

Without a sound the beefier one—who I was pretty sure was the guy who'd assaulted me—came over and motioned me to stand.

"And I'll need my hands," I said. "Unless you want to handle things. And I do mean *handle* things."

This produced a snort from the one just watching. My escort found no humor in it whatsoever. But after a pause he did three things: He replaced my hood, then raised me up from the chair and cut the zip tie behind my back. I guess the hood was to keep me disoriented and make it harder for me to lash out at him.

A second later, through the tattered remnants of my shirt, I felt the cold press of a gun against my skin. Just as quickly it was removed. This way I knew it was there, but it wouldn't be in a vulnerable position.

He pushed me toward the door. Once outside he guided me down the steps and over dirt covered with pine needles. My bathroom would be in the trees. We marched about 30 feet before I was treated to two more words.

"Go ahead."

I unzipped my fly and, at the risk of another blow from Rocky, couldn't help admonishing him. "And no peeking, all right? I can't see you, so you're on the honor system."

The truth was, I didn't even have to go that bad. I just wanted to get off the hard chair, move around a bit, see if I could stir anything up, catch a few stray words. Well, I *did* get other words, but not exactly what I had in mind. While I did my business I wondered what else I could do to stall the return inside.

And that's when I heard the shots. Two of them, a pause, and then two more. Then voices carrying through the cold night air.

"Shit," I muttered low enough that my escort wouldn't hear it. Absolutely nothing good could come from shots fired. If agents truly were following me, they wouldn't take out the bad guys until we had Devya and her granddaughter safely in hand. Gun shots meant things had not gone well for the good guys, unless they were simply defending themselves. My gut told me that was a desperate hope.

My bulky friend behind me hadn't moved, and that was also a bad sign. It meant I'd been right about them waiting for activity, and that these three were not acting alone.

"Let's go," came the voice behind me, and he punctuated the command with a jab from the gun.

We went back to the cabin, where I was pushed back into my seat. The hood stayed on.

It wasn't long until I heard more shoes on the steps outside. The door opened, followed by the sound of someone else being shoved to the floor. Whoever it was had survived the shootout, because I heard their heavy breathing. There was a muffled discussion in the corner, and then one of my captors came over and pulled the hood from my head.

I blinked a couple of times, then made eye contact with my fellow prisoner, who was also zip-tied, lying awkwardly on the wood floor.

It was Parnell.

CHAPTER TWELVE

Neither of us spoke. Neither acknowledged knowing the other. Agent training, whether it's Q2 or British Intelligence, always handled situations like this. Don't let shock betray anything, and give the enemy nothing. In seconds Parnell and I understood the shittiness of the situation and then broke eye contact.

So this was Quanta's play. Separate us before Butler made his move with me, and use Parnell as the tail. And don't tell me about it so I don't accidentally do anything to blow it. Which was insulting but also, I had to admit, rational. In her place I probably would've done the same thing. It didn't endear me to Quanta at the moment, but I'd been annoyed with her lately anyway, and she with me.

And in a flash it occurred to me: Is this how she and Butler began to grow apart? Did it start with minor irritations and fester to the point where a gun went off and an agent went into hiding?

I pondered if this was yet another piece of evidence that I

was turning into Butler. First by losing a grip on my humanity through multiple investments, and then with a wedge driven between me and the boss. Our pairing was odd anyway: The Asian superstar agent who gave up field work to run a covert American agency, and the smart-ass former special ops soldier with discipline issues. Things like this—teaming me with Parnell, then giving her a new task without alerting me—might not have bothered me as much a year ago. But lately I'd been on edge, questioning my own soul. My relationship with Quanta could just be collateral damage from my personal mental battle.

I shook the thought away for now; much more pressing issues were at hand, including a new question that arose. Why was Parnell, and not one of the other Q2 agents, chosen for this assignment? Or were there other agents teamed with her and they hadn't made it to the cabin? Four shots had been fired in the woods. How many bodies might be out there? And how many of them were my Q2 brethren?

For the first time I noticed that Parnell had been the recipient of at least one of those slugs. She was bleeding from her left thigh. She pressed a hand over it, trying to staunch the wound, but a small pool formed beneath her. Another streak of blood ran along her forehead, stretching up into her hair, but that looked to have come from her hand, probably rubbing away sweat and grime. She was a professional and had put on a strong game face, but I knew she had to be in agony.

Without giving anything away, I spoke to the smaller guy, the one who'd perched near the window. "You know she's bleeding pretty good here. Think you might at least wrap it or something, try to stop the flow?"

The response, predictably, came from my personal tormentor. He walked over and cracked me against the skull with the side of his gun. My ears rang from the blow, and now I was bleeding, too.

My casual tone belied the fact that I was genuinely concerned about Parnell's situation. With a leg wound like that she could bleed out unless she got treatment. And the lax attitude from the goon squad didn't inspire confidence that they'd hurry to help. If the odds had been even slightly more favorable, I would've lashed out. But making any kind of move right now, with so many armed opponents, would only get both of us killed.

One of the new arrivals, another solid side of beef with a shaved head covered with graphic tattoo work, answered a call. He said, "Yeah," then stared back and forth between me and Parnell. His expression said, "*I will take great pleasure in killing you*," but maybe this clown walked around with that expression 24/7.

After grunting a few replies he walked over next to me and switched on the speaker to his phone. I heard a voice that could only belong to one person.

"Mr. Eric Swan," came the greeting.

"I'm assuming you're Butler," I said.

"We'll have a chance to talk face-to-face soon," he said. "And I can't tell you how much I've looked forward to it. For years, actually. But before that can happen, I was hoping you'd spare everyone some time and yourself some pain."

"Oh? And how could I do that?"

"By telling the gentlemen who are keeping you company where to find the tracking device on your body."

"The what?"

He chuckled. "Swan, this is part of the time-wasting I was

hoping we could eliminate. My friends went to great lengths to prove there was no tail, either on the ground or in the air. The only way this woman and her dead companions could've found you would be with a tracker. Now, we know it's not in your clothes, which means Quanta had you personally violated somewhere. And if she's still the Quanta I remember, she took great joy in ordering that violation. But regardless, that leaves you two choices. One, you could get even more violated by men who are searching blindly, tearing you open in places that might hold the device. You know, random incisions, probes, that sort of thing. That would be extremely painful, and messy, and so unnecessary. See, the thing is, they're all barely a step above wild animals and they won't stop until they locate it. By that time you might look as if you'd fallen on a grenade."

"Or," I said, "the other option is that I just tell you."

"Now, see, even just saying the words shows you it's the sensible thing."

I took a deep breath. This wasn't a bluff, and Butler knew that I knew it. Prolonging the inevitable would be stupid.

"All right," I said. "But how about some quid pro quo?"

The voice on the speakerphone conveyed a tinge of impatience. "Swan, this is far from a give-and-take situation. You placed yourself in my hands with no expectation of receiving anything in return. Not information. Certainly not God Maker. When you get right down to it, not even your life. And still you showed up. So it's much too late to begin bargaining. Please stop procrastinating, or else my employees will happily carve away patches of your skin until they find what they're looking for. And . . ." He laughed again. "And the closest any of them has come to surgical skill is Byron. He worked in a meat processing plant as a young man. To make matters worse, I believe he was fired from that job."

The comment had exactly the effect I'm sure Butler counted on. I envisioned giant slabs of meat that once were cows, hanging from hooks and getting sliced into ribeyes and New York strips.

I looked up at the grunt holding the phone, the one with the intricately-decorated bald head. "Are you Byron?" He returned the iciest stare he could summon.

"Your boys don't talk much," I said to Butler. "Listen, they brought a woman in here. She's been shot, and she's bleeding. Quite a bit. Before I tell you where to find the tracker, I'd like her to get some help. You can do that."

"Yes, I *could* do that," he said. "But we'll do things the other way around. You give us the device first and then we'll deal with the young lady."

I again made quick eye contact with Parnell, who began to show signs of weakness, the kind I'd seen with other gunshot victims. Her wound needed attention. More negotiating would mean lost minutes that were critical for her. I still didn't know the British agent well, but what I knew I liked. And, more importantly, I trusted.

Granted, trusting someone who only months earlier had been on the team trying to kill me was unorthodox. But situations in my business consistently led to unorthodox methods and outcomes. Many times those were the only solutions that worked.

I could only steal glances at her now, maintaining the illusion that I didn't know her personally, that she was just another FBI agent backing up a Q2 case. But I had to get her stitched up soon.

"All right," I said. "One place they threatened to put the tracker was in my rectum, but your numb-nut friends here will be happy to know they don't have to venture in there.

It's on the back of my neck, just above the hairline, slightly to my left side. And don't let Byron do it. His hands look filthy."

"Thank you for your cooperation," Butler said. "Once this little business is taken care of we'll get you on your way again."

"Ask them to be gentle, will ya?"

Butler snorted. "Oh, I don't believe any of these men have experienced a gentle day in their lives. Especially after being called numb-nuts."

It was indeed Byron who cut into the back of my head, but he and the rest of the crew must've been warned not to let anything serious happen to me. The big guy's punch and the crack across my skull was probably as far as they dared go. I helped my wanna-be surgeon by feeling for the STC with my fingers and pointing it out. His cut was actually done well, and soon he had the little device in his hand.

"What, no Snoopy bandaid?" I said to his back as he walked away. I put my hand against the incision and pulled away bloody fingers, but it wasn't too bad.

Byron held the chip in one hand and dialed his phone with the other. When the call answered, he mumbled something that sounded like, "Yeah, piece of cake." Then he was back again, holding out the phone on speaker.

"Very nicely done, Swan," Butler said. "I'm glad we've established a history of cooperation. Now, we're going to take you for another ride, and make sure no more of your friends show up. And, if things go well, like I'm sure they will, you and I can sit down for a nice dinner tomorrow night and compare war stories."

"Dinner sounds good," I said. "But you probably won't find me in the mood to share too much with you. You have some people and some property that don't belong to you. I'm here to get those people back, and hopefully the property, too."

"That's not very friendly."

I gave a loud sigh. "Butler, I don't have friends. Neither do you. So let's just get together and hash things out, okay? The sooner we begin the sooner we can wrap this up without any more people hurt."

"You may change your mind after a while," he said. "There's so much you still don't know. But we'll see. In the meantime, please behave yourself for the next 18 or so hours. I don't want Byron and the boys to have to work too hard. You know how it is; they'll come back wanting combat pay, or overtime, or something."

"It sounds like you're preparing to hang up," I said. "But you haven't helped out this woman yet. Like you promised."

"Oh, that's right, the agent. Byron, will you please take care of the lady for me?"

Without hesitation, the bald asshole pulled out a gun.

And shot Parnell right through the heart.

If I was frozen in shock it lasted only a second. I bolted from the chair and threw myself against the murdering bastard, knocking him to the floor. I got in two quick blows to his face before the rest of the mob descended, pulling me off and landing enough shots of their own to subdue me. Whipped and bleeding on the floor, I lay on my side and stared into the lifeless face of my partner.

Death had been instantaneous. Her face was almost peaceful, her eyes vacantly staring at me with a single tear settled upon one cheek. I felt my own eyes well up, and fought to keep it together.

The mob dispersed, but not before Byron took the chip he'd cut out of my head and dropped it onto Parnell's body.

Then he got his childish revenge by kicking me hard in the stomach. The air rushed out of me as I doubled up.

The phone call with Butler was still engaged, and his voice now drifted down to me on the floor.

"I don't make promises, Swan. To anyone. And, as you see, I don't leave loose ends. I'll see you tomorrow night."

CHAPTER THIRTEEN

I 'd been back on the floor of the van for at least three hours, blindfolded and zip-tied again. I didn't care. I never uttered a word.

Rage swelled inside me, stoked by the image of the tear on Parnell's face. It was the tear that got me, as if everything wrong with this case had condensed into that one simple, poignant frame, magnified and enhanced in my mind.

And, what had been a crucial assignment, the most important of my career, had turned a corner. This wasn't the first time I'd lost people I cared about; one of the reasons Quanta had recruited me rested on the fact my immediate family members had all died tragically.

This was a different kind of pain. I hadn't known her for long, and our thin partnership had barely begun, yet Parnell was the closest thing to a professional soulmate I'd encountered. Even through our disagreements I respected her and, in some way, envied her professionalism. Where I could admittedly be prone to drastic swings of emotion, she was much better at modulating those feelings in the line of duty.

It didn't make her a robot; it made her a dependable intelligence agent. One of my flaws happened to be one of her greatest strengths.

Now she was gone.

My numerous experiences with death hardened me when it came to my own mortality, and the killers I killed didn't haunt my dreams one bit. The death of Parnell, though, was a savage wound.

Since I was the one who championed her entry to the Q2 program, and because she was gunned down by a coward while she attempted to keep track of me—for *my* safety—I felt responsible, and rightly so. What stung the most, however, was the fact that she hadn't yet uploaded. I wasn't a religious man, and I had no idea where her consciousness had traveled to when the flicker of life left the eyes that stared at me from the cabin floor.

But that consciousness wasn't stored in some complex hard drive in Washington. Parnell had expressed concern to me about the process, curious yet fearful of it all. I'd been somewhat cavalier with her on the subject, an approach I now regretted.

And I cursed Quanta for sacrificing such a valuable agent before she could upload, when three perfectly capable—and properly uploaded—agents could've taken on the assignment.

Another mark in my ledger against the woman in charge. Another warning flag that my simmering animosity toward Quanta was pushing me closer and closer to becoming a rogue agent. To becoming Butler.

And that terrified me.

The van made several turns, throwing me against the hard metal sides a few times before smoothing out and accelerating onto what must've been a highway. In the darkness all I could do was stew on the anger I wanted so much to release.

A meeting I'd had with the Q2 shrink, Miller, replayed in my mind. He'd always been curious about my insistence that something within me was changing, a change that was not for the better. He was a pro, and before I was really aware of it he'd slowly led me down a path where I found myself talking about some of the not-so-pleasant thoughts I'd collected.

"You say you're irritated," he'd said. "Are you sure that's all it is?"

I'd shifted my gaze from his window to where he sat across from me. "I don't know. What's next up the ladder from irritation?"

"Anger."

I didn't answer, so he asked me directly: "Are you angry, Swan?"

This was dangerous territory, and I knew it. Miller was a friend, but he also reported to the woman who decided my fate as an agent. As coy as I could be without appearing that way, I said, "There's only one person I'm really angry at, and even that's on the back burner."

Miller knew about my obsession with one particular bad guy, perhaps the baddest of the bad, even worse than Butler. But he also knew I was avoiding his question. He set his coffee mug on the table between us and crossed one leg over the other.

"When I was a young man, about 21 or 22," he began, but I cut him off.

"I hear a touching story coming on."

"Shut up, Swan. Mostly *you* talk in these meetings, but right now it's listening time. Anyway, I was home from college for a holiday, and alone in the kitchen one morning with just my dad. The rest of the house was still asleep. He was in his rattiest pair of jeans with one of those Dickies work shirts, sort of his work-outside uniform when he was in project mode around the house.

"He asked me about something I'd briefly mentioned at dinner the night before. I didn't think it was a very big deal, just some story about a professor who continually pissed me off about one thing or another. I'm sure in front of my family I'd simply thrown it out there with a sarcastic footnote, but I remembered at the time my dad looking at me before going back to his dinner. It must've been on his mind ever since. Now twelve hours later, with just the two of us in the room, he had me explain the whole story.

"So I did. I talked about the shitty professor and his shitty rules, and how often I walked out of his class pissed off. And then I waited for my dad to offer sage advice on how to handle this asshole."

He paused in his story and I saw the ghost of a smile play across his face.

"Well," Miller continued, "he did indeed have advice. But it had nothing to do with the professor. Instead he leaned across the table, the way he did when he was imparting advice that he really wanted his kids to hear. And since I'd been the lucky recipient of his timely shots of wisdom, I kept my mouth shut and listened.

"'You're a smart young man,' he told me. 'You could have everything you ever wanted. And not just from the schooling.' He kind of waved as he said that, as if the education he was helping to pay for wasn't the education that counted in life—which it probably wasn't. Anyway, then he said: 'But as smart as you are, and as gifted as you are in terms of talent and judgment, there's one thing that'll wreck everything you've worked for, and everything you could be someday.'

"Well, shit, he had my attention now. I waited for the grand announcement, to find out what this magic component was. And when he told me, I thought he was kidding."

"What was it?" I asked. I was embarrassed to admit I'd been completely sucked into Miller's story.

The Q2 therapist had turned his attention back to me. "He said I was in danger of becoming an angry young man."

I remember sitting in that room with Miller, a little let down by the answer. "That's it?" I said.

He laughed. "You know, that's exactly what I thought. *That's the big reveal? After that build-up?* But something in his voice kept me quiet. And then he explained. 'There's a big difference between getting angry and being an angry young man. We're human, we're bound to occasionally have something that rubs us raw, and we'll have a normal reaction. We get mad.

"'But we get over it,' he said. 'It doesn't stick with us, doesn't define us. You . . .' And it was here that he paused, kind of shifted his jaw a bit. 'You're at a crossroads for your life, son. Because I see you getting angry more and more. You act like it's no big deal, but the more you slide into anger to deal with issues in your life, the more you'll become an angry young man. And it *will* define you. Believe me, you don't want that. Too many people live an angry life, and that's no different than a cancer.'"

Miller fell silent, letting the wisdom of his father sink in. Then, in a softer voice, he said, "Swan, I see you at the same crossroads. You're like me; you don't see it. You rely on humor to deflect your anger, so you don't notice the damage it's doing."

After a moment I laughed. "I mean, it's a great story, Miller, and I don't want to shortchange your father's wisdom. But it's not like I'm walking around with a perpetual scowl."

"No, you're not. You have a pretty good mask. A clown's mask. But remember: I know the details of your past, and I know how you channel your anger. Especially toward Beadle."

It wasn't often that the name came up in our sessions. The man I swore to find, to capture, and to kill. Without turning him in. Beadle had caused damage and heartbreak to me personally, and not just because he'd killed more than one version of me as a Q2 agent. He'd slipped away from me before; a time would come when he wouldn't.

When I didn't answer, Miller continued. "And now it's not just Beadle. In the past you've expressed some frustration with Quanta and the other powers within Q2, but it's more frequent now. And at times it targets more than one person or one thing at a time."

He leaned forward. "I'm giving you something to think about. Become aware of your feelings, and when you find yourself slipping into that shell of the angry young man, look for something to help you change course. Anger can motivate you in short bursts; but the longer you hold on to it and use it, the more it begins to use *you*. It changes from motivation to a cancer that eats you up from the inside. Until you're completely miserable. Or dead."

That conversation had taken place only five weeks earlier. Ironically, it pissed me off at the time. Nobody likes to be labeled a generally angry person, and I resented the implication. All because I'd expressed a few complaints about the organization and its leadership.

But I wasn't being honest with myself then. I could be now.

Miller's assessment had, as usual, been on target. Too often I camouflaged the brewing anger I felt with a laugh, and usually with a smart-ass comment. Some of that was motivated by fear, mostly fear that I'd never catch the one person I wanted to track down, which would make me a loser. And I had low tolerance for losing.

But it also was fueled by my inability to use the gift of investment technology to answer certain questions. They were questions I'd had since the first moment Quanta explained how the investment process worked. That I could be that close to an answer for the ultimate question that plagued our species:

What happens when we cross the veil? What is that moment like, and, more importantly, what waits beyond?

What did Parnell experience the moment her ruptured heart stopped beating, the moment her last conscious thought drained away? Those eyes, which had expelled a single tear, weren't really looking at me; what *were* they seeing? What did she, at that exact moment, know?

Because if I knew what Parnell had experienced, I'd finally know what my parents and my sister had experienced.

Investment allowed me to tiptoe right up to the answer. It actually gave me a glimpse before snatching it away, slamming the door on the knowledge of it all. Letting me live it—and die with it, I suppose—and yet forbid me to keep the memory of that journey.

It angered me, which in turn drove me back into the line of fire. I did not seek death, I had no fantastical death wish. I didn't have to; in my line of work it would eventually find me whether I sought it or not. But it also gave me an edge in that I carried no fear of the transition. Because one of these days I *might* somehow hold on to that memory, that final experience, and have peace at last over a tortured past.

For now, though, I was tied up and blindfolded in a van moving toward a meeting with a dangerous man. He not only controlled my personal fate, but he was grasping for control of a power that could impact the country—hell, the world—in a catastrophic way. For Butler was a killer who thought of himself as an angel. A justice-dispensing angel whose insanity was the worst kind.

Because he was on *a mission*.

People had already died from this mission, including my partner, my friend. And many more would likely die if and when Butler persuaded Devya Nayar to build his factory of soldiers.

The stage was set for the showdown between two allegorical entities: The angel of death and God Maker.

Pursued by an angry young man.

CHAPTER FOURTEEN

The van stopped. I heard the beep of a gate intercom, followed by a muffled conversation between the driver and someone on the other end. Then the van lurched forward again, and we crawled up what must've been a long, twisting drive.

When the sliding door crashed open, hands took hold and I was pulled out. They were not gentle hands.

With an escort on each arm they led me inside a building and down a carpeted flight of stairs. A right turn, then a left, then another door cranked open. When you're blindfolded you try your best to memorize the geometry of the trip, as if somehow those details will be helpful later. It's the tiny bit of control you feign in an out-of-control environment.

At the end of the march I was pushed down onto a small bed. My hands were freed, and the hood, which had become sweaty and smelly, was finally removed.

The three goons included the tatted-head man, Byron, and two others. The need for masks was apparently over. I gathered as much detail on them as quickly as I could.

Byron was perhaps 25, muscular, and clearly Butler's lead dog. The second was shorter, stocky, with a look I'd seen on plenty of hired guns. It was the look of stupidity, someone who could follow orders but would never have a single unique thought of their own. The third guy was lean, almost wiry, with stringy hair and some of the worst teeth you could imagine. I mean so bad I had to look away.

After glancing around the room, Byron indicated with a nod that the others should leave. Then he gave me one of his death stares, obviously intended to intimidate the hell out of me. Which meant I couldn't let him win.

"I need to leave a wake-up call for 6:30," I told him. "And when you bring coffee, throw in a croissant with butter and raspberry jam, all right?" I mimed looking for cash in my pocket to tip him, but then held my hands out, palms up, with the *What can I say?* look.

I thought it was good stuff, but all he did was maintain the death stare for another few seconds before walking out and dead-bolting the heavy door.

It was late, I'd had one of the shittiest days ever, and I still felt the physical effects of getting my ass kicked back at the cabin. I'd need to explore my new home, but that could wait until the next day. For now I just kicked off my shoes, shut off the light, and collapsed into a dreamless sleep.

THE CLUNK of the door opening woke me with a start. I no longer had a phone, so I didn't know if Byron was honoring my 6:30 call with breakfast or if I was about to get roughed up again.

To my surprise a rather small woman waltzed in, greeting me with a smile. She couldn't have weighed more than a hundred pounds sopping wet, but carried herself like a general. Her skin was a deep mocha, her hair jet black, and her outfit impeccable. You sometimes just get a feel about someone the instant you see them, and whoever she was I already liked her. I hoped I wouldn't have to eventually kill her.

"Mr. Eric Swan," she said, standing beside the bed with her hands clasped in front of her. I was still sprawled across the bed, in my clothes from the night before, and probably with hilarious hair.

I sat up. "Hi." After blinking a couple of times and rubbing my eyes, I added: "Are you the innkeeper?"

She had a pretty laugh to go along with her pleasant disposition. "You know, I did work for the Hyatt corporation when I was in college, but my hospitality days are well past. No, I keep Mr. Butler's schedule and arrange his business affairs. My name is Marta."

I tried not to laugh, but failed. A business manager for a criminal mastermind, what Shakespeare called a *serviceable villain*. Butler was already unlike any other knave I'd tangled with, and he continued to raise the bar.

"Well, good morning, Marta," I said. "Uh, what time is it?"

"It's time for you to get up. There's a washroom right over there, and you'll find toiletries arranged for you. In the closet there are some comfortable clothes. When you're ready, I'll take you to see Mr. Butler."

Interesting.

"All right," I said, standing and stretching. "Any chance I could get some coffee?"

"It'll be here waiting when you come out, along with something to eat." With that, she gave a professional nod of her head and spun around, leaving me alone and wondering just how long the courteous treatment would continue. Probably not long. It was a fairly common tactic: weave the good with the bad, keep your prey confused, unsure of what would come next.

No matter what, I told myself, never forget what happened the night before. All the hospitality in the world wouldn't change the fact that I was a prisoner of a man who'd ordered the execution of a government agent before my eyes. A platoon of pleasant minions couldn't gloss over the evil behind it all.

Snapping on the light in the bathroom I saw towels and assorted hygiene products laid out. There was no mirror, probably to keep me from having anything sharp to use as a weapon. But I'm sure any image would simply be that of a man who'd been beaten and tossed around. A wince was unavoidable as I gently fingered the abrasion on my forehead where I'd been clocked by the gun barrel. I showered, hoping to wash away some of the fatigue and body aches that had set in. I settled for simply scrubbing off the blood and grime, then stood under the hot water for a few extra minutes, my hands against the tiles.

Stepping out, I debated whether or not to shave, which was somewhat challenging without a mirror, but something I'd done in my special ops deployments many times. I decided that, since the products were there, why not? In the modest closet I found a package of underwear, socks, and a small assortment of T-shirts and sweaters. My own pants, although scuffed and dirty, would suffice.

When I came out of the bathroom a tray with coffee, water, and an omelet sat on the table, along with a small bowl of fruit. I devoured it all. One of the rules of spy craft was simple: No matter how stressful the situation, eat and sleep whenever you can, because there's no telling when you might get the chance again.

While finishing the fruit I glanced around the room, taking in my temporary home. It was about the size of a hotel's junior suite, with a bed, sitting area—no television, of course—a table and chair, and the separate bathroom and closet. There was no window, and I knew without inspecting it that the door was thick and secure. Besides, trying to bust out would be senseless for two reasons. One, I'd volunteered to meet with Butler, so why would I try to leave? And two, my host would have at least one creep sitting outside, armed and ready to inflict pain at the slightest provocation.

And although I couldn't spot them, cameras had to be watching my every move. Hopefully not in the bathroom, but, yeah, probably there, too. I decided to not give anyone a show. I wouldn't scuffle around the room, inspecting and analyzing, behaving like a zoo animal desperate for freedom. I just sat comfortably, waiting for company.

It didn't take long. Marta returned, still beaming her sweet smile. It dawned on me that I was living scenes from the first James Bond movie, when 007 and Honey Rider were captured by Dr. No. They were treated to the same courtesies and happy faces. Until the mad scientist decided to kill them.

"Ah, you look so refreshed," Marta said, clasping her hands again, this time as a sign of joy. "And you must feel so much better after bathing and eating."

"Yes, it was quite good," I said. "The clothes, too. Thank you."

She inclined her head in a swift bow. "It's our pleasure. If you need anything else, just let me know. Now, if you're ready, I'll take you to see Mr. Butler. I know he's anxious to talk."

I stood up. "As am I."

She led me out of the room and down a hallway, trailed by

an armed guard. "How long have you worked for Mr. Butler?" I asked.

"Oh, not that long. Were you able to sleep all right?"

"Sure," was all I needed to say. Marta was friendly to the max, but made it clear with her redirect that she'd reveal nothing about her employer.

We climbed what struck me as a servants' staircase, arriving at the back of whatever home we were in. Marta tapped on another heavy door, then opened it and gestured for me to walk past her into the room.

It was large and opulently decorated with dark wood and bookcases. Ceilings soared to probably 18 feet, and one entire wall was glass, providing a glimpse outside that duplicated the one at Devya's estate. When the weather improved the view would be magnificent. Today, however, was gray and misty, a cold, wet cloak covering the landscape. In the center of the room a large aquarium was the obvious conversation piece, bubbling away with several exotic fish and other creatures. The room held a distinct sense of calm.

I recognized Butler from the short snippet of video taken during the Q2 break-in and the photo in his file. The crooked nose, and especially the aggressive tattoo over his eye, jumped out. He sat behind an impressive desk, opening a package with one of those old-fashioned letter openers. Two more of his muscle men stood nearby, one making sure I saw the gun held to his side. Butler set down the package and opener as I came in, got to his feet, and walked up to me with his hand outstretched.

Instead of shaking it, I hauled off and punched him hard across the jaw.

He stumbled backward, and in a flash both of the goons

were on me. One punched me across the face and the other placed his gun against my forehead.

"That's all right," Butler said, regaining his balance. "Let him go."

The two men were obviously not happy with the order, and hesitated before stepping back.

Butler laughed, rubbing his jaw. "Quite a greeting."

I dabbed at the fresh cut on the side of my mouth, then put my hands on my hips. "Well, that was just in case you kill me before I can do anything about the people you've murdered. It's not much. Hopefully I'll get a chance to do more later."

He looked amused. "Fair enough. Actually, you'll be happy to know I've planned on going a few rounds with you. I do my best to stay in shape, but nothing like working out with a fellow Q2 agent. Especially someone schooled by Quanta. Have you even come close to kicking her ass? I never did."

"You came close to shooting her, though."

He raised both eyebrows. "She told you about that? Yes, well, it wasn't meant to kill her. Just an exclamation point on our, uh, disagreements. Of course, looking back, I suppose I should've gone ahead and placed that shot right between her eyes. I may regret that moment of courtesy."

"You will."

Indicating chairs by a fireplace, he sat down. After exchanging scowls with the hired help, I joined him. Nodding toward the window I said, "This is nice property you have. Where are we?"

His smile was back, but he ignored the question. "Swan, you have no idea how good it is to finally talk with someone who's walked the same path I have. Someone who's had the same experiences, who knows what it's really like when you pull back the curtain on the big, bad world."

"We may have walked a similar path at one point, but one of us veered way off track."

"I won't quibble with you, because right now you're in company-man mode. But I will say that veering off that path didn't take me into the weeds; it just put me onto a different path. A better one. A much more honest one."

It was my turn to chuckle. "Honest? Is a murderous path an honest one?"

"It is if you're truthful about the reasons for killing. As long as you ultimately accomplish the right things."

"In other words, to borrow a cliche, the ends justify the means," I said. "And killing federal agents, in your mind, can be justified."

Butler turned to look out the windows into the gray gloom. "Killing the FBI agents in the woods was not something I wanted. But you'll recall the instructions stated you were to come alone. It wasn't my fault that your team broke the rules. If they'd stayed away, as I asked, they'd be alive right now. It's two more deaths you can place at the feet of your boss."

"That might be the weakest attempt at validating murder I've ever heard."

"Again, you're being a company man. But I *am* sorry about the FBI agents. I'm sorry for a different reason for the Q2 agent who died with you."

I just looked at him. How could he know that—

"Her name was Parnell, I believe?" he said. When I didn't respond, he kept going. "Parnell, former British Intelligence, and the latest recruit by Quanta. It looked, at the Nayar estate, like you were partners."

When he saw my surprise a slight smile played across his face. "C'mon, Swan. Once a spy, always a spy. You should know that. And once inside a compound's surveillance office, well, how hard is it to, uh, borrow the tools?"

It dawned on me. "You hijacked the surveillance cameras at the estate."

"Very easily. Took my IT specialist about three minutes." He grinned. "It was great fun watching you and your partner investigate the crime scene. I took particular delight in the discovery of the ceramic message I left for you."

I let out a long breath. "And from the video it was easy enough for you to search Parnell's image for a match. Well, maybe not easy considering she was a foreign agent, but not impossible."

"Depends on the helpful people you know," he said. "And I know a lot of them from my time in the field. For an exchange of funds most of them are very willing to help."

I felt like an idiot, an idiot with a sinking feeling about the entire case. Butler was a deadly criminal, who may or may not have been certifiably insane. But he was also wickedly brilliant, thinking steps ahead and harnessing all of the skills he'd been trained to master. Trained by the people who now hunted him.

In the silence that followed it was clear that Butler was letting me sift through all of this, probably reveling in the fact that he'd rattled me. And at this point I didn't care that he knew. As professional athletes say, you tip your cap to the ones who whip your ass and you summon the courage to get better.

"So," I said. "Why am I here? Surely not just for you to gloat."

"As hard as it may be for you to believe, my style isn't to gloat. And if I *were* to gloat, it would be to Quanta, not to you. No, my style is to simply keep winning. And to do that I need to use every scrap of training and every tool available to keep my edge. I already have the greatest possible weapon in my arsenal, and that's God Maker—whom you'll meet at dinner tonight. Such a lovely person. And now I have you."

I squinted at him, thinking about that. "What's the big deal in having me? I'm surprised you didn't kill me when you killed Parnell."

"What?" he said, looking genuinely surprised. "Why would I kill *you*? Oh, Swan, I can't believe you don't understand what our time together is all about."

"Enlighten me."

He leaned forward, his elbows on his knees, and looked into my face. The slight smile had returned.

"Swan, my friend, you're here to join the winning team."

CHAPTER FIFTEEN

I don't think I exactly laughed, but I must have at least snorted. It was the last thing I'd expected to hear from the man I'd been sent to kill. When finally able to speak, all I could manage was, "That's a good one."

He leaned back in his chair. "It's true. As far as I'm concerned—and as far as *you* should be concerned—you're a free agent. Free to sign on with any team. I think, given enough time and information, you'll choose this one. In fact, I'm sure of it."

"And why would I do that?"

He stood up and went around to lean on the back of his chair, facing me. "Why? Please, if our talks are going to have any substantive value, you have to drop all the posturing bullshit. The *why* couldn't be more obvious. Because deep down you know you're not a Q2 agent. Oh, sure, you were at first. Gung ho military assassin, strict obedience to discipline, the excitement of a new challenge. All quite thrilling; I know, because I was that man. Even the first couple of times you try on a new body, you're captivated by the whole experience. Maybe even long for a little more."

Now his voice lowered. "But you've spent enough time to know your talents are wasted. The incessant uploading and downloading is starting to weigh on you, and the whole process has you worried." He paused. "And don't play dumb, Swan. If the investment process *doesn't* have you concerned then you're of no use to me. I can't have morons on the team." His eyes flickered briefly up to his guards, then he added, "Well, at least not on the varsity."

Now he straightened up and his face went cold. "But you're not a moron, are you? You know exactly what I'm talking about. The old Swan may have never considered it." His eyes bored into mine. "But that Swan disappeared long ago. I suspect you already know that."

I didn't answer. Too many of his depth charges were hitting their target.

After a moment the cold, dispassionate face morphed back into the Cheshire cat smile. He said, "But this was just a get-to-know-you meeting. We'll have lots of time to talk. Besides, tonight's a social occasion, just you, me, and the legendary God Maker."

I noted that twice he'd mentioned Devya without a word about Tisha, her teenage granddaughter. The omission was especially troubling.

THE NEXT TEN hours dragged by, nine of them alone in my cell. Yes, it was a smartly-furnished room, but it was a cell. Marta granted me a one hour reprieve where I was allowed to run on a treadmill in the small home gym just across from my room. Of course, two armed monsters never took their eyes off me.

One was the clown who'd hit me right after I clocked Butler, and he looked anxious for another swing. I didn't bother to waste any witticisms on them, and was grateful to work up a good sweat.

Every minute of my time on the treadmill, and most of the time in my room, was spent contemplating what Butler had said before dismissing me.

His pitch shouldn't have surprised me at all. Since the case had begun I'd struggled with two mysteries: Why was he interested in me, and why wasn't he going after his personal nemesis, Quanta? The man had a reservoir of hate for the diminutive head of Q2, and yet had made no move against her since the infamous slug in the wall.

Now everything clicked into place. By coming after me, Butler was aiming for the ultimate revenge against Quanta. If he could turn her senior agent, and, from what I gathered by my assignments, her *best* agent, it would be a crippling blow. I imagined the consequences of her first two operatives defecting. It would not only rip her professional heart out, it would undoubtedly cost her everything: her job, her career, and that once-golden legacy. All with one turn.

It truly was a brilliant plan. Kidnap Devya Nayar, acquire the investment technology, and recruit me. The first step was done and he was closing in on the second. Converting me certainly wasn't the most damaging, but it completed a sinister triple play, adding a vicious twist of the knife. Try as I might to damn him straight to hell, I reluctantly admired his scheme.

That final piece, however, was a ridiculous reach. Butler had no chance of turning me against Q2, no matter how disillusioned I might be with management. I was no traitor, especially if it meant assisting the man who'd killed my partner.

And yet Butler was no fool. He wouldn't even attempt such

a play if he felt there was *no* chance. And what had he said at the end of our talk? *That Swan disappeared long ago.*

He'd verbalized exactly what plagued my thoughts, daily. Said it succinctly, said it confidently. Like he knew.

Because he *did* know. He'd been the pioneer, breaking the trail that I followed. There was likely nothing I'd told Miller that Butler hadn't confessed himself. Which would explain why Miller was so insistent on working through the issue with me. He'd seen this movie before.

Alone in my room with my thoughts, I kept from shaking my head or expressing any kind of despair, because I knew of my host's penchant for surveillance. His plan was to toss the mental grenade into my head and then wait and watch the thing go off. I refused to give him the satisfaction.

I got back to my cell after the workout at about two, and Marta announced that dinner would begin with drinks at six. The charade of a friendly dinner date between old friends was galling, but I said I'd be ready. After another shower I stretched out on the bed and forced myself to catch an hour or two of sleep.

A LARGE FIREPLACE roared in a study just off the dining room. The view through these windows revealed only trees dotting well-manicured grounds. It would grow dark soon, but I gathered even a sunny day would give no clue as to our location.

After my muscled escorts deposited me it was barely a minute before Butler breezed in, accompanied by the woman responsible for my many lives.

Devya Nayar looked almost unrecognizable from the pictures I'd seen. She was gaunt, and a shadowy despair hung about her face. Immediately I felt the pang of sympathy. She was terrified. Somewhere her granddaughter was being held, surely threatened with torture and death if Devya did not come through. Butler guided her into the room, his hand on her elbow, and it seemed his touch repulsed her.

It took her a moment to notice me in the room, but there was no flicker of recognition. And how could there be? She'd probably never seen a picture of my new identity. For that matter, she may or may not have heard my name—and that thought had never occurred to me until this moment. Did the woman known as God Maker even know the names of her disciples? Did she stay abreast on the doings of the men and women using her technology in service of the country?

Just as we were isolated from knowing our fellow agents, God Maker was kept hidden away. More than once I'd squawked about this to Quanta and Miller, saying that a nice pep talk from the inventor could be helpful. You know, let us know what changes might be coming around, or special tips for dealing with the transitional period. Something.

But we got nothing. Devya Nayar was our own great and powerful Oz, kept behind the curtain. Only now I was standing in a room with her.

Butler led her over to me, his arrogant smile locked in place.

"This should be interesting for both of you," he said. "Dr. Nayar, I'm very pleased to introduce another of your, um, subjects? Yes, that's probably right. Dr. Nayar, this is the pride of Q2, Mr. Eric Swan."

She stared up into my eyes, and the first emotion I saw was fear, perhaps tinged with anger. And that's when I realized: *She thinks I'm his partner in this crime. What has he told her?*

Because of this she kept her hands to her side. I made no move to shake her hand, or touch her in any way. Instead I gave a slight nod of my head, and, because I felt the situation needed to be addressed, said, "I'm very sorry you and your granddaughter have gone through this, Dr. Nayar. I'm here to get you both home as soon as possible."

Her expression went from fearful to disgusted. She didn't believe me. It didn't help when Butler leaned next to her ear and said, "Don't let him raise your hopes, Doctor. Swan is a guest here, too. He and I have lots to discuss, so I'm afraid he won't be available to be anyone's knight."

He walked over to a bar and proceeded to pour a glass of white wine and make two cocktails. I hoped to say something to Devya, but she turned away, her arms crossed. Forcing anything right now would've been the wrong play.

I joined Butler at the bar. "No goons in here to protect you? I'm a little surprised."

He handed one of the cocktails to me. "Makes the conversation so awkward with meatheads standing around. But two things you should know: Your violent greeting in the office was the only free shot you'll ever get. Remember, I've been doing this longer than you, and I'm probably much better at it. And two, my friends are right on the other side of both doors, watching everything through a monitor. They can be inside, ripping your head off, in less than five seconds."

Picking up the other two glasses, he added: "So can you try to go just one evening without saving the day? After dinner we can talk again and you can puff out your chest all you want, hmm?" With that, he carried the glass of wine to Devya, who took it from him but made no move to drink it.

"I think everyone will be more comfortable at the table," Butler said, indicating a set of double doors. "Shall we go in?"

The doors opened and a small staff of servers stood at attention as we walked into an elaborate, stiffly decorated dining room. The table, beneath a gaudy chandelier the size of a small car, could seat twelve. More large windows let in the last of the gray afternoon light, and huge tapestries that were someone's idea of class hung from the walls. It was meant to be impressive during entertaining. To me it was a caricature straight out of a Richie Rich comic. I would be sure to drip gravy on the carpet.

We sat at the end of the table nearest the windows. I looked across at Devya as we flanked Butler, who'd placed himself at the head of the table. There were already salads at each setting.

"I feel like I'm at a banquet every time I eat in this room," Butler said, smiling. "But don't worry; the food is exquisite, and the wine is remarkable."

"I'm surprised you own a place like this," I said, sipping my drink.

He shook his head. "Oh, I don't own this. I would never buy anything like this." He gave a quick, denigrating look around the room, then back to me. "To tell the truth, Swan, I don't own a damned thing. Not even a car. I never stay anywhere very long. Basically live out of a suitcase; sometimes don't even have that. Owning nothing makes it much easier to disappear. Or to never have existed in the first place, which is even better."

One of the servers filled the wine glasses, though I'd barely touched my cocktail. Butler was way ahead of me.

"No, I have this place just a little while longer," he said, digging into his salad. "Probably won't surprise you that the people who rent it are not the most honest citizens themselves, and they love that I paid in advance with cash. Those are the kind of people who stay out of your hair and ask no questions. As long as you don't trash the place, and my rock star days are long past." He gave a laugh. "Look how early I eat dinner these days. Then I'm usually in bed by ten. So boring."

"Except for the night you broke into Q2," I said.

His eyes lit up. "That was *such* a good time. I've waited years for that one, brief visit home. *Years*, I tell you. I thought I'd be ready long ago, but you know what they say about finding good help."

During his excited rant, I threw quick glances at Devya. She was looking away, ignoring her food, her wine, and both of us. I didn't blame her at all. But that was a problem. If there was any chance of breaking out of here, I'd need her cooperation. It's harder to rescue someone you have to drag or carry.

The answer was to get her alone and make her understand that I was one of the good guys, and that I wasn't going to betray her. But there was little chance Butler would give me that opportunity.

I turned back to him. "So where did you wind up finding your helpers? Attica?"

He'd stabbed a cherry tomato with his fork and now wagged it at me. "That's funny, coming from a man currently walking around in a convict's body."

"Touché," I said. "But the software controls the hardware, doesn't it?"

"Ah, and that's why I'm so glad we have our favorite scientist with us," Butler said, turning to Devya. "I know you couldn't possibly explain the entire process over one dinner, Doctor, but I'm sure Swan is as curious as I to know how you ever came up with the ability to transfer human consciousness. Please, tell us at least one secret."

Devya didn't acknowledge he'd even spoken to her. She kept her attention turned to the far end of the room, the closest she could come to turning her back on him.

Butler leaned over to me and lowered his voice, although Devya would easily hear him. "She's been like this the whole time. Easily the worst dinner guest I've ever had. I have to carry every conversation."

"Seems like what you were born to do."

"Oh, don't be snotty," he said. "You'll find deep down inside that you and I are practically the same person. So condemning everything I do will only paint you as a hypocrite."

I put my elbows on the table, straddling the salad plate, and leaned forward. "Putting aside that ridiculous assertion for just a moment," I said, "tell me this: Where have you been for the last few years? Why disappear for so long?"

He actually seemed to grow pensive, a look I hadn't noticed before this. Then he said, "You could say I went through stages. Very similar to the stages of grief. Familiar with those?"

I dug deep. "Uh . . . anger, denial. Remind me of the others."

"First is the denial, which I'm sure I did. Denied that I'd allowed myself to be used by the government, denied I enjoyed it—when, really, I did. See, that's a subtle bit of their manipulation that you eventually figure out. They only bring you aboard if you're the type of personality that will easily take on the shape that they're molding. If you're not clay, they're not interested."

He grabbed his glass again. "Then, yes, anger. Well, as you pointed out, I did fire a weapon in Quanta's general direction. So anger's a given." He took a drink and patted his mouth with his napkin. "The ones you forgot are bargaining, depression, and acceptance.

"Bargaining?" he mused aloud. "Yes, there was some of

that. You know, *If only I'd realized sooner what was happening I could've done something about it.* Or maybe, *If I'd requested a move from field work to management I could've helped shape the program differently.* That sort of tripe."

"Depression?" I prompted.

"God, yes," Butler said. "Prolonged. Deep. Dark." His eyes focused on something only he could see, and he remained in that haunted space while long seconds ticked off.

Then he shook himself out of it. "But for me there were only the four stages. Acceptance? No, not for me. If I'd accepted everything we wouldn't be sitting here together at this lovely dinner, you and I talking while the pouting doctor just listens and judges."

He raised his glass to his lips, but before drinking he gave me a hard look. "No, Swan, I do not accept any of the shit that happened. That's for weak, gutless fools. The strong don't accept what's wrong; they fix it."

This finally drew a reaction from Devya. She turned and threw a quick, nervous look at our host, then glanced at me, probing, perhaps curious about my reaction. I kept my face passive, simply held eye contact with her, until she again turned away. I wanted desperately to know what was racing through her mind.

But I also wanted to keep Butler talking.

"Tell me more about your helpers. How many do you have working for you?"

He finished his first glass of wine and refilled it from the bottle on the table. "Not enough at the moment. But I intend to have hundreds."

"Hundreds of do-gooders, is that right?"

"More like hundreds of *make-righters*," he said. "People

are sick of being afraid to go out at night, tired of having to lock every door, install security systems, carry pepper spray. They want to just live their life, work hard, play when they can, and not have to worry about having everything taken away by someone who respects nothing. Respects no privacy, no personal property, and certainly has no respect for law. My people will encourage the return of a safe lifestyle."

"Sounds like a nice fantasy," I said. "Butler, there have been bad people since we first picked bugs off our cave mates. Just like that, you're going to ride in and clean up the world?"

"Just like that," he said with a nod. "With the doctor's help."

"And you'll oversee all this make-right activity as the biggest criminal in the country."

"Judged today, maybe. But that's not how I'll be judged in a hundred years."

I gave him an amused smirk. "You think in a century people will sing songs of praise about you, is that it?"

"I'll find out," he said, holding up his drink to me in a toast. "I intend to be there to hear the songs myself."

CHAPTER SIXTEEN

I t was the strangest dinner I'd ever attended. Butler pontificating about the glorious good his team of immortal superheroes would bestow upon the world, while I continually lampooned his ideas and Devya Nayar ignored everything.

I picked at some of the food—which, true to Butler's praise, was delicious—and barely finished one drink. Our host, meanwhile, put away one cocktail and at least four large glasses of wine, followed by an after-dinner port, then left in a very happy state. And why not? He held all of the cards at the moment. And besides, throughout history every plan drawn up was golden until the first thing went wrong. I'm sure the CIA big shots who first scratched out the idea for the Bay of Pigs invasion thought they were total bad-asses. For at least the first couple of hours.

So far Butler had experienced no setbacks. Both of his commando raids had gone off without a hitch, and he'd managed not only to capture me, but also to eliminate my tracking device. He could afford to get loopy on whiskey and wine with his primary objects of interest sitting impotently beside him, listening to him preach.

Watching Butler get drunk made me ponder whether or not an alcoholic—or any addict, for that matter—would have their addiction transfer with them through an investment. Would it carry over with the consciousness, or would it remain behind in a physical body? Or did it take both components? I wanted to ask Butler if he could shed any light on this.

He left the room without saying good night or farewell, and after a few minutes some of his guards took me and Devya back to our rooms. Apparently the dinner party had ended and our host had passed out.

It was late afternoon the next day before I saw him again. I'd done my time on the treadmill and was thinking about a shower when Butler appeared in the doorway to the home gym and motioned for me to follow him.

"How's your head?" I asked.

"I feel terrific, thank you. I don't get hangovers in this body, if that's what you're asking. Some strange physiological thing. You've probably had some unusual experiences of your own with different bodies. They each seem to have good and bad, don't they?"

Escorted by my usual guards, we left the main house and made our way into a large metal building that seemed part oversized garage and part work area. The object of our visit dominated the center of the space.

It was a boxing ring. Nothing elaborate, but at about 18 feet per side it was a good training size. Butler grinned when he saw my reaction. "When I knew you'd be coming, I had this delivered. Figured we'd want to get a couple of good workouts to stay sharp. Come on."

He climbed onto the platform and through the ropes, then stripped down until he was wearing only gym shorts.

"Well?" he said, still smiling and doing a boxer's dance around the ring. "Get a move on. It's a chance for you to get some more punches in. Let's see how you do when it's not a chickenshit sucker punch."

As strange as it was, I couldn't deny I was intrigued. I was also anxious to kick his ass. I'd never counted on an ass-kicking that was practically sanctioned.

I was still in my gym clothes, so I climbed up and in and removed my T-shirt. He pointed down to my running shoes and socks, so I slipped those off as well. We were grown men, living in strangers' bodies, preparing to hit each other. His hired henchmen helped us with professional training headgear and regulation gloves.

He finished before me and banged the gloves together, then whacked himself in the headgear a couple of times. "I'll trust you not to kick me in the groin," he said.

We met in the center of the ring and he held up his gloves for me to tap, the gentlemanly way of greeting before a match. But as soon as I reached out to tap his gloves, he pulled back and landed a wicked punch to my head. Even blunted by the gear, it still rocked me backward.

"Your shot in the library was bare-knuckled, but I'll consider us all square now," he said. "Let's see what Quanta has taught you."

I shook off the dizziness, banged my own gloves together, and assumed a stance. He grinned and moved in.

At first neither one of us landed much in the way of kicks

or punches. Once his foot connected with my sternum, which put me down, but I bounced back up before he could pounce.

"You're nimble," he said. "How do you handle combinations?"

With this he let loose with lefts, rights, and assorted kicks. He was good. He was really good. It wasn't just that his technique was solid; he was also creative in the way he fought. After toying with me for a bit, he got serious and landed two hard shots. I fell back against the ropes and went into defensive mode, absorbing a few more punches and kicks.

Then he pulled away, and let out a small whoop. "I love this. Thank you, Swan. I've needed a good sweat."

I lowered my hands and caught my breath. "Oh? You're sweating?"

Butler put his gloved hands on his hips. "I tried telling you before: I've done this for a long time. Quanta's training was great, but I did follow-up lessons on my own. Let me ask you: Do you find a lot of difference between the bodies when it comes to your martial arts?"

"Oh, no doubt," I said. "This one totally sucks. With my last body I would've knocked you out in the first minute."

This produced a big laugh. "Well, then I'll consider myself lucky. All right, bring it."

He moved in and released another volley. But although I may not be the best fighter in a ring, I'm observant as hell and a quick study. I'd paid attention and learned his favorite moves, even a certain tell with a bob of his head. So I laid back, waiting for him to telegraph. He did. And I knocked him on his ass.

Recuperating for a moment on the canvas, he nodded up at me. "All right. I feel the beast now. Good. Very good."

Climbing to his feet, we engaged in another full minute of

combat, with Butler connecting on three or four shots for every one of mine. Then, both of us panting, we stopped and hung against the ropes.

"Tell me something," I said. "Where's the girl?"

He glanced at me, then pretended to be very interested in something overhead. "The granddaughter? She's, uh, staying with some friends. *My* friends, but still. Don't worry; she's perfectly okay."

"Everything you've done qualifies you as a complete asshole," I said. "But involving a child adds total shithead to your scorecard. You know that's about the lowest thing you could do, right?"

He made a 'meh' sound and shrugged. "The people who win the award for Miss Congeniality never win the crown, though, do they? I'm not interested in playing nice, Swan; that's for losers. And I don't mean social losers, I mean ultimate winners and losers. In everything that really counts. Besides, the girl's just a few years away from being an adult. It's not like I took a baby."

"It's shitty, Butler. Why don't you call your friends and tell them to let her go? You have me and you have Devya. You don't need her."

He turned to face me, still holding on to the ropes. "The girl's future is dependent upon one thing, and that's the level of cooperation I get from God Maker. As you saw last night, she has a long way to go to reach anything close to an acceptable level."

"What threats have you made so far?"

"I haven't made *any* threats."

I blinked. "Right."

"No, seriously. Not a single one. I separated Dr. Nayar

from her granddaughter, and I've been nothing but a gentleman toward both."

"Then I'm confused."

"Yeah, well, I know what I'm doing. And I have all the time I need. No one will ever find her, or you, or the girl. Everybody's sealed up tight, and we can maintain a lovely life-style here for quite a while. Eventually I'll get what I want. And, in the meantime, I'll use the time for us to get acquainted. We're like brothers separated at birth, you know? Finally thrown together as adults. Right now the only thing we have in common is that neither of us likes Mom."

There were so many small, idiosyncratic twitches of his sociopathic personality. His festering hatred of Quanta, his bizarre obsession with me—now I was a brother—and his need to convince me that Quanta was the enemy. Then there was his warped blueprint for rescuing the planet from crime by using an immortal army of vigilantes. He smiled a lot, he spoke of grandiose plans, and envisioned a future world that idolized him as a savior. But he also fought like a crazed demon. The thin veneer of friendliness spread over the top of Butler only masked a raging maelstrom of insanity swirling beneath. When the surface ruptured, I was afraid of what terrors might escape.

With no chance of outside help and a team of armed defenders around him, I had to accept the idea that this would not be a quick battle, but more of a prolonged war.

But in every war, generals made mistakes. So would Butler.

"It's getting late," he said, pushing off from the ropes. "I'm going to finish kicking your ass, then go have a steak. You can sit in your room and enjoy a TV dinner tonight."

"Tell me one thing first," I said. "Is this exalted plan of

yours really about saving the world from scum? Or is it more about just getting you new bodies so you can live forever?"

He did the boxer dance, hopping from foot to foot as he answered. "Well, those are not mutually exclusive propositions, Swan. Yes, I'm going to clean up as much of the filth as I can. And if I happen to get sublime, perfect bodies to witness the evolution through the years, that's just a premium bonus. In fact, the first thing on my list is to upgrade this model."

"Seems pretty strong to me," I said. "And, considering the way you drink, do you really want to give up a life of no hangovers?"

"Yes, I'll certainly miss that. But there's a little matter of identification. Quanta has photos of me for now, but not much longer. That's why I gave her one last look when I violated her secret underground vault at Q2. I was letting her say goodbye to this face. She won't recognize the one that comes up one day and turns out the lights for good."

He took a step toward me and I was just able to block his first punch. But after that Butler went berserk. Like a Tasmanian devil, he was spinning, kicking, punching, and basically landing almost every shot. He put on a demonstration with a martial arts style all his own, an MMA version of shock and awe. Once or twice I parried with a blow of my own, but mostly I backed up, protecting myself.

All for naught. With a combination kick and punch, he had me on my knees. Then, stepping to the side, he crushed me with a hammer blow to the head. Even with my protective gear, a bolt of pain rocked me, and I fell to the canvas, rolling onto my side. Every square inch of my body felt like it had been bludgeoned. It took all I had to stifle the groan that so badly wanted out.

A moment later Butler was down on one knee, his headgear

off. "I enjoyed the hell out of this workout, Swan. I enjoyed the talk, too. Thank you. I knew we'd have a lot of ground to cover, so this was a good start."

Standing again, he dropped his gear and gloves onto the mat beside me. "Get some good sleep tonight. And think about what I've told you. You can join me and help me create a brighter future, you know? If not, this little punishment will seem like a tea party. Remember, I have a way of torturing you for eternity."

He walked out, whistling, leaving me wincing in pain, gasping for breath, and wondering just what the hell I was going to do.

CHAPTER SEVENTEEN

I didn't see Butler the next day. I was granted my one hour on the treadmill, but I still ached so much that all I did was walk, and not very quickly. The rest of the day I was alone, trapped in my cell with whirling thoughts and an aching jaw and ribs.

There was a decent selection of books on the shelves, and a couple of times I picked one up and flipped through it. Whether they'd been selected by Butler or came with the property, I didn't know. I found it humorous, though, that the majority of titles were traditional hardback spy thrillers: Greene, Forsyth, le Carre, and Ludlum, so someone was a fan of the classics. So was I.

But I couldn't shut off my mind long enough to absorb anything I was reading. I kept going back to the oddest thing about the kidnapping. Butler apparently wasn't asking anything of Devya. He wasn't threatening her, wasn't screaming at her that he was going to kill her granddaughter. Nothing.

He'd said, "*I know what I'm doing.*" So I wanted to know,

too. He obviously had different plans working simultaneously, seeking one outcome from Devya and another from me. Somehow I needed to draw more information out of him. To that end I did have one good thing going for me: Butler liked to talk. Granted, most of it was bloated self-admiration and pompous proclamations, but he was a Chatty Charlie nonetheless. If you played the part of fascinated listener long enough, people like that would usually offer all the information you wanted. They couldn't help themselves.

Complicating my situation was the fact Butler had split up the grandmother and granddaughter. Without knowing where Tisha was being held, defeating Agent One could potentially lead to the death of the young girl. It wouldn't surprise me if Butler had an arrangement for her to be killed if he didn't check in with her captors every so often.

And then there was the issue of the grandmother. If I couldn't get Devya Nayar to cooperate with me soon, things would be twice as difficult.

Locked in my room all day certainly took its toll. It frustrated the hell out of me. It was a completely wasted day, and I didn't have many to work with in the first place. Butler knew the impatience would grind my gears, which is why it was part of his Swan Plan. He was already a formidable opponent physically—as I'd painfully discovered in the ring—but now I understood just how much he relied on psychological tactics. And how good he was at using them.

Besides being windowless, my room had no clock. That combination will make a day interminable and really screw with your head.

Eventually I drifted off to sleep with one of the heavy Ludlum books tented on my chest. I didn't remember a single word I'd read.

MARTA DELIVERED BREAKFAST, which was the only clue it might be morning. But who knows? It could've been midnight. When I asked her what time it was, she smiled and gave her standard response: "It's time to eat."

The smiling smart-ass.

I didn't see her the rest of the day. There was no visit to the gym, either, and one of the meatheads delivered both a light lunch and a very unsatisfying dinner. We exchanged no words.

All I could do to keep from going crazy was to pace the room. I would've done sets of pushups, but my sides still ached where Butler had pummeled me. A couple of times I went to the door and contemplated banging on it, demanding a chance to get outside for a few minutes. But I couldn't bring myself to beg like that.

I went to bed too angry to read Mr. Ludlum.

WHEN THE DOOR BURST open I was awake but still lying in bed, an arm thrown over my head, preparing myself mentally for what might be another day of isolation. To my surprise Butler flipped on a light and bellowed good morning.

I sat up on the edge of the bed and watched him strut around the room, surveying the books I'd pulled out and sniffing around the remains of dinner still on a tray.

"What, didn't care for the stew?" he asked. Then, looking back at me and lowering his voice in a conspiratorial tone, added, "That's okay. I had some when I got back last night and I didn't think it was very good, either. And after I built up the cuisine around here to you. Disappointing."

"Where have you been the last couple of days?"

He came over and sat down next to me on the bed. "Did you miss me, Swan? I'm touched. Well, I missed you, too. To be honest, I felt bad about whupping your ass the way I did. I should have gone easy on you. You looked so beaten and demoralized, lying there on the mat. Like a sad, broken doll. Have you sufficiently recovered?"

"Nothing a rematch wouldn't cure."

This brought a laugh. "Oh, yes, after you're healed up we'll go a few more rounds. I mean, that's why I had the ring delivered. And no worries, I'll hold back next time. Don't get me wrong, you're quite good, but it'll take years for you to really compete with me."

Before I could give a pithy response he was back on his feet, heading toward the door. "I'll tell you what," he said. "The day you beat me, straight up, with me giving 100 percent, we'll celebrate. But for now get dressed. I feel like a stroll, and I'm sure you do, too. When you're ready just knock. I'll wait outside."

The man was a walking tornado, with words and gestures spinning out of control. I didn't know if it was his natural state, if it was a result of the data corruption I feared, or if he was chemically altered in some way. But as an introvert I could only take small doses of manic personalities like his before my circuits blurred.

Ten minutes later I was out of my room for the first time in two days. Butler led me outdoors, trailed by his usual two-man escort. It had warmed a little, the sun and blue skies a welcome sight. If I felt this joyous after only two days in solitary confinement, I wondered what it must be like for prisoners who spent 30 days or more in the hole. It was an effective strategy, because in just 48 hours I'd been climbing the walls.

This was also my first opportunity to see the grounds of

his base, although it didn't reveal much. The home's exterior appeared to be mid-century modern, with modest landscaping around its sizable footprint. I heard waves dashing over a rise. I couldn't ascertain a thing from the neighboring homes, which were obscured by trees and hedges. Nothing I saw could identify our location, but I surmised we were in Connecticut.

I didn't bother to ask.

"Did you read the paper I sent to Quanta?" he asked, turning toward the water.

"Your manifesto? Yeah, I did."

He made a face. "Ugh, I detest that word. Sounds so . . . trite."

"Oh, I don't know. The Declaration of Independence was a manifesto."

His face brightened. "That's true." He thought about it for another moment. "And, you know, that's actually a fair comparison. Two documents, both espousing revolution. Damn, why didn't I see that?"

"Well," I said, my tone as condescending as I dared, but I didn't finish the thought.

Butler, however, was fired up. "In a way I'm proposing the same thing the Founding Fathers were: a sort of independence from tyranny. Only in my case, it's the tyranny of crime lords."

We were silent as we cleared the rise and I saw the gray waters of what I took to be Long Island Sound. He stopped and surveyed the shoreline, hands in his pockets and a smug look across his face.

"I suppose I should've asked this already," I said. "But what the hell is this obsession you have with crime lords, or whatever these targets are? Or tell me now if this is all some bullshit cover."

He didn't answer right away. Just stared at the water. Then: "Swan, you ever married?"

A jolt of ice water shot through my veins. Butler had taken the photo outside my condo in the Stadler Building. Either he already knew about Christina next door and this was just him screwing with my head again, or . . .

Or maybe he didn't know. Maybe he simply tracked me home one time and had no idea about the connection between our units. How could he? If ever I was grateful for the idea of putting in the secret panel, it was right now. For this very reason.

He'd turned and looked at me, puzzled by my silence.

"As a matter of fact," I said, "I thought I was engaged back in college."

"*Thought* you were? Where is she now?"

"Awaiting trial for murder."

Butler grunted. "Well, good thing you didn't marry her."

"Especially since she killed her husband."

"She what?"

"And I'm the one who busted her."

"You're shitting me."

"I shit you not." I turned and met his gaze. "Not that long ago, actually. Cleaning up a little poisoning cabal in the Southwest."

It took a moment, then he let out a long laugh. "Oh, Swan, we're going to need some alcohol in us and then you're sharing this story in full."

"We'll see. So why'd you ask?"

His smile faded. "Because I was married."

The comment hung there, as if suspended just above our heads by the stark breeze coming off the water. I stayed silent, understanding that this simple statement might be at the crux of everything. There are times when you intuitively know your role in a conversation has shifted, and the only thing required of you is to listen.

After a long wait, he continued. "I was too young, of course. Everyone says that to you when you're 18, and they're probably right in most cases. We're foolish, idealogical creatures at 18. We have no idea what we want out of life, but it's the time when we're the most sure that we do. It's almost comical; never again will you be so thoroughly convinced of something based on so little experience. Which is why we make impetuous decisions, *life-altering* decisions we later come to regret. Because we're so *sure*, and then so surprised at how wrong we were. Surprised and angry, really, because everyone else was right. And if there's anything universally true about youth, it's that we resent the absence of experience and wisdom that others have accumulated before us. We want to stubbornly believe we were born with that wisdom, like it's an inherent trait, and we can't stand the idea that everyone else watches us stumble without it."

He remained motionless, hands still in his pockets, the wind buffeting his hair in crazy circles.

"So I got married. I probably thought it somehow automatically elevated me to manhood. You know, as if a marriage license was actually an *adult* license." He gave a sad laugh. "Like I said, we're so sure of things at that age, and the whole time all we're doing is grasping at anything to validate us.

"And it was even more true for me because I was alone. My parents were gone, I'd barely finished high school while living with friends, and college was out of the question. Didn't matter, because I grew up with the mentality that the street was my school of higher learning. It taught you some perverse form of respect, and it taught you about survival. I think taking a wife also seemed like a way to show that a street kid could just as easily have the American dream; a home, a family, a foundation of normalcy."

He glanced at me to see if I was listening, and I said, "Go ahead. I want to hear this."

"Well," he said, looking down at the tufts of wild grass mixed with dirt and sand, then back out toward the horizon. "We did pretty well for the first few months. A little bit of fighting, nothing major. But it began escalating, to the point we'd go days without a word between us. I remember once we went weeks without even seeing each other. Some nights I wouldn't come home, some nights she wouldn't. It was obvious we'd jumped into something before we were even close to understanding it. I guess we both thought it was some ticket to a picket-fence future.

"At 19 I got into trouble with people you don't want to get on the wrong side of. I'd done a few minor jobs for them, nothing too important, but I got careless. Maybe a little greedy. I don't know, I think my defining characteristic back then was impatience. When these people found out what I'd done they roughed me up pretty good and threatened even more. I spent weeks trying to make it right, and for a while I thought I did. But then I did something stupid again, and this time they put me in the hospital."

I'd had a taste of this in the file Quanta had given to me, but it was interesting to hear the details now from him. "Organized crime?"

Butler nodded. "Organized to the extent that they were more than just street hustlers. It wasn't a big-city crime family, but they were powerful enough to scare the shit out of anyone. The kind of people you think you wanna have on your side until you're on the *other* side and you see just how evil they really are.

"When I got out of the hospital one of their lieutenants came to see me, and he offered three options. I could join them full-time if I'd learned my lesson; I could get the hell out of town and never come back; or they could kill me. Simple as that. And I had to pick before he left."

"So you left town?" I asked.

"I did. But not before I busted his head with a softball bat."

My eyebrows must've shot up. "Oh."

"Yeah. My wife came home right then and found me standing over him, deciding whether or not I should finish the job. A big-shot with a crime organization, and he's unconscious and bleeding on the kitchen floor. My wife grabbed the bat out of my hand and screamed at me. *What have you done? What are we going to do now?* She knew the position I'd put us in.

"So we each packed a bag, stepping over this guy on the kitchen floor while we hurried, loaded the car, and sped out of town. Never looked back."

Butler looked over at me. "And you know what? As horrific as that was, and as close as I came to my first killing, it somehow repaired the shit in my marriage. I mean, our life couldn't have been worse: no money, no home, no place to go. Neither of us with family to turn to, and even if we could, we couldn't, you know? I'd made a mortal enemy out of a group of nasty people. But even with all that stress, we started getting along again. Like it took a crisis to finally mature us.

"We drove clear across the country. I couldn't put enough distance between us and the family that wanted to kill me. We laid low. We both did menial jobs for cash, several times lived on the kindness of strangers. And found a different kind of spark between us. Not like newlyweds, because I don't think we'd ever feel that again. This was more of a soul-mate kind of thing. We'd survived something catastrophic and knew we could rely on each other.

"About eight months later, when I turned 20, I told her I was going to join the military. And to her credit, she supported it all the way. Said it would be good for me. Good for us. So I joined up, went through training, found I had a knack for certain things the military found useful." He gave me a slight smile. "Probably the same things you discovered.

"Anyway, got transferred a few times, served on some pretty intense missions in some pretty awful places in the world, and developed a skill you can only use two ways: In service of your government, or in service to slime.

"I wasn't seeing my wife hardly at all. She'd settled in a small town in the south, held a pretty good job with a small local business, still supported what I was doing. We'd become more like best friends. Even when I got leave to go home, we didn't behave like husband and wife. We slept in the same bed, but that's it; just slept. Had good times together, but I think had realized we were better off this way. I know most people wouldn't understand it, but we loved each other more as friends than we ever had as lovers. And we'd gone through that nightmare together. We'd always have that secret between us."

I sensed something tragic was coming in his story. It was.

"I got called in to see the XO while I was in Central Asia. I'd been idle for about a week, so I thought he was going to brief me on a new mission. Instead he told me that my wife was dead."

Now Butler knelt down and scooped some sand into his hand, and let it slide through his fingers.

"She'd been killed. The police listed it as a break-in and random murder. They never solved it, and I suppose it's still an open case in that town. But I knew immediately who'd done it, because they used a bat. Didn't take a thing from the house. Didn't do anything else to her. Just came into the apartment, killed her, and left. Left the bat next to her. Sent the loudest, clearest message they could: *You can't hide*. It had been years, but they'd found her, and they'd find me, no matter how long it took."

I stood there and looked down at him. He scooped another handful of sand, then tossed it away and stood up.

"You know what, Swan? Not long after that, when Quanta approached me about helping her start a new government agency, I couldn't sign up fast enough."

"And as far as she knew," I said, "your wife was the victim of a random murder, leaving you with no family whatsoever, so Quanta—or anyone—never knew you had your own score to settle."

His stare was cold. "She didn't know at the time. She learned later. When I took out that crime family."

I stared back. "You did this as a Q2 agent?"

He broke eye contact, and turned back toward the house. "C'mon, Swan. You need to spend some more time thinking about things, and I need to talk with my other guest. Her easy vacation is just about over."

CHAPTER EIGHTEEN

F our more days passed—or at least I thought it was four days. I'd completely lost track of time, which I'm sure was part of the plan. I was allowed to go to the gym on two of those days, but otherwise I was again confined to my cell. I didn't want to think I was so constitutionally weak that I could be beaten with solitary confinement, but the isolation definitely influenced my thoughts. I found myself considering radical ideas.

On what I guessed was day three, I contemplated waiting just inside the door for Marta to arrive with dinner and then attacking her. By this point, I reasoned, I must have lulled them into a false sense of security with my docile behavior. If only one guard accompanied her, I could slip behind Marta, through the door, and be on him before he knew what was happening. And if Marta called out, I could silence her quickly, too. But I didn't think violence with the sweet lady would be necessary; a finger to my lips to shush her would probably be enough before locking her inside my room.

I don't know if I telegraphed my intentions, or if the

kidnapper playbook prepares them for wild stunts at this point on the timetable. Marta was cautious entering the room, and two goons came with her now, not one.

I spent the next day pouting. Got downright pissy, you could say. That morning I took the plate of scrambled eggs from Marta and hurled it against a wall. One of the guards advanced, ready to reach down my throat and rip out my heart, but Marta raised a hand to stop him. She gave me the saddest smile you can imagine, left the broken plate on the floor and the greasy eggs dripping down the wall, and walked out. The brute squinted a warning at me that I answered with an extremely juvenile gesture. His partner in the doorway found it all quite funny.

As punishment for my tantrum, I received no more food that day and no exercise outing. It was just me, the cold, rubbery eggs, and a growing sense of failure. Not only was I disgusted by my inability to do anything with the situation, I had no idea what was happening with God Maker. Butler had initially left her in peace, but his pronouncement on the beach indicated that he'd begun turning the screws. All while I was kept on ice, slowly growing more and more desperate. I'd read about the technique of solitary confinement, how quickly it impacted two areas of the brain. The hippocampus, which affects memory and spatial awareness, begins to shrink, while the amygdala, which governs our fear and anxiety, grows more active. In other words, social aloneness jacks us up pretty badly.

Before this case began I'd battled a growing concern about depression. That fit nicely into my hypothesis that continual cycling through the investment process was corrupting my mental abilities. The isolation, mixed with a sense of dejection over a failed mission—the most critical mission Q2 and I had ever tackled—was taking a monstrous toll. Throwing a fit with my breakfast wasn't an act; it was exactly what I felt like doing at that precise moment. Looking back on it I was appalled at my lack of control, but at the time I didn't think twice about it.

Lying on my bed and staring at the ceiling, I forced myself to calm down and apply critical thinking skills to the problem at hand.

What *could* I control? Not much. But I was still hopeful a mistake would be made by the people holding Devya and me, and I needed to be sharp in every respect to take advantage of it. Losing my shit over scrambled eggs was not only unproductive, it bolstered the enemy's confidence that I could be broken.

With God Maker there was a chance for controlling the situation. She was frightened, she was nervous, and she was distrustful of everyone. But given some time with her, I believed I could get her to understand my role. Another reason I had to remain sane.

Butler? As unlikely as it seemed, there was *some* control at my disposal there, too. Sure, he was physically superior, and had lots of heavily-armed helpers around him. But he'd already taken a deep dive into the psychotic pool, and I had to use that to my advantage before the gap between our respective sanity levels closed.

And, no other way to put this: he seemed to like me. He treated me like a little brother, one he had to guide through a tough adolescence. He even likened us to brothers separated at birth. I got the feeling that converting me was meaningful to him. Maybe he looked upon it as a measurement of his spy craft abilities. Or maybe he wanted to recruit me to his side as validation of his scheme, as if he was trying to convince himself of its viability as much as he tried to convince me. If that was true, I was in for a full-court press. Winning me over might be what he needed to assure himself he wasn't crazy.

Well now, wasn't *that* a depressing notion. The fate of the mission rested in the hands and minds of two government agents, each battling self-doubt and insecurity as much as they battled each other. I'd say *may the best man win* except neither of us could pass for the best.

I'D FINALLY CALMED my brain enough to get decent rest, even though I'd gone probably 36 hours without food. I woke up determined and in control of my emotions.

Marta and her relentless smile returned, this time pushing a cart with a larger tray. It was loaded with eggs, bacon, waffles, fruit, and a side plate of flaky croissants still hot beneath a linen napkin. A carafe of coffee sat beside another full of cranberry juice. A breakfast feast for a king.

"You must be starving," she said, her voice conveying the tone of a worried mother.

"Starving," I echoed. "And this looks spectacular."

"Good." She sounded genuinely pleased. "Let me know if you need any more."

Before she could leave I called out to her. "Wait a second, Marta."

She walked back over and I indicated another chair at the table. "You haven't spent any time with me other than bringing my meals and walking me over to the gym. You should have some coffee with me. Or have one of these croissants or something."

"You are very kind, Mr. Swan, but I've already dined this morning."

"At least sit down and keep me company while I'm eating."

She seemed to waver, unsure if she should accept the offer. I pushed out one of the chairs and gave her my best puppy dog look.

"Well, just for a moment," she said. The guards looked very unhappy about this turn of events, glancing at one another. But they also didn't contradict her. That was interesting. With a single slight gesture Marta had stopped one of them from attacking me before, and now they didn't utter a peep when she was obviously breaking protocol. I filed away this piece of information.

I began with an innocent entry point. "Tell me what's going on outside. Is the sun still out?"

"It's beautiful today. Even the breeze is warm. I think springtime is anxious to make an appearance."

"Well, then I hope you get some time off to enjoy it. Does Mr. Butler give you days off?"

Her smile picked up a few extra watts. "Oh, yes. He's very good to me."

"Where did he find you? I can't imagine it was on a job-search web site."

This caused her to hesitate and her smile to falter just a bit. I think her role as beneficent housekeeper was legitimate, but I wondered if she managed other duties for Butler as well.

"I was actually referred to Mr. Butler by another employer of mine. They have . . . done some work together."

"Oh?" I said. "Together on this particular job?"

She opened her mouth to answer, then stopped and playfully swatted my arm. "You are a sly one, Mr. Swan. You know I can't discuss anything like that. In fact, I have work to do." She pushed back her chair and stood. "I hope you enjoy the rest of your breakfast. I'll be back to take you to the gym in a few hours, okay?"

I gave a small salute with a piece of bacon. "You bet. Thanks for chatting. Sorta."

When the door closed I stared at it, wiping my fingers on a napkin and thinking. So Marta worked primarily for Butler's partner, obviously the partner who'd helped him with the kidnapping. The one who'd overseen the taking of Devya and Tisha while Butler was in D.C.

Someone I wasn't supposed to know about.

I DID NOT GET my treadmill workout after all. Instead, Butler and his entourage showed up and we trooped back over to the boxing ring. My mind was happy for the jail break, but my ribs and jaw reminded me there were some things worse than mental discomfort. Butler, meanwhile, was subdued, relatively speaking.

After adjusting the protective head gear and stuffing my hands into the gloves, we met at the center of the ring. I was prepared for another cheap shot, but he only nodded, tapped my gloves, and went into his fighting dance.

This time there wasn't nearly as much talk. My host wanted only a good workout. It was clear this was all part of a choreographed game: Give me some freedom and exercise, then isolate me, then freedom, then extended isolation. Now I was out again, with the threat of another long confinement unspoken but implied.

Butler, true to his word, held back. He fought well, but was expert at matching my skill level so that we applied equal pressure and absorbed equal punishment. In the back of my mind I wondered if another beat-down loomed.

During a short break I worked him for information, but he declined to reveal anything. When I brought up Devya, he said she would join us for another dinner, but left it at that.

My lack of progress on the case began to subtly affect my fighting. I gradually ramped up the intensity, which did no good at all because Butler only matched my energy. The entire workout was a stalemate. I'd worked up a solid sweat, but had no victories, either physically or in my search for intel.

"Let's do one more round," he said. "Then I have some things to take care of before dinner."

Another glove tap initiated another succession of blows and strategic parries. As the time ticked by, though, Butler seemed to grow antsy. I could tell he wanted a decisive finish, and the restraint was slipping away. Twice he hit me hard, and when I managed to land a pretty solid punch he immediately countered, putting me in my place. Just as I felt him revving up, I backed away and raised my hands.

"That's enough for me," I said.

He didn't know what to make of my surrender. I'd denied his chance to hurt me again, and he responded with a hard look. But instead of moving in for a cheap kill-shot, he just turned around and walked away, grabbing a string on one glove with his teeth.

I followed and stood next to him, both of us removing the gear. His mood puzzled me, but I wrote it off as another sign of his volatile personality. One minute the manic, jolly host, the next a quiet, calculating machine. Before being led back to my room I wanted to wring something out of him. Anything.

"Hey, tell me something," I said as I pulled the protective head gear off.

"I really don't have time to talk this afternoon," he said. "Why don't you save your questions for tonight."

"Just one thing. Something I've wondered about since I first saw the ceramic swan at Devya's estate."

With a sigh he turned, the very image of impatience. "All right."

"As clichéd as it is: Why me? I know I was the second agent in the program, but there are three others. Why would you single me out?"

At first his expression was puzzled, as if I'd just asked the dumbest question of all time. Then it morphed into one of a shrewd smile. He said, "Has this really been bothering you?"

"*Bothering* might be too strong. But yeah, I'm curious. Wouldn't you feel the same way?"

Now he gave a soft laugh. "Oh, Swan, of all the questions you've asked, this has to be my favorite. And you know what?"

He squeezed through the ropes and dropped down to the floor, then looked back up at me.

"I'm going to milk your curiosity until dinner tonight. I want you to ask God Maker. She should be the one to answer that question."

CHAPTER NINETEEN

During our first Christmas together, Christina and I exchanged only one gift each. Both were small, both professionally wrapped, and they sat under the tiny silver tree she kept on a corner table in her family room. Neither of us went all-out with holiday decorations; not because we disliked the occasion, but because at this point we'd each spent many holidays alone. You tend to not get too extravagant when you're flying solo.

"Is the suspense killing you?" she asked on Christmas Eve.

"About what's inside the box?"

"You haven't peeked while I was out of the room, have you? Should I check to see if the wrapping has been tampered with?"

"I'm not that way."

"Never? You never peek?"

"Never. Why, do you?"

She eyed me with suspicion. "Should I trust a spy? I mean, isn't it your job to sneak around?"

"That's a fair question," I said. "I *am* damned good at

stealth. But, at the same time, no criminal has ever tempted me with a gift-wrapped box with a sparkly bow, either. Should I be worried about what's inside?"

We'd had four glorious months getting to know each other —as much as I could manage with my schedule—and all she knew about me was that I worked in the field of espionage. She knew nothing about Q2, and by default assumed I was with the CIA. The time was rapidly approaching when I'd have to either tell her everything and swear her to secrecy, or end things. How many people could accept that the person they were seeing could come home at any time in a different body? Besides, the longer I put it off, the greater the chance I'd have no choice in the matter. If it had been anyone else, I'd have been convinced they wouldn't take the news well.

But this was Christina, and I'd learned right away that she was unlike anyone else in my limited relationship experience. She was her own person, with her own life and her own dreams. That in and of itself didn't make her unique; lots of people were all about themselves. What made her interesting was the ability to maintain her own world completely intact while vacationing in mine. At least that's how I saw it. Without giving up any of her independence, she managed to step into my life for as long as we were together, giving me her heart and her soul. Then, when I left, she was instantly back in her reality, the vacation over.

Nothing was fake or phony; she loved our time together and made me feel infinitely special. And yet, if I pulled back the edge and looked underneath, I'd find the world of Christina Valdez humming happily along.

On this snowy night, however, I was sure I was in love with this woman. I wanted her to know about *my* world, and see if she could incorporate it into her own.

"I'll tell you why I don't peek inside presents," I told her. "Because a gift isn't about the person receiving it. It's about the grace and the generosity of the person giving it. They're giving something of themselves to the other person, and for that they deserve the joy of seeing it received. I want to wait until the right moment so I don't rob them of *their* happiness."

She took a sip of her red wine. "Whew, that's quite a speech. If I drill down into it, I think what you're saying is that a person who peeks at a gift is an asshole."

"A *giant* asshole," I said.

"And spies aren't assholes?"

I took my own sip. "No, spies are pretty much the biggest assholes on the planet. But I'm different."

"Oh, you're different?"

"Babe, you have no idea."

This exchange, one of my favorite memories from a life outside Q2, played across my mind as the armed men led me from the metal building, back across the grounds of the property to the main building and my cell. I missed my wife, and knew she'd be worried. There were several occasions when I'd been out of touch for days, and Christina had come to almost expect them. But she also knew how unusual this case was. She knew it involved Agent One, and that I was unable to upload until things were back to normal. Which meant I could die.

But I'd also recalled the Christmas scene because not all secrets were easy for me to ignore. Butler's enigmatic smile and the cryptic reference to Devya Nayar only served to stir up my emotions again. There was a story behind the story. If it served as a clue to help solve this case, I didn't want to wait. I wanted it now.

AGAIN I WAS the first to arrive in the dining room. I served myself a cocktail and looked around to where one of Butler's meatheads eyed me with open hostility. I raised my glass toward him and gave a wink. I hated to think what these guys would do to me if their muzzles were taken off.

I wandered over to the same seat I'd occupied before, assuming these were now assigned seats.

When Butler entered with God Maker he seemed back to his jovial ways. It was almost scary how his moods flipped.

"You've started without us," he said, nodding toward my whiskey. "Good for you. Let me pour the doctor a glass of wine and we'll get the party started."

She was seated across from me again, but other than one quick glance my way she kept her eyes averted. Butler was in the next room, at the bar.

"Dr. Nayar," I said. She ignored me. So I repeated it.

"What do you want?" she asked.

"I want you to look at me."

Reluctantly, she turned her gaze my direction. Her eyes were bloodshot and swollen.

"No matter what Butler has told you," I said, "I'm not on his team. Do you hear me? I was sent here to get you out. If you choose to not believe me, just think about how difficult that makes my job. That's all. Okay? If I do anything that even remotely seems contrary to that outcome, then I'm a liar. Otherwise, I can't succeed if you continue to live behind a wall. For the sake of your safety and your granddaughter's, I need your cooperation. If not tonight, fine. But think about it. The time is coming when you'll need to quit moping and step the hell up."

I didn't want to be cruel, but things were getting desperate. It was time she climbed out of the self-pity well.

Her eyes flashed something, perhaps anger.

"You're mad?" I said. "Good. Use that. Being a zombie doesn't help a goddamned thing. You might think I'm luring you in and will just betray you. But right now you've got no choice, Doc. Either help me get us out of here, or prepare for the worst. I can't have you sleepwalking through this. I need you to be an active partner. Snap out of it."

My voice was more firm than I'd originally intended, but I was tired of sitting on the sidelines while the game moved into the second half. Devya Nayar might be devastated over what had become of her granddaughter, but I couldn't worry about that right now. The order of business was Butler, his silent partner, and then rescuing the girl. It sounded harsh, but there was no other way.

Butler came back into the room, setting a wine glass in front of Devya. Her eyes remained locked on mine, and I did everything in my power to send some sort of telepathic signal to her: *I'm on your side. Work with me.*

"You're both going to love what's coming out of the kitchen tonight," Butler said. "I almost sacked the chef after that horrendous stew the other day. Apologies for that monstrosity. Tonight it's Chicken Marsala, and I guarantee its perfection." He took a drink from his cocktail. "And if it's not perfect, well, I'll have a new chef tomorrow night."

Servers came out with an appetizer I wasn't familiar with, but didn't bother to ask about. My mind was on more pressing matters.

Butler, however, would not be rushed into business. He enjoyed the role of dinner host, and insisted on small talk. Endless small talk. Which was difficult since Devya refused to participate, no matter how often he attempted to draw her out.

That left me as the foil for our host's inane chatter. I took a deep breath and decided to relax.

"Doctor," Butler said, "did you know that my friend Swan is an excellent student of the martial arts?"

She didn't respond.

"Of course," he said, "he's still just a student. As the master, one of my jobs is to keep him from being discouraged. Which, I have to say, is quite a challenge when he's on his back, looking up at me."

He chuckled at his own wit, and Devya glanced at me again. This time she appeared confused. Butler wasn't helping his case with her by humiliating me. I don't think that occurred to him at the moment. Good.

The entree was served, and it lived up to the hype. I wasn't shy about cleaning my plate. Throughout the meal Butler peppered me with questions about my military background, my early assignments for Q2, and endless enquiries about the bodies I'd inhabited. I answered some of his questions, deflected many others. I was growing bored waiting for the real action.

Later, when the plates were taken away and we were left with after-dinner drinks, Butler sat back and addressed Devya.

"You know, Doctor, Swan and I had a nice workout this afternoon. Have to stay in shape, you know. And when we were finished he asked me a very interesting question."

If he hoped to evoke a response from her he was disappointed. She sat stone-faced, staring down at the table.

Butler said, "He asked me why I had approached him about this whole affair instead of inviting the other Q2 agents."

This had an immediate effect. Devya looked up at him, then at me, then back to Butler, who wore his usual smile.

"Of course," he said, "I could've answered his question.

But, since you're the inventor of the investment program, I told him it would be much better if he heard it from you. Wouldn't you agree?"

She still didn't speak. I had to.

"Listen," I said. "I don't know what the big secret is here. And I don't really care *who* gives me the answer. But could someone tell me what all the fuss is about?"

All Butler could do was grin and twist the whiskey glass in his hand. For a moment I wondered if the mystery was that he'd murdered the other agents. Perhaps his mission had begun with taking them out, so he only had to deal with me. But that didn't add up. The basement hard drives he'd stolen, other than mine, were only those of felons who'd donated their bodies. So killing the other agents would mean nothing once Quanta recovered the ability to download their minds into new shells.

Killing a Q2 agent didn't solve anything, which was the whole point of the program. We could be relentless.

Then another thought flashed through my mind, and I winced. Had Butler already managed to convert the other three agents? Was I the holdout, the prize he'd been unable to win? With three impeccably-trained Q2 agents on his team—and with his own talents and psychotic drive—it would make for a formidable unit.

The sense of dread I'd felt before was back.

"For God's sake," I finally said. "Enough with the drama. Someone answer the question."

There was silence another few moments. Then, at last, Devya Nayar cleared her throat, and in a very faint voice spoke to me across the table.

"There *are* no other agents in the program, Mr. Swan. You're the last one."

CHAPTER TWENTY

The sound of laughter finally registered. It came from our gregarious host sitting to my right, but I must not have heard it for the longest time. Everything around me had faded away as I watched Devya's face, trying to arrange this new piece into the grand puzzle of it all. Butler's glee was simply annoying and didn't aid my thought process a bit.

Devya held my gaze, her expression neither brash nor apologetic. The facts were the facts. I'd asked the question, she'd answered.

I was the only Q2 agent.

But I couldn't be the only Q2 agent. For the last few years I'd heard from Quanta that we . . .

Heard from Quanta.

The boss in charge of the organization. The woman who'd sent me from one deadly conflict into another. Who arranged for a shrink to analyze my every thought and gauge any degree of psychosis he might root out.

Quanta, who kept me from interacting with other Q2 field agents. Why? Because . . .

She never told me why. It was positioned as a standard need-to-know situation, and to her I didn't need to know squat. If what Devya had told me was true, though, the *why* was now obvious.

There *were* no other agents to interact with.

These thoughts zipped back and forth across my mind, answering so many questions that had raged within me for years, while at the same time prompting new ones. If this was true, then why bother to even *say* there were others? Why the subterfuge? What did Quanta accomplish letting me believe I was part of a tactical team, rather than a lone ranger? It was yet another wedge in my relationship with the woman at the top of the organizational chart. Yet another reason for me to fume.

It was at this point the laughter seeped into my consciousness. I turned to face Butler. He muffled his amusement by taking another drink.

"Okay," I managed to spit out. "It would be nice if someone would please explain this to me."

Butler lowered his cocktail, wiped at his mouth with a napkin, and gave Devya a look that said, *Be my guest.*

She was obviously unnerved by the topic, but at the moment I gave zero shits about her discomfort. For once during this mission she had a chance to *do* something, even if it was as simple as providing information.

"Well?" I said, this time with force.

For the first time Devya took a sip from her wine glass. Then she laced her fingers together on the table and looked at me.

"It's true," she said. "You are the only current field agent using the investment technology."

Another muffled guffaw from Butler, but I ignored it.

"So why would Quanta tell me there were four of us?" I asked. "What good does that lie do anyone?"

Devya shook her head. "It wasn't a lie. There *were* four of you. Well, five if you count Mr. Butler, but after he left the program you were brought in, and over the next year three more."

"But you said—"

"I said you were the only *current* field agent. The others have retired from active duty."

There was silence for a few seconds before Butler joined the conversation. "Well, Doctor, I think the word *retired* is somewhat misleading, wouldn't you?"

"What's a better word?" I asked, looking back and forth between them. "Were they killed? Did they somehow die permanently? Did their backups fail? Come on, out with it."

Now Devya took a longer drink of her wine. She said, "There were some minor flaws in the application of what I call the Deep Limbic Control Center."

"Limbic," I said. "That's the area of the brain that controls emotions."

She sighed the way someone who's skilled in a particular field does when asked to become a teacher.

"Well, yes, but it's much more complicated than that. It's not just emotions."

"What minor flaws are you talking about?"

"It's much too complex to explain in an abbreviated fashion."

"Try."

Now she was beginning to look angry again. I still didn't care.

"The uploading process is essentially flawless. When you send your uploads, you're emptying the contents of your mind fully, and the hard drive captures all of it. There's no, um, leakage, I guess you could call it. But going the other direction there can be irregularities in the receiving system."

"In plain English, please?"

She gave a frustrated groan. "I'm trying to tell you, it's not easy to explain." When I only stared back, she looked around the table. Grabbing an empty glass from my side, she turned to Butler. "This will cause a mess."

He seemed entirely amused by the conversation, so the prospect of a mess only added to his joy. "Whatever you need, Doctor. We have people in the next room who are more than happy to clean up after you. Besides, I'd love to see a demonstration. Wouldn't you, Swan?"

I ignored him.

She took her own water glass, topped it up from a carafe on the table, and held it up. "Let's say the water in this glass represents all of the data that you're uploading from a body. And this—" She indicated the empty glass, which was an identical size. "—is the hard drive storage system."

She poured the water into the empty glass, simply transferring the contents from one vessel to another.

"Simple enough, understood?"

"Yes," I said.

Now she took the freshly-emptied glass and held it up again. "Now assume that this is a new body, a new mind to be processed. The data transfer from the first body has been successfully completed, and it's awaiting a new home. Under normal circumstances it would be easy. Well, relatively easy. We simply pour it from the hard drive into the new body."

She did that, pouring the water back from the second glass to the first.

"All right," I said. So far I saw no issues. But she wouldn't be going to the trouble of this demonstration if there wasn't a point.

"What we've learned," Devya continued, "is that there are two factors that complicate this otherwise simple process. One has to do with compromised volume."

Before I could ask what that meant, she picked up a small salt shaker and placed it in the bottom of the empty glass, then held it up to show me. "The receptor, this new body, will have differences in capacity. They could be remarkably slight differences, but differences nonetheless. If, in this case, there's not as much volume to fill with data, there's a possibility of data loss."

She poured the full glass into the one holding the salt shaker. It filled to the rim and then overflowed onto the table.

Devya let go of both glasses and all three of us looked at the small puddle on the tablecloth.

"This was an extreme example, just to make a point. It generally isn't much loss at all. I'd even call it negligible, which is why we saw no problems throughout testing and the first few field uses."

"But it's cumulative," I said.

She nodded. "Yes. But, again, I want to stress that in a real scenario it's not as bad as this looks. And, I should point out that the mind compensates. It's similar to a lizard regenerating a new tail that has been cut off by a predator. Our mind regenerates most of the matter that's been lost."

"*Most*," Butler said, still having the time of his life.

I kept my eyes on the glass that had overflowed, watching the water droplets running down the side, disappearing as the tablecloth absorbed them. For a crude demonstration, it was powerful. And chilling.

"So what you're saying," I said, drawing out the words, "is

that the other agents had a critical amount of spillage during transfers."

Devya gave an almost imperceptible nod.

I looked at Butler. "And the same with him."

"Hey," Butler said with a grin. "I'm perfectly fine."

"Uh-huh," I said, then turned back to the scientist. "Four out of five have washed out. Congratulations, Dr. Nayar, that's an 80 percent failure rate."

Disgusted, I threw my napkin onto the table and stood up. Looking down at her, I asked, "Or is it 100 percent?"

"No," she said without hesitation. "You are the success story of the program. Which is what makes you so valuable."

"Uh, you both know I *am* in the room, right?" said Butler.

This time we both ignored him. I walked a few feet to the window, where outside the trees bent under a heavy wind assailing the coastline. My mind was reeling, digesting everything I'd learned. For years I'd harbored a deep, brooding fear that I was somehow degrading, deteriorating in a way that I couldn't explain. Miller had made it the root of all our psychiatric discussions, consistently bringing me back to that fear, forcing me to slog through the implications of everything I laid out.

Why was it so important to him?

Because Devya Nayar had realized the inherent flaw in her miraculous technology and reported it to Quanta, who, in turn, gave marching orders to Miller: Get to the bottom of this. Eric Swan is our last agent, and he's expressing doubts as to how intact his circuits are. Probe. Explore. Quantify. Report.

So we can get it right next time.

I whirled back to face Devya. "Are you aware what I've reported to Miller?"

She said, "Yes and no. He doesn't reveal details of conversations. But he does report on general concerns."

"So you know this is exactly what I've told Miller was happening to me. And yet he and Quanta have told me I'm worried for nothing."

"You *are* worried for nothing," Butler interjected.

"Shut up," I barked at him, which only made him laugh again.

Devya leaned forward on the table. "I wasn't lying when I said you were our success story. Would you like to hear why?"

I started to scream *No*, and storm off like a petulant child. But of course I wanted to hear it.

Without waiting for my answer, she continued. "I told you before that there were two factors complicating the investment process. One is the compromised volume I demonstrated for you. The other involves something we don't exactly understand yet, but it's what has made you different from every other agent so far."

She had my attention—and, clearly, Butler's—so I regained my composure and sat back down.

"It's not just a matter of the proper volume in the receiving brain. No two brain sizes will ever be identical, and data doesn't necessarily take up much physical space anyway. I told you, the differences are minute. The problem is in the storage structure of each individual brain mass, especially where the limbic system operates.

"But for some reason, it's clear to us now that certain individuals have a type of, oh, um . . ." She struggled for a word. "A type of elasticity to their data. So this water I poured into the glass with the salt shaker would actually be structured differently itself. Not just the receptacle, but the data is malleable. Elastic, as I said."

I pretty much followed this, but didn't want to assume I

completely understood. "So wait a moment. My data—my water," I said, pointing to her glass, "is, what? Fundamentally different than his?" I jerked a thumb at Butler.

"Yes," she said, her face showing relief that she'd explained it properly. "To use another analogy, you can move your furniture into any size apartment because the furniture itself acclimates and adjusts to the size of the room. Your data compresses on its own, and expands on its own, depending on the system it's inhabiting. Which is why you haven't displayed the same issues the other agents experienced."

"But then why do I feel like I am?"

Butler couldn't help himself, it seemed. "Maybe you're a limbic hypochondriac," he said.

Although it was meant as a joke, I wondered if what he said might have an element of truth to it. We do tend to talk ourselves into symptoms of whatever we fear the most.

Or, in the glow of what Devya had said about my own peculiar wiring, was I now leaping at any chance to feel normal again? She'd offered an explanation for why I was okay, why I didn't suffer from the deterioration that Butler and the other three agents had dealt with. Was I just so eager for a clean bill of health that I'd swallow anything Devya Nayar told me now? For that matter, was she even telling the truth about *any* of this? There seemed to be a climate of lies and deception running throughout the Q2 program; why should she, the mother of the whole thing, be an exception?

And wouldn't she be more likely to spill misleading and false information in front of our biggest threat?

"What happened to the other three agents?" I asked. "The ones who washed out?"

Devya shook her head. "I don't know."

"How could you not know? Quanta didn't tell you?"

She didn't respond.

I looked at Butler. "Do you?" Before he could open his mouth I waved him away. "No, never mind. I wouldn't believe what you said anyway."

The whole thing was headache-inducing. I was mentally fried, physically tired, and weary from carrying the burden of it all. I wanted to drive out of here, rush back to Christina, and forget everything: Quanta, Devya, Q2, and the technology that had created more than one nightmare.

But that fantasy lasted only a moment. The real nightmare sat to my right. Butler wouldn't go scurrying home to mama. He was on a mission, driven and determined, and somehow I had to blow up his plan to build an army of vigilante thugs.

He, at least, seemed to have no concerns whatsoever about any degradation of mental skills. And why was that? Could I just chalk it up to the fact he was already damaged, and therefore unable to adequately judge the risks involved?

I didn't think so. For whatever bruising had taken place within his data, Butler was smart. He was a chess master working out his tactics three or four moves ahead of his opponent. He knew everything that Devya was talking about. Which meant he must know of a solution.

Butler finished off his port, set down the glass, and placed both palms flat on the table. "Well, my friends," he said, without a trace of humor left in his voice. "Tonight has been great fun. Dr. Nayar, I suggest you get some rest, because your vacation is officially over."

Pushing to his feet, his face hardened and his voice became cold steel. "Tomorrow we'll be getting down to work."

Before I stood up, I made eye contact again with Devya, and tried to telegraph another mental message.

Stay strong. I won't let him win.

CHAPTER TWENTY-ONE

Three excruciating days followed. I was back in solitary confinement, with a single trip to the gym my only outing in those 72 hours. And even the workout was abbreviated before they hustled me back to my cell.

I did not see Butler.

This left me wondering what mental anguish he'd begun applying to Devya. She would naturally resist his demands to cooperate. She knew the potential dangers inherent in the investment technology, and she was no doubt terrified at the possibilities of her precious invention in the hands of a homicidal maniac.

But no matter how strong she may have been when she first arrived, I knew it was only a matter of time until she conceded defeat. Butler had to know it, too. He held the winning hand, and would merely wait for her to fold. His entire scheme made sense to me now. Rather than immediately pressuring her for information and for assistance in building his own program, he let her sit idly, alone with her thoughts,

thoughts that would of course be focused exclusively on her granddaughter.

Butler told me he hadn't issued threats. He didn't have to. One week with a total blackout on information would wear on the doctor. Her own imagination would be the tool Butler employed the most; the thought of her 14-year-old grand-daughter sitting in another home somewhere, guarded by some of the worst villains on the planet, would be enough to tear down her defenses. By the time Butler got around to turning the screws, Devya would be much more compliant. His plan of simply keeping her in the dark would work wonders.

On the third evening Butler sent for me. I'd given up on the Ludlum book and instead had settled onto my bed with an old Elmore Leonard novel. Given my chaotic mind, the pacing was easier and the dialogue was a fun distraction. Besides, I had to do something other than just think.

Butler had me brought outside where we went for a walk around the grounds. His primary goon, Byron, and the one with horrible teeth followed twenty paces behind, just out of earshot but within striking distance should I misbehave. For the first ten minutes I simply soaked in the fresh air, the pleasant slap of a breeze against my face, and the salty ocean smell. I wondered if the isolation was working its wonders on my own compliance.

We approached the rise that afforded a view of the water and Butler turned to me. "You've had time to think about everything. I'm wondering where your head is."

"About which part? You've thrown a lot at me."

"Which part? We could start with your outdated and misguided loyalty to a person and a program that's used you, abused you physically and psychically, and completely deceived you. The fact that Quanta has treated you like a lab specimen. A *lethal* lab specimen, but nothing more."

I looked out across the water. Its grayish-blue color melded into the hazy sky, making it difficult to spot the line of the horizon through the light mist. Normally I would spit Butler's words right back into his face. I wasn't easily manipulated, and I generally resented someone's effort to do so.

This time, though . . .

"I'll answer your question," I said. "But you go first."

"All right. What do you want to know?"

"If what Devya said at dinner the other night is true, why would you even want to continue to invest in new bodies? Why take a chance you'll do further damage to your conscious mind? That makes no sense to me."

"So you're telling me you won't ever invest again." he said. His tone was matter-of-fact.

"I . . ." The words died out before they could be uttered. Butler had managed to hit on the very conundrum that plagued me. The war that had raged within me for years, through so many bodies that I'd lost track of the count. The hypocrisy I could never overcome, no matter how many ways I found to spin it.

I didn't *want* to invest anymore.

But I *would* invest. I *had* to invest.

He was looking at me, dispassionately, reading my thoughts. At least that's what it seemed like.

Especially when he said: "Not an easy answer, is it?"

I shook my head. "No, it isn't." I looked to my right, gazing down the shoreline. "How far can we walk this way without trespassing on someone's property? People around here don't shoot strangers, do they?"

He grunted a laugh and started walking that direction. I fell in beside him.

"You know what I find funny?" he asked. "Your naive inner turmoil. If it wasn't so pitiful it would be adorable."

"First of all," I said, "you know nothing about what goes on inside my head."

"Really? You think you're that mysterious? Of course I know. I know because you couldn't answer the question. You're frightened of the technology, what it's doing to you, and you probably have been for a long time."

"Well, that doesn't take an oracle to figure out," I said. "Everyone who's volunteered for this program has probably wrestled with those same concerns."

"True. But I studied your face when Devya told you about the other agents. You were so dialed in that you didn't even blink. That wasn't someone simply getting confirmation about *concerns*. It was the face of someone who just found out their worst nightmare was real."

"And the turmoil?" I asked.

He reached over and touched my arm, almost excited. "Now *that's* what interests me the most, Swan. The turmoil. The inner battle. The thoughts that make you crazy. Because I know you *will* keep investing—otherwise, with all those fears, you would've quit long ago. But you didn't. And you won't."

"And why do you think that is?"

Butler gave a soft laugh. "That's exactly what I want to find out. I know you know, but I also know you'll be a stubborn jackass and refuse to tell me. At least at first. Pretty predictable, actually. You treat it like it's some intimate thing only you can be privy to. Which is horse shit."

Now it was my turn to chuckle. "Oh, really? It's horse shit

if I keep something deeply personal like that to myself and don't share it with the psycho who's kidnapped and killed?"

"Oh, Swan. This is the naive part I mentioned. It's horse shit because there are five people in history who have done what we've done. Five. Hell, more than twice that many have walked on the goddamned moon! Everything you and I have done is simply data to make the program better and safer down the line. And yet you act like you're on a crusade of one. You're not. You just happen to be one of the early specimens in a science experiment."

"I'm a killer for the government."

He stopped walking and spread his arms. "And the government has had thousands of killers over the years, hasn't it?" Then he held up one hand, his fingers splayed. "But, remember, only five of us. Face it, Swan, you're a lab rat. Get rid of any high-and-mighty delusions that you're a superior being just because an MIT genius figured out the right keystrokes and the quantum calculations. Because that's all you and I represent: mathematical calculations."

He lowered his hand and stepped closer to me, so we were practically face to face. "And that's why you should reveal that inner demon troubling you, my friend. It's important data. If you die and I erase your hard drive, all of that experience dies with you."

I studied his face. "And why do you care?"

"Because I'm the new caretaker of this system and I want it perfected. You heard what the good doctor said the other night: You're a success story. But that only means you haven't gone completely crazy like the other three."

"And you."

"Don't be an idiot, Swan. Right now you don't *think* you like what I'm doing. But you don't have any evidence I've lost my mind. And you're especially uncomfortable with the idea that I might be right."

He nodded, looking back and forth from one of my eyes to the other. "And we can probably add that onto your stack of turmoil. You want to believe what Quanta told you, that I went off the deep end. You're troubled because there's a seed of doubt. And every day you spend with me that seed grows a little bit more. Pretty soon you'll have enough of the facts to figure it out on your own."

Butler grew quiet and turned to stare out at the waves. Then, in a voice that barely rose above the sounds of the surf, he said, "There are times you're probably not even sure where to draw the line between good and evil. Not just regarding yourself; probably with some of the people you've hunted. Am I right?"

I didn't answer, so he went on.

"But don't you see how blurred that line has *always* been? For thousands of years people have been confused about who to cheer for and who to condemn. Doesn't matter if it's fiction, like Robin Hood, or real life, like Bonnie and Clyde. People who began as criminals evolved into folk heroes."

He turned and touched my forearm, his voice becoming animated. "Did you know that the first comic book featuring Superman—at least the first one the two creators came up with —portrayed him as a villain? A bald-headed Superman who used telepathic powers for evil. And yet, just a couple of years later, the world had no problem embracing this character. He went from being booed by people to eventually representing truth, justice, and the American way."

I looked down at his hand on my arm, then back up to his face. "Just because a few people are morally-bankrupt morons doesn't mean shit," I said. "Women threw themselves at Ted

Bundy, too. Did that make him a hero? No, it made him a goddamned psychopath who knew how to turn on the charm. There's a big difference, you know."

He let go of my arm and made a scoffing sound. Then, raising his voice, he said, "You're missing the point."

After a pause, he turned and started back toward the house. I followed.

We walked in silence for a minute. I stared down at the two sets of footprints marking our outbound walk, and found myself subconsciously stepping into my set on the return trip. Retracing my path. Using a mindless exercise to cleanse my mental palette, hoping for something resembling clarity to filter in. Butler's earlier words had struck the most sensitive nerve possible, cutting to the core of what drove me: The *why* behind my need to keep investing, to keep searching.

"Listen," he said, his voice much calmer. "You have some personal reason why you keep investing. And if you don't want to tell me today, fine. But you'll tell me. You'll tell me because talking to me is more enlightening for you than talking to Miller. If you're an NFL quarterback, the only person who's going to really understand what you've been through is another quarterback. Someone else who has taken the hits. Reading about it ain't the same thing, now is it?"

I couldn't disagree. I enjoyed my talks with Miller, and had even come to think of him as a friend. Yet it was true: How could Miller possibly understand the depths of mental frenzy that came from continually reinvesting in a new body? He couldn't. Oh, sure, he recognized that it was difficult, that it took ages to acclimate—if that was ever really possible—and that agents carried a burden that was damned hard to even verbalize.

But until you'd awakened on that table in the basement at

Q2, staring up at the ceiling with eyes that hours earlier weren't yours, feeling entirely new physical sensations, hearing differently, smelling things differently, your goddamned voice different . . .

That was very likely one of the reasons I'd been excited to have Parnell join the team. I didn't know any other agents, and this would be someone I could share my thoughts with. God knows she would want someone to talk to after her very first download.

Which, because of the man next to me, was never going to happen. Parnell was gone.

Damn it. Butler had a way of sucking me in, connecting with me, bonding with me. He was a murdering sociopath brilliant enough to play me. He knew every switch to throw and every lever to pull, relying on psychology gleaned from textbooks filled with data on interrogation techniques. He'd isolated me, then saved me, briefly exposed me to other victims, rewarded me, punished me, physically beaten me, and . . . hell, taken me on a long walk on the beach.

But was I really being *played*? More importantly, how many times during this mission *had* I been played by different puppet masters? Was I now snapping back into Quanta's way of thinking, following a sort of Manchurian Candidate programming? Who was right in all of this? Who was wrong? Who were the heroes and who were the villains?

Stop it, I told myself. *You just said it: Butler killed Parnell. He didn't pull the trigger, but he killed Parnell.*

Through all of these cascading thoughts and the conflicting ideas struggling for dominance; through the reminder that I did indeed have my own personal agenda for continuing to invest, even when I knew it was likely stripping away vital parts of my consciousness; against a backdrop that lulled me into an almost melancholy mood, the hypnotic sound of waves rushing up to the shore . . .

I realized that at some point I would have to kill Butler.

And for the first time since the mission had begun, I felt something about that possibility that, days ago, I never would've imagined.

I felt regret.

CHAPTER TWENTY-TWO

M arta arrived with breakfast two days later, her usual cheeriness intact. It made me wonder again about her backstory. She worked for the silent partner, who I was dying to know about, but there was so much more to learn about her. How does a woman whose personality comes drenched in honey and sugar end up tending to a group of thieves and murderers? Wouldn't she, by nature, be appalled by their brutish behavior? She obviously made good money with lavish perks, but her Glenda-the-Good-Witch spirit should've precluded her from having anything to do with Butler.

She couldn't possibly be unaware of the atrocities he and his partner had committed. I was being detained by gunmen, kept prisoner and often subjected to solitary confinement. And yet she continued to waltz into my room with her 100-watt smile.

If she wasn't so damned likable I could've hated her guts.

I decided it couldn't hurt to keep digging.

"Hey, Marta, how about we play 20 questions?"

Her hands did their usual clasp in front of her. "Mr. Swan, you just won't give up, will you?"

I sat down at the table where she'd laid out an omelet with toast and a random assortment of fruit.

"It's your own fault for being so mysterious. Come on, tell me this: What can it hurt for me to know little things about you?"

"But you don't tell me anything about yourself, either." She punctuated this with a light tap on my shoulder, like she was making a point to a pre-schooler.

I instantly warmed to the challenge. "What would you like to know? I'm a bachelor who lives in Washington with no pets and no friends. I used to ski in the winter until I decided I didn't like snow down my pants, and my musical taste could best be described as pop alternative. I like jigsaw puzzles, but I can't stand crossword puzzles, and I don't understand why that is. My mother was a music teacher, mostly stringed instruments, who passed along none of her skills to me, although I used to fancy myself a good singer until I got a good look at the pained expressions on my audiences."

She laughed. "You don't expect me to believe that, do you?"

"I know, you'd think I'd be great, but I guess I can't carry a tune."

"No," she said. "I mean the part about being a bachelor."

It took every ounce of my composure to maintain a cheerful, nonchalant attitude and hope that she didn't notice the quick twitch around my mouth. Did she know about Christina? Once again the image of Butler's photograph from outside my condo flashed through my mind.

"Why do you say that?"

Another tap on my shoulder. "You're one of the most

charming men I've ever met. It's not possible that someone hasn't scooped you up. If you're really a bachelor I'll have to let some of my good friends in Washington know about you."

My courtesy laugh camouflaged the sigh of relief that escaped me. If Marta was an actor, she was damned good.

"I would never inflict myself on friends of yours," I said. "So now you know something about me. Your turn. Where are you from?"

The hesitation and barely-noticeable break in her smile revealed her conflict. It was clear she'd been instructed to keep each moment of contact brief and free of information. I convinced myself that pure charisma could overpower her orders.

She settled on what she thought was a sufficient response.

"I'm not from America," she said. "But I've been here many years."

"Enough to be contaminated?" I asked with a grin.

"Oh, I like to think I'm a citizen of the world. You know, so much to see, so many wonderful people to meet and get to know. Like yourself."

I stabbed a piece of strawberry. "Tell me more about your usual employer. Last time we talked you were in a big hurry. Is he also not from America?"

She leveled a genuine smile at me this time. I could tell she pitied me somewhat, my lack of detail regarding my captors; but she also found it cute that I wouldn't give up my quest. In some ways I think Marta saw me as a wayward puppy.

"I'm afraid I just can't discuss these things," she said.

"Okay. Can you at least tell me anything about the young girl they've kidnapped."

At last the smile faltered, and Marta seemed concerned. She surprised the hell out of me by pulling out the chair next to me and sitting down. Again, I tried to act like everything was normal and went about my business with the omelet.

"I'm sure I'm not speaking out of turn by telling you that the young lady is perfectly safe and being treated well."

"Treated well?" I said with a touch of scorn. "Come on, Marta. She was abducted from her bed in the middle of the night, separated from her grandmother, and kept locked away. Not sure how anyone could think that's first-class care." I paused. "Have you even checked on her?"

"I have," she said, the smile fighting its way back. "I try to visit her every two or three days."

This was more valuable intel. If Marta was dividing her time between the two camps, it couldn't be more than a couple hours away. Probably less than that. I opened my mouth to ask another question, but she cut me off.

"You really are a dear man," she said, this time her small hand on my forearm. "And I won't lie: Because I've grown fond of you, I worry about *your* health and safety. I hope you'll be smart and reasonable over the next few days."

"Smart is easy enough," I said. "I'm a virtual Einstein. Otherwise how could I ever get this job?" I took a bite of toast. "But as for reasonable; well, not even my own boss thinks I'm reasonable."

"Are you a problem child, Mr. Swan?" she asked with her big smile.

"Yes, ma'am. I've been known to piss in the Post Toasties from time to time." I set down my fork and steepled my fingers, lowering my voice. "But I've also been known to help people who were in very difficult situations. People who had no idea how to get out of a tough bind. I pretty much specialize in that help, Marta."

I kept a level gaze on her eyes. She appeared on the verge

of responding when her pocket buzzed. She pulled out a cell phone, held it up to her face, read something, then replaced the phone.

Then she patted my forearm again, stood up, and beamed. "Thank you very much for the nice talk, Mr. Swan. I'll let you finish your breakfast."

She turned toward the door, then stopped and looked back. "And I sincerely thank you for your kind words. They mean a lot."

After the door closed and I heard the lock engage, I took a look at the remnants of my food and pushed the tray away. Marta was what a former special ops lieutenant liked to call *inscrutable*.

And I wondered just how appreciative she really was for my offer.

By now Devya had given Butler exactly what he wanted. At least that's what I had to assume. And it wasn't her fault. She was a scientist, not a specialized secret agent. She'd never been trained in how to withstand torture, whether it be physical or mental. One moment she'd been lounging at her palatial Rhode Island compound, and the next a former operative who she'd helped create was holding her granddaughter's life over her head.

Naturally I assumed she'd been lounging, only because if I lived there that's what I'd have been doing.

It had been five days since she'd spilled the beans at dinner about how the investment technology was, by my estimate, a cerebral disaster. Everything about this hostage situation had changed with that dinner. Devya had opened up for the first time and Butler had shifted gears from docile host to determined soldier. I was kept out of the way, other than the little beach chat. And even that served no purpose other than to crank my concern up to DEFCON 2.

Something was bound to happen soon.

It did.

The door flew open and Butler entered far enough to wave me outside. I assumed I was about to get my ass handed to me again in the ring. Butler's blood lust was like a sports car engine that needed regular tuning and maintenance. At my expense.

We did indeed march over to the large metal building. But this time the ring was not empty. Standing inside it, holding onto one of the ropes, was a large, beastly hulk of a man. Head shaved, shirt off, muscles that menaced. The man gave me a look that implied I'd slapped his mother's ass. And all I'd done was walk in the room.

"Swan," Butler said, "I'd like for you to meet Mr. Bolt."

I said, "First name Thunder, no doubt."

The man in the ring spit his first words out. "No. Edwin."

I turned to Butler with raised eyebrows. He responded with a slight roll of his eyes, and dropping his mouth next to my ear whispered, "Physically he's a god. But, as you can see, he utterly lacks any *savoir faire*."

"Since you brought me here, am I to assume his job is to beat the shit out of me? What the hell did *I* do?"

Butler clapped my shoulder. "Swan, you've done absolutely nothing wrong. You're an enchanting guest, and I've enjoyed all of our talks. I hope we have more. Assuming you survive the night."

Now he walked up to the ring and turned to face me, his face alight. "No, Mr. Bolt needs a test, and I want you to administer it."

"Let me guess: A blood test, with my blood."

"Oh, don't sell yourself short. I've sparred with you, and you're excellent. I think you'll acquit yourself quite well. Now get your shoes off and climb in there with Edwin. I need to see how he performs."

I looked around. "Where's the gear?"

"No gear."

"What?"

Butler gave an oh-well shrug. "Not this time. Now go on, climb in before Mr. Bolt starts drooling on himself."

There wasn't anything I could do. Butler was serving me up to a guy who looked like a pro football linebacker 'roided to the max. The fact that he had the brains of a spatula didn't do much to comfort me. As I walked—slowly—toward the elevated platform and prepared to climb through the ropes, I wondered how far Butler would really let the punishment go.

He certainly wasn't too concerned; he'd pulled up a folding chair and sat down, ready to watch the show. If popcorn had been handy I'm sure he'd have been munching it.

Inside the ring I sized up the competition as I slid my shoes off and removed my socks. Edwin glared at me, of course. They always do. I looked up and down his Mr. Universe body, hoping to spot a weakness.

There was no weakness.

God, I thought. This was the last thing I'd expected. Why would Butler bring me all this way, spend all this time, only to execute me in such a cruel way?

Well, screw it, I thought. I wasn't going to just roll over for the beast. I'd been trained for years in hand-to-hand combat. This guy was simply a weight-lifting monster. He probably didn't know shit about real fighting.

I thought that right up until the point where he slugged me.

Jesus Christ, it was probably the hardest punch I'd ever felt. I'd managed to go with it, which probably saved my jaw from being broken. But I still went down, my head buzzing and my cheek pulsing with pain. His hands were on me, trying to lift me to my feet so he could punch the shit out of me again. Bastard.

The moment I was off the mat I kicked him square in the balls just as hard as I could. His knees buckled and he lost his hold on me. I dropped to my feet and scampered backward. The monster, however, had not gone down.

Butler was applauding. "This is marvelous," he shouted. "One point apiece. Although, I have to say, Swan, yours was very ungentlemanly."

I spat blood onto the mat and a tooth went with it. "Son of a bitch," I said, then looked over at the ox in the ring with me. Now I was in the right frame of mind. Fear usually dominates in situations like this until you just get good and mad.

"Come on, asshole," I said, beginning one of Butler's patented boxing dances. Rather than waiting, I scooted forward and dodged first one punch from him, then another. I countered with a hard blow to his side and kidneys.

It was like punching a roll of carpet.

Stepping back one pace, I watched him take another lumbering cut. It passed just in front of my nose and I felt my hair blow back. This guy could literally kill me with his fists if given the chance.

Now I funneled the anger, bracketing it with my training, the things Quanta had drilled into me. I feinted to one side, and when Edwin reacted I weaved the other direction and placed a hard kick to the side of his knee. He let out a mangled cry and dipped to that side. In a second I was landing punches to his neck and head, then retreated as he swung wildly toward me.

We were both injured animals now, fighting for survival. But I'd noticed something. Mr. Bolt may have been the most imposing physical specimen I'd ever seen, but something was way, way off. It wasn't just that he lacked a significant IQ; his eyes had a lost look to them, and his movements were even jerkier than I'd expect for a muscle hound.

I circled, utilizing my speed advantage. My head was beginning to really ache, the effects of Edwin's first blow coming home to roost. I had to finish him off because I was starting to slide downhill. And if he connected again, I was done. Survival instincts rushed in.

I baited him by moving backward, enticing him to follow. His hands were up in traditional boxing style, and blood oozed from the cuts I'd inflicted around his nose and mouth. A bloody snot bubble expanded from his nose and popped. The entire scene was downright gruesome and sickening.

When I had him moving the way I wanted, I suddenly planted my right foot, launched myself at him and raised the heel of my left foot into his chin. His head rocked back and, in almost slow motion, he fell onto his back, the mat shaking like a San Andreas quake.

And yet, though he was down, the big galoot wasn't out. Unbelievable. He started to push himself to his feet, so I sliced in and jacked him hard with my right foot, straight into his jaw again.

This time he collapsed. And didn't move.

The entire fight could not have lasted two minutes, and yet it seemed like an eternity. I bent over, hands on my knees, sucked in some air, and then glanced through the ropes. Butler was standing now, applauding again.

"Well done," he said, and put his fingers into his mouth to emit a loud sports fan whistle.

I flipped him off and staggered over to where my shoes and socks lay.

"Oh, don't be sore," Butler said. He was now ringside, leaning on the lower rope. "He only hit you once. Look what you did to *him*."

I spit out another bloody wad of phlegm. "Yeah. He only hit me once. And almost caved my goddamned head in."

Rolling out of the ring to stand next to Butler, I contemplated smacking *him* right in the mouth. Instead I went over to his folding chair to put on my shoes.

"You wanna tell me what the hell this was about?" I asked.

He knelt beside me. "I told you, it was a test. I had to see how Mr. Bolt would perform in his first full day. I'd say it was mostly a disappointment, but at least there's something there to work with."

I had two socks on and had grabbed a shoe. "First full day of what?"

Butler blurted it out. "Life!"

I froze, the shoe suspended in the air. "What the hell are you talking about?"

He sounded almost giddy. "You know what I'm talking about. Mr. Bolt was my first invested soldier."

The shoe fell onto the floor and I stared at him, suddenly unaware of the throbbing pain in my cheek.

Devya had caved.

CHAPTER TWENTY-THREE

"Let's grab lunch."

Butler said it with a flippant tone, like Gina from the payroll office chatting you up in the break room instead of a psychotic terrorist who'd just sicced his attack dog on you.

"Screw you and your lunch," I said.

"You know, for a trained killer you can be such a baby sometimes. Quit pouting and come to lunch. There's so much exciting stuff going on, and you know you wanna hear about it."

I ignored this, even though it was true, and paid attention to tying my shoes.

"Or," Butler added, "I can always just send you back to your room for a week. Would you prefer that?"

For the sake of pride I kept up the silent treatment for another five seconds. Then I said, "Your Frankenstein's monster knocked a tooth out. I hope you have milk shakes."

He laughed and walked toward the door. I gently probed the side of my face with one finger, wincing, then followed him out. Nobody bothered attending to Mr. Bolt.

As a goodwill gesture Butler had a servant bring an ice pack for me while he went off to make a phone call. I assumed it was the mysterious partner.

By the time he returned there was a plate of cold pasta salad at both seats. I had no appetite.

"Dr. Nayar not joining us?" I asked, still holding the ice pack to my face.

"She is much too busy," he said. "And after what I saw today, I intend to keep her much busier."

"Gonna leave a one-star review, I guess."

He picked up a basket of bread sticks from the table, offered them to me, and when I shook my head took one for himself.

"How well do you remember your first new body?" he asked. "Does it still register?"

"Of course," I said, flexing my jaw a couple of times. "It's like your first kiss or losing your virginity. It was not that good."

"Mine either," he said. "The thing is, the body itself was maybe one of the best I ever got. And it was wasted because it was my first time, which is always a bad experience. Took me a while to figure out why, but I'm pretty sure I know the answer."

"I'm all ears."

"You see," he said, slathering butter on the bread stick. "It's not nearly as simple as Dr. Nayar first imagined. I'm not talking about the science side of it; that's so damned complicated I wouldn't be able to figure it out in a hundred lifetimes. I'm talking about the acclimation part of it."

I nodded, but kept quiet so he'd continue.

"The way I see it, it's like driving a manual transmission. After you've done it for a long time, it doesn't matter what car you get into. You can just naturally drive it without fits and jerks. The first time you're downloaded into a new body, it's like going from automatic transmission to a stick. Fits and jerks. You have to learn what it's like to not just live in a new body, but really *live* in it. You know what I mean, right?"

"Yeah." The pain in my face was getting worse. "Hey, I hate interrupting a good simile, but could I get some Tylenol or Advil or something?"

"Oh, of course." He looked up at one of the servants, who hurried out of the room.

"Go on," I said. "If you know the first time is awkward, what has you so concerned about Edwin?"

"Because I've watched him the last two days. At first, of course, he was beyond freaked out. I expected that. And once I explained everything to him, he accepted what was happening. But it just wasn't . . . right. I'm sure you saw it."

I frowned. "Butler, it's not the same as you and me. We knew going into the program what was going to happen. Maybe you can't prepare for everything, but you at least know it'll be weird. This guy, Bolt? He was under the impression he was donating his body to science, so he'd probably prepared himself for that, made amends to his maker, whatever. Then he uploaded without even *knowing* that he was uploading; to him he was just lying there for 90 minutes. Then he went to sleep in a prison infirmary, and the next moment he opens his eyes in a different room somewhere, *and* he's inside a different body. I'm surprised he didn't die of shock."

"I understand that. We're doing the best we can to bring them out of their sleep gradually. Edwin was barely lucid at first, and we spent an hour just talking him through what was happening before he had complete sensory control of his body."

"Didn't help though." I said it matter-of-factly.

"Well . . ." Butler took a bite of pasta salad. "Who knows? It may have helped immeasurably. But even so, he was really misfiring. I saw it in the ring. He was strong, but he must've been especially clumsy."

"Why? Because that's the only way I could've beaten him?"

He smiled at me. "Judging from the grapefruit blowing up on the side of your face, I'd say so."

The pain medicine arrived and I gulped down four of them.

"Maybe the felon you downloaded wasn't that bright to begin with," I said.

Butler shook his head. "We did some research on them. We only took ones that we were confident would make the transfer well." He waved a hand. "Doesn't matter. The hard drives we took were only intended as test subjects anyway. You know, to make sure the technology worked well. When the time comes to build the army, I'll have much better subjects to use."

"Oh? And where will you find them?"

"Swan, there are more people who'd love this chance than you might think."

"People like Byron?"

"Great example. He doesn't even know about the program yet—none of my employees do—but I'd love to have him available for investment. And he'll jump at the chance."

"And the bodies?" I asked. "Where will you get those? Now that I think of it, where did you get the beast you put Bolt into?"

Butler smirked. "That body came from a gym in Mass-achusetts. Probably doesn't surprise you. We wanted to start with someone who was remarkably fit. May have gone over-board, I admit."

I leaned forward on the table. "You just kidnapped some guy from a gym? So you could practice downloading?"

"Byron found him for me. I suppose he might be partial to overly-muscled types."

For a moment all I could do was stare at him. "And all of this still sounds noble to you? That you'll improve the world with your little program?"

He let out a long, exasperated sigh. "Please, Swan, I know you're not stupid, so don't put on this act. The history of our species has always included painful, short-term sacrifices to pave the way for major advances. Marie Curie and others gave their own lives so that we could learn about radioactivity, which led to things like X-rays. The early test-pilots and the early astronauts were sacrificed so we'd have all the advances we enjoy from the space program. Short-term pain—and death, I should point out—for the luxury of technological advances. All I'm doing is focusing the advances on ridding the world of its worst citizens. The average person would be grateful."

I closed my eyes and put my head in my hands. There was no sense arguing with him. In his mind it made perfect sense. And I honestly believed he was convinced that his cause was virtuous. That the family of the young man abducted from a Massachusetts gym would be thankful Butler had essentially murdered their son so he could march across the globe, righting wrongs.

With my face hidden behind my hands, I asked, "What about this partner of yours? Does he or she agree with every-thing you're doing?"

I heard the clink of a fork against his plate, but there was no answer. Finally I peered at him around my hand.

"That is another matter entirely," he said, chewing. "I hesitate to tell you because you're already so troubled. Maybe we should let you rest and wait for the swelling in your face to go down. You might feel differently if you're not in pain."

"No, don't keep me in suspense. Each new thing you announce lowers the bar a little further."

A servant walked in and Butler nodded toward his glass, indicating that they should bring a refill of tea. Then he pushed aside his plate and crossed his arms on the table, leaning toward me.

"You're already put out by the way I've prepared everything, so I guess one more bit of news won't make much difference. Besides, you'll see everything my way before long."

"I'm sure. So what's the story?"

"The story is that I needed help to pull all of this together. Finding the right properties to stage everything and to hold Dr. Nayar and her granddaughter. Setting up the proper help; that's a much more delicate matter than you think."

"Right," I said. "You don't just stumble across someone like Byron at the arcade. Or maybe you do. Anyway . . ."

"Anyway, from the day I escaped Quanta's control I've worked solo. Sold my services around the world, made good money, honed my skills a little more, but only with assignments *I* chose, not someone else choosing them for me.

"The key," he added, "was working alone. By doing that for years I didn't have to worry about someone blabbing. I didn't have to square my plans with some moron. I could up and move anywhere I wanted when a job was done. And the whole time I was doing it—the *whole* time—I put the ultimate assignment together in my mind."

I gingerly took a sip from my own tea, hoping the pills

would kick in soon. "So your little murder and mayhem plot against Q2 has been brewing for that long?"

"Every damned day. I don't like to think of myself as obsessed, but with this I was. Made and rejected at least a dozen plans, because none of them fulfilled the three goals most important to me: Take over the investment program and run it my way; hurt Quanta to the point she'd never work in espionage again, anywhere; and, by extension, recruit a fellow agent to make the program nearly perfect."

"But suddenly you had a mission that was too big for just you," I said.

"Correct. I needed one ally, someone to grab Dr. Nayar and her granddaughter while I paid a visit to the Q2 basement lab. The two things had to happen simultaneously, because either one of them would've set up massive security alerts that would've prevented the other. Not only that, but I needed someone who was professional enough to not ask too many questions. Someone who would do it for the money and not worry about the ideology."

This took a moment but it finally dawned on me. "They don't know anything about investment."

He smiled. "Nothing. Nobody does. Yet. I wanted someone to take care of their part of the plan, keep an eye on the young-ster for a bit, and then go away."

I couldn't help it; as malicious as it all was, I had to chuckle. "You're going to kill your partner before they find out what's beneath all of this."

Butler shrugged and spread his hands, weighing the idea and his response. "Oh, I doubt I'll do it myself. Might be good practice for one of my new soldiers, though. Who knows, if you haven't damaged Mr. Bolt too much he might be up to the task."

He welcomed his new glass of iced tea, and when the servant left he raised it to me in another toast. "I told you on the phone; I don't leave loose ends."

The reminder of Parnell's execution sent a hard, cold flash through me. But I couldn't afford to be distracted by that right now, with so much happening so quickly.

"And what about Devya?" I asked. "Is she a loose end?"

"Oh, I would never harm the doctor unless she became a brat about everything. That's why her granddaughter is so important. Leverage."

"How long can you keep that poor girl as a hostage? Forever? You couldn't be that monstrous, could you?"

He gave a faint sigh. "That's a fair question. And I don't know the answer. I *do* know that being unable to see or talk to her granddaughter has been extremely beneficial. But you get to the point where it has the opposite effect. So the next phase will reunite them and use implied pain to keep the doctor, um, motivated."

"So we'll all be one big happy family here?"

"No, there. In fact I'm leaving in an hour or so to go visit sweet Tisha and make sure everything is prepared. We're moving our base of operations there for its semi-permanent home. I've learned to not stay too long in any one location. While I'm gone my so-called partner will be coming here to oversee the movement of you and Dr. Nayar."

"Then," I said, "once we're all under the same roof, you'll kill your partner but keep Devya and the girl alive. What are your plans for me, Butler? Other than having ogres try to beat me to death."

He rubbed at the condensation on his glass and didn't make eye contact with me. After a lengthy pause he said, "That's been up to you this whole time, Swan. I'm willing to bet that after enough time you'll not only agree with the way things are going, you'll want to actively participate."

There were a lot of things simmering behind those words. What stood out the most was the subtle reference to *enough time*. It meant I was to remain locked up, with long episodes of solitary confinement, until my mind was pliable. Until either the Stockholm Syndrome or my own mental degradation took a toll and I succumbed to his will.

What frightened me the most was the distinct possibility that Butler would win his bet. In only a matter of weeks I'd found myself questioning Quanta and her organization, as well as feeling sympathy for Butler, the former agent who understood exactly what haunted me the most about investment.

My mind was a battleground, two sides warring over a decision that had to be made. One side jubilant that someone who felt what I felt, who lived what I lived, was right there, speaking to me in language that not only resonated, but moved me.

The other side tamped down that excitement, making it clear that the only way it could end was with me or Butler dead. Or both.

And for the first time in years, dead meant dead.

One way or another, the time for action had arrived. Regardless of the manpower—and subsequent firepower— aligned against me, I'd have to make a move. I feared that once we were all encamped at the new site, it could be weeks before I saw the light of day.

And by then Butler's crusade would be well under way.

CHAPTER TWENTY-FOUR

F ans of mystery novels are familiar with a particular niche within the genre, one that serves as the ultimate test for great detectives and private eyes. It's known as the Locked-Room Mystery. Basically, a murder victim is found inside a locked room, with no possible exit for the killer. How did they do it, and how did they get away with it?

I always admired the writer who could craft one of those tales. To invent not only the scenario but the eventual solution that left a reader slapping her forehead, saying *Of course*!

Now I faced my own locked-room dilemma. There were no windows in my comfy cell, and the door was thick enough that there'd be no crashing through it. You might think the answer would be crawling through an air duct, but unfortunately I wasn't in a big-budget thriller movie, which is the only place that happens. Ever. Outside Hollywood the rest of us have vents that could hold, at most, a cat or maybe a porcupine.

That left me with an equally-challenging alternative: How to overcome two large, pissy, armed men, especially when they never let down their guard. On top of that, they always appeared itching for a fight, hoping for any chance to wallop me. The two who'd witnessed my fight with Edwin had seemed genuinely disappointed that *they* weren't granted the honor of beating the hell out of me. I have no idea what I'd ever done to them. Just animals, I guess.

Complicating my situation was the fact I had no weapon, and the prospects for MacGyvering one out of the meager furnishings in the room were slim. And yet that seemed the only option. With Butler gone and a new warden stepping in to oversee moving day, everyone would likely be on high alert. That meant I probably wouldn't be going to the gym. The attack would have to take place in my room, and soon.

In the morning there was no sign of Marta. Three soldiers showed up with breakfast, two to stand guard while the other placed it on the table. Well, *tossed* it, to be more precise. Toast skittered off the plate onto the floor, eliciting a snort from one of the men watching by the door. I felt like I was back in middle school. But, worst of all, from the moment they entered the room until the door was re-bolted from the outside, about twenty seconds had elapsed. They were quick, with no wasted movements, and stood dispersed in a way that made any hand-to-hand combat impossible. At least one would always be stationed at a distance, happily ready to gun me down at the first sign of trouble.

The no-show by Marta bothered me the most. Escaping would be difficult as it was, but one ploy that might work involved wrapping an arm around her throat and using her as a negotiating tool. I recalled the image of her controlling the guards with a single look, which led me to believe she was very esteemed in their eyes. Or perhaps she was so valued by

Butler that his other employees feared getting on her wrong side. If that was the case, there was a good chance I could use the threat of violence against her to disarm them.

I'd feel like a complete shithead strong-arming the sweet woman, but this was war.

When she didn't show up with breakfast it occurred to me that she might have accompanied Butler to the other compound. And if that was the case, it meant I'd have to scrap that idea and start working on another plan.

I walked over and glanced at the breakfast tray, uninterested in the sloppy arrangement of fried eggs and an overdone sausage patty. The two pieces of toast were on the floor, buttered-side down. I kicked at them out of frustration, and went back to the bed to ponder my predicament and come up with a solution.

At least that's what I'd intended. My thoughts instead drifted toward the one thing I'd managed to keep tucked into the recesses of my mind, as if by ignoring it I could pretend it didn't exist.

But it did. And as I lay back with an arm behind my head, looking up at the ceiling, I realized I couldn't push it away any longer.

In Washington, Christina was getting ready for her day, either preparing the restaurant's menu for that evening, or perhaps out on a walk. She carried a child, acting as surrogate for a couple unable to get pregnant. It was one of the most generous acts I could imagine, and it didn't surprise me at all that Christina would volunteer to help Antonio and Marissa fulfill their dream of having a family.

It was something she and I had briefly discussed for ourselves, but ultimately ruled out. How could a child ever understand a father who sometimes came home in a different body, with a new face? Or, like now, went weeks without coming home at all? What would a child tell her friends when asked what her parents did? *Oh, my mom's a chef, and my dad's an assassin for the government.* Not exactly a storybook upbringing.

And yet there were many times, at moments like this, that I wondered if not having children was one in a long line of poor decisions I'd made. Could it be one of the things that subconsciously caused me to continually question my association with Q2? Did I, on some level, recognize that there were much more important things in life than tracking down bad guys?

Now I'd left Christina alone during the most emotionally-charged and physically-demanding period of her life. She took on the noble challenge of carrying a couple's child for nine months, while I was locked in a room in . . . in who knows where? Christina harbored a new, innocent life, while I'd watched a friend die on the floor in front of me. One of us was intimately involved with creating a life, the other specialized in death.

Pretty soon one of those deaths could be my own. The investment program was temporarily shut down in Washington, and Butler had control of the technology and the vault where my digital self resided. At any time he could unplug the machine *and* put a bullet in my head, thus ending the long, winding journey of Eric Swan. For good. Staring at the bland ceiling above me, I accepted the fact that this was the most probable outcome of the mission. There were but two things that could potentially save my life: Joining Butler, or killing him. And neither was a guarantee of my safety.

And if this episode ended with me finally drawing the

curtain, I imagined it would be Quanta who broke the news to Christina. I couldn't call to say goodbye, to apologize for not being there to help. To tell her I loved her.

Instead, Quanta, in her cold, business-like manner, would show up at Christina's door, introduce herself, and then explain that I was gone. With my current state of mind regarding the boss, this rankled me. I hated the idea of it. I could visualize it, and that made it even worse. Making it exponentially worse was the timing, during Christina's pregnancy. Of all times for a case to go rotten.

Until lately my thoughts on death held no fear. Curiosity, perhaps, but not fear. Since losing the three people closest to me—family members all deprived of long, happy lives—I waffled between an angry quest for revenge and a deep longing to understand what death even meant. The investment process supplied me with a laboratory of sorts, one that provided countless opportunities of crossing that veil, but never holding on to the experience. A tease, a brief glimpse during the lights out moment before it was ripped away, leaving no memory, no imprint. No answers.

It was difficult for me to talk with anyone about this struggle. It made it sound like I had a death wish. But that wasn't right. It wasn't a death wish; it was a desperate search for an answer to the ultimate question. I wasn't ashamed of my obsession; I just didn't expect anyone else to understand. It was my own holy grail.

But I was also selfish. I wanted the answer while still being able to hit the do-over button through investment. For the time being, the game did not come with that option.

And *was* this all a game for some people? When that select group of national defense types had gathered years ago to create the country's stealthiest and most technologically advanced security agency, were they entirely committed to the version that spun out of those meetings? Or did the reliance on new, mind-boggling technology leave Q2 stuck in a vague, peripheral file, languishing for now in a type of governmental purgatory? What Devya had admitted to me at dinner suggested that the organization was far from having a permanent line in the budget. Until God Maker perfected the investment process, it wouldn't surprise me if Q2 became trapped in perpetual *prove-it* mode, dependent on results, which we'd so far delivered—or, at least *I* had—combined with proof that the science actually worked properly.

Without the right political muscle on our side, it would be just like Washington to yank our charter, disband the team, and stop making Frankenstein's monsters down in the basement.

For another few minutes my thoughts returned to Christina. I wasn't sure I believed in soulmates, and had perpetually rejected the romantic notion that there's just one individual suited for us. And yet, given my remarkably convoluted, crazy life, I couldn't imagine anyone else better suited for me than Christina Valdez.

And goddamit, I needed to get home to her.

WITHOUT THE LUXURY of a gym at my disposal, I did as much as I could in the room. After all, stretching, pushups, and other assorted exercises didn't require fancy equipment, and could be done almost anywhere. The shell I currently inhabited was pretty much middle-of-the-pack when compared to bodies I'd test-driven before, but it handled the workouts well. If things went to hell, it wouldn't be because I was out of shape, even after two weeks of captivity.

I was in the middle of a stretching maneuver using one of my dining room chairs when the door was unlocked and pushed open. Byron, his regulation scowl in place, said, "Let's go."

Exhibiting the only form of revolt left to me, I moved as slowly as I could get away with, like a teenager doing chores. I took my time changing into a clean shirt, then smirked at Byron as I breezed past him and through the door. Outside, two more armed escorts awaited, looking somewhat bored with their ongoing guard duty. If they were going to triple-team me at every turn, breaking away was going to be nearly impossible. Which, I'm sure, was exactly why Butler had set it up that way.

But something in that thought tickled my frontal lobes, igniting a small flicker of hope.

They marched me down a hallway, then up the same flight of stairs we took to the dining room. But instead of turning left, we turned right, and a few moments later I was back in the same library office where I'd slugged Butler the first time I'd seen him.

Devya sat in one of the chairs facing the desk, but other than one meathead guarding her the room was empty. Byron and one other shithead from my own escort team took up places against the wall near the door. My assumption was that I was about to meet Butler's partner, the one he planned on eliminating once the move to the other complex was complete.

While we waited I leaned over and said to Devya, "I don't know if you heard, but we're going to be taking a road trip."

She stole a quick glance at me, but it was enough to see this was news to her.

"And I think you'll have a chance to see your granddaughter," I added.

Relief washed across her face and some of the tension in her shoulders seemed to evaporate.

"But," I said, leaning closer and lowering my voice to a whisper, "don't get too comfortable yet. I'm still planning on getting us free from these clowns."

This brought another look from her, and this time her eyes remained locked on mine, unsure of what this meant in the grand scheme of things.

I went back to a normal speaking voice. "Hey, I saw one of your creations. Mr. Bolt. I gotta say, Doc, I wouldn't put him on your resume. Not your best work."

She still didn't speak, but now her eyes flitted back and forth with mine, trying to convey something. I took a wild guess what it was.

She had intentionally not given her all in creating the all-new Edwin Bolt. I gave her a small smile to show the message was received and understood.

"I think I'm meeting the substitute teacher today," I said. "You've already met him, though. The guy who stole you and Tisha away in the dead of night."

Now she turned away, a cloud returning to her face. Good. I didn't want Devya too complacent, thinking that everything was cool just because she'd given Butler what he asked for. Well, *mostly* what he asked for. When the time came, I needed a little high-octane juice flowing through her veins.

The wait dragged on. Five minutes. Then ten. Just as I was about to complain to the charm school graduates guarding us, the door opened and two more people entered. One carried himself like a leader, walking around from behind us to take his place across the desk.

When he sat down and turned his cold, lifeless eyes my

direction, my breathing stopped and every muscle in my body went rigid.

Sitting five feet away from me was the man I'd sought for years.

Beadle.

CHAPTER TWENTY-FIVE

One of my earliest missions for Q2 took place not far from where I currently was incarcerated.

Supporting a handful of FBI and NSA agents, I'd spent a week in Boston on a case involving a congressman and a violent extremist group. The politician wasn't directly tied to the terrorist organization, but there was talk that he'd accepted a few too many donations without fully vetting all the people behind them. Now he was anxious to disentangle himself before the whole dirty mess caught up with him. So far the press didn't know anything, and he wanted to keep it that way.

The problem is, really bad people aren't known for humbly bowing out and letting slimy assholes off the hook. Debts are repaid, either in cash, influence, or blood. The congressman, we were pretty sure, was trying to decline the first two options and somehow thought his high-ranking position would spare him option number three. The FBI had suggested he arrange a talk with the offended parties, where the authorities could hustle in and make the appropriate arrests.

On my sixth day after arriving in Boston we got word that

a meeting would take place during the politician's annual end-of-summer bash hosted on another donor's yacht. Two dozen of New England's most powerful and affluent people embarked from Boston and sailed to Cape Cod. The trip, it was whispered, always began as a high-society shindig and ended up a drunken orgy of food, booze, and more than a few assignations between people who normally went home to someone else.

Sounded like a swell time to me.

I was one of six federal agents who'd mingle in plain clothes during the party. Two of the FBI agents were responsible for staying within eyesight of the politician, while three NSA agents kept watch on the guests. My job was to take out anyone who caused trouble, using deadly force if necessary. I had a short but solid history of successfully doing that sort of thing.

About six hundred yards back, close enough to keep us in sight but far enough to not cramp the party atmosphere, a Coast Guard vessel monitored the activity.

An hour out I bumped into Whitstone, one of the NSA agents. "Heard anything?" I asked her.

She gave a slight nod toward the stern. "Helipad," she said, under her breath.

A moment later I pretended to sip from a cocktail while glancing at the back of the boat. The large, stark white landing pad was empty.

"Rumor floating around that some big shot is flying in," she said.

"*Our* big shot?" I asked. She only shrugged and walked away.

Made sense, though. Rather than navigating the dock and

throngs of people, the head asshole would zip in, have his talk, and zip back out in a chopper.

I felt a tingle of excitement, the kind that told me the fun was about to begin.

At dusk it did. But it was far from fun.

It began innocently enough with a helicopter passing over-head, although much lower than it should've been. It caught everyone's attention, but only briefly before they went back to impressing each other. When the chopper came back around, it didn't approach the landing pad; it did the unthinkable.

It rained gunfire down on the boat.

I don't know how many people died during those first few bursts, but I personally saw three people cut down. A woman not ten feet from me had shells go through her chest and neck, and an eruption of blood covered the man she'd been chatting up. For a split second people were stunned into silence. Then pandemonium broke out. Screams pierced the air and people rushed to find cover. A stampede toward one of the stairwells leading to the lower deck resulted in a logjam as people stumbled, piling up on each other. That only created a massive target for the gunman's next spray, and five or six more guests lost their lives in that instant.

As soon as the gunfire began I instinctively dove to the floor. Now, as the screaming and bloodshed exploded, I keyed the mic on my lapel and sent an urgent message to the Coast Guard ship. Meanwhile the helicopter had moved a little higher, repositioning itself on the other side of the yacht. It was only a matter of time before they cut loose with another salvo.

Whitstone appeared, and I got to my knees and tugged her down beside me. "Get over the side," I yelled. "Find a life vest and get to safety."

She yelled back in my ear, over the sound of the chopper and the terrified screams. "Gotta find—"

A slug tore through her arm, spraying me with blood, and ricocheted off the metal bulkhead behind her. She screamed and I pushed her to the deck, then covered her with my body.

The helicopter now centered itself over the boat, and I could tell what the murdering bastards had in mind. They dropped an explosive onto the deck.

The entire craft shuddered, and flames sprouted everywhere.

I lifted Whitstone to her feet and eyed her wound. It was bad, but not deadly if she got help soon.

"You've got to get off the boat," I said into her ear. "Find a vest, get into the water. Now. Hurry!"

I stumbled back toward the place where I'd last seen the two FBI agents. After a minute pushing my way through the bloodied, staggering survivors still on their feet, I found the congressman. His eyes were wide open, staring toward the darkening sky, a look of surprise still etched across his face. Most of his torso was a sick, bloody mess of exposed organs and torn tissue.

His nefarious donors had successfully completed option number three.

"Shit," I said, but had no more time to assess the situation. With a roar the boat shook from an explosion below deck. I was thrown off my feet, colliding with another man. It was Gallo, one of the FBI agents assigned to shadow the congressman. He was bleeding from one ear, and a long gash ran from his scalp to below his jaw. He was in bad shape, and there was no time to waste. I grabbed two life vests off the outer wall of a cabin, thrust one into Gallo's hands and pushed him against the railing, yelling at him to jump. He wanted to stay and look for the other agents.

"It's going down!" I shouted into his ear. "Get out of here."

He hesitated and looked back, sure that he could still do something. With a burst of adrenaline I lifted him off his feet and tossed him overboard, then began slipping into my own vest. At that moment another explosion ripped through the boat, and I was catapulted into the water.

The impact momentarily knocked me senseless, but the vest somehow stayed on. It brought me back to the surface, where I watched an inferno boiling around me. I saw Gallo 30 feet away, scrambling into his vest. I heard another explosion, this one from farther away, and saw the Coast Guard vessel engaged in its own battle with a second helicopter. The terrorist group had planned for everything.

The yacht was going down fast.

But the chopper that had attacked us wasn't satisfied. Appearing like a ghostly specter through the smoke and flames, it hovered not far over me and the others floating in the water. A face I couldn't quite make out through the smoke peered down. The man holding the machine gun.

And he began firing again.

Bullets ripped through the group nearest me, immediately killing two people. I ditched my vest, and dove to escape the fire.

And drowned.

AT LEAST THAT'S my best reconstruction of the events, based on second-hand accounts. I didn't survive the attack, and neither did the congressman or three of the federal agents. A total of 19 people died; 17 survived, including Whitstone and

Gallo, who filled in many of the details. Gallo provided the detailed description of the man with the machine gun.

It was the same man who now sat across from me and Devya Nayar. Beadle. The man who'd killed me more than once, and who was also responsible for killing my sister. Which is another story for another time.

Beadle rarely pulled the trigger himself anymore; he'd morphed into more of a planner, what you might call an underworld consultant. Q2 and the FBI had him connected with multiple jobs, all of which had two things in common: They paid him an exorbitant amount of money, and they involved a lot of death. He was a mastermind for hire, with no idealogical restraints to prevent him from accepting any job. If you could afford him, and if the project was big enough and flashy enough to suit his ego, then Beadle didn't care about your ethnicity, your politics, or your religion. Deposit a substantial amount of money in his offshore account and he was your devil.

He was also number one on my to-do list, and had been for years. Quanta and Miller both regarded my interest as an unhealthy obsession. I considered it goal-setting.

At this particular moment I wanted to lunge across the desk and drive something sharp into his heart. But three armed men would likely cut me down before I could do the job. And, in the excitement they'd likely shoot Devya, too.

Butler had said he planned on killing his partner before they learned the true nature of the technology they'd helped him steal. And until discovering the associate's identity I would've considered that execution a slam dunk. Butler was skilled and ruthless. But now? I gave it a 50 percent chance of success. Maybe 40.

I'd learned through the years it was foolish to bet against Beadle.

My mind raced, wondering why Butler would saddle up with someone this high on the criminal food chain when all he needed was a smash-and-grab job. Granted, the assignment required detailed planning and cold-blooded precision—all of which were in Beadle's wheelhouse—but he'd purchased a Porsche when a Lincoln would do.

Then it registered. Butler was already planning to make a major statement backing up his manifesto, all right off the bat. He'd get his technology working and use it to do something Q2 had never been able to accomplish: Take out Beadle. He'd not only validate his intention of cleaning up the scum, but he'd debut in a way that once again would humiliate Quanta. It was Butler's way of saying, *You've had years to get this guy; I got him right away, using the technology you've always had at your disposal.*

Again, as much as I hated what the man had done, I had to admire his determination in going after what he wanted. And doing it with such flair.

Beadle's cold stare at me and Devya lasted long enough that it became awkward and uncomfortable. Then, without removing his eyes from us, he held out his hand to the man who'd entered with him. That guy placed a SIG Sauer pistol into Beadle's palm. The gun was set on the desktop. Then Beadle laced his fingers together and finally spoke.

"You're going to be leaving this place in approximately three hours. You'll be in separate vehicles. The journey will not take long."

His voice was mild and he clipped his words, a type of enunciation often used to try to drive home a point.

"What you need to understand," he continued, "is that you

won't see or talk to me again after this. There's no need for it. You'll do as you're instructed, and you'll waste no time. Others may be flexible in their discipline; I am not. I'm explaining this to you now so you'll be very clear on how I do business."

I raised a hand to ask a question, mostly to throw him off his rhythm. They always hated that.

He fixed me with a hard look, then said, "There are no questions. Nothing else needs to be explained to you. You'll get no second chances at following directions."

Standing, he picked up the gun. "It's possible that you're under the delusion you're too important to be killed. That is not the case. Regardless of how you've been treated up to this point, the only thing that matters moving forward is that you remain quiet and do as you're told."

With the gun he gestured at the man who'd handed it to him. "This gentleman has been with me almost nine months. And he's served well."

Beadle brought the gun up and shot the man in the forehead.

Instinctively I jumped halfway from my seat as the assistant, the top half of his head gone, toppled to the floor. Devya screamed and reached out for me. The other men in the room came to full alert, obviously stunned by what had happened. A sickly smell, one I'd encountered too many times to count, reached my nose. It was the acrid scent of gun propellant mixed with blood.

My eyes wide, I looked up at Beadle. He turned back to face us. His expression hadn't changed at all.

"As I said, he served me well. But not perfectly. His latest mistake today was the last I'll tolerate." He now raised the gun so that it lined up with *my* forehead.

"I think the lesson is clear," he said. "If this is how I handle problems within my own team, you can imagine how little patience I will have for yours. Do not cross me, do not cross the men who will be in charge of your move, and do not waste anyone's time. Again, there are no second chances."

This time his eyes did not shift between me and Devya; they stayed locked on mine. In instances like this I always wondered if Beadle somehow sensed the history we shared. He wouldn't recognize the body I inhabited, of course, but that didn't stop me from believing it was possible he *felt* our connection, or at least felt the waves of hatred radiating from me. After the momentary jolt from the unexpected blast of the gun, I'd gone statue still. My own gaze matched his cold glare. Not a muscle on my face twitched.

I had every intention of finishing this son of a bitch before we left the house.

His speech finished, Beadle turned and stepped over the corpse with the mutilated head without so much as a glance at it. He handed the gun to one of the other startled guards and left the room.

CHAPTER TWENTY-SIX

Three hours. I didn't know if that was an honest itinerary or if Beadle was bullshitting, but neither would surprise me. As far as he was concerned we were no better than baggage loaded into the belly of a plane.

Assuming it was accurate, however, meant I had next to no time to get my shit together and figure out an escape plan. For the moment Butler's forces were divided, but once we were transported like cattle to the next holding pen his armed detail would be fortified. It was time to improve the odds.

Except the escape plan suddenly had a wild card I couldn't have foreseen. Was my assignment to stop Butler, save Devya and her granddaughter, and retrieve the investment gear? Or was it all of the above *and* a side order of Beadle's head on a platter? I could only imagine the look on Quanta's face when she discovered the identity of the silent partner. Probably the same look I'd worn when he'd walked into the room.

Normally she poo-poo'd my less-than-subtle efforts to glean intel about Beadle's location or his current activities, afraid it would distract me from any casework I'd been assigned. But throwing himself into the heart of the Nayar case had elevated my number-one knave into complete relevance. He'd voluntarily added himself to the whole wicked stew, and while I was stunned, I was also grateful. It was as if Beadle had done me a favor without even realizing it.

Of course, there was still the matter of getting to him. And, prior to that, getting out of my cell.

The tickle of hope I'd felt earlier continued to linger, however, and the act Beadle had staged in the library only reinforced the idea. Butler was a former Q2 agent, which meant he knew exactly what I was capable of doing in a situation like this. That was why he'd beefed up security around me, often using three armed guards when he himself wasn't there to supply additional muscle. Three gunmen for one hostage was something most criminals would feel was overkill. Not Butler. He took no chances with his prize.

I had to hope Beadle still knew nothing about the workings of Q2, that Butler had kept those particular details from his partner. If so, Beadle probably wouldn't send three men to look after me. It was also possible he felt his loud demonstration would sufficiently terrify his two captives into meek submission. It could even be classified as pride; assigning three men might be interpreted that I was the world's most supreme badass, and someone he should fear. And if I knew anything about Beadle it was his complete disdain for everyone he worked with and everyone he sought to crush. He was the coolest of the cool, and elevating anyone's status to anything near his was unthinkable.

Devya had been sobbing as they led her away. She looked back at me over her shoulder, a pleading request for help, but she was immediately jerked around to face forward, and I heard her give a small cry of pain. Jesus, these guys were all such complete assholes. Nobody would catch a break from me if I got the chance I wanted.

But there was one bit of good news: The look God Maker had thrown my way confirmed that she finally trusted me, and looked upon me as a good guy. That would help when the time came.

Strong-armed into my room, the door was slammed shut and I heard the bolt turn.

First things first. I made a circuit of the room, looking once again for anything that could conceivably be used as a weapon. The closest thing I found with a natural shape to it was my toothbrush, but I didn't put much stock in that. It would have to be something sharp, even *somewhat* sharp, unless I found a suitable blunt object that could be concealed.

But there was nothing. Again, Butler was no fool. I had no silverware—Marta brought that with each meal and took it away when she left. It was plastic, anyway.

No curtain rods because there were no windows. No mirror, not even in the bathroom. The bed rested on a simple platform, so there were no wooden slats to manipulate. The table's legs were a possibility, but they were also large and unwieldy, not easy to shield from view of a wary guard. The element of surprise was critical.

What the hell was in this room that could work? It was damned frustrating. I could, of course, take my chances with plain hand-to-hand combat, but I'd feel a lot better about the odds if I could quickly disable one of the goons.

For once I cursed the fact that my cell was a comfortable suite, with a soft bed, toiletries, and even books to pass the time.

I stopped.

Books.

As a general rule books are not deadly, although in high school Faulkner nearly killed me. But today, just maybe . . .

Walking over to the book shelf, I studied the titles on the spines. With a grunt of laughter, I removed the Robert Ludlum book I'd used to pass a few hours. I pulled open the hard, heavy front cover and ran my fingers along the top corner. No, it wasn't ice-pick sharp, and it would never cut a loaf of sourdough bread. But that corner could be refined enough that perhaps a well-placed, solid stab would create a sufficient hole in someone's throat.

Yeah, it was stupid. But it *could* actually work. And since I had jack shit other than my reading material, the beggars-choosers rule came into play.

Flipping the hardcover book over, I fingered the two corners on the back, then compared them to the front. The front seemed less worn. I gripped it with one hand while holding the bulk of the novel with the other. Then, after muttering an apology to both Mr. Ludlum and Ms. Appleton— our fussy high school librarian—I tore the cover away. Of course, it didn't come off without a fight, and required some aggressive manhandling before the heinous deed was done. What remained was a mangled mess of liberated pages, many of which fluttered to the floor. The other handful I tossed onto the shelf. The room's next occupant would be left to wonder what poor Robert Ludlum could've possibly done to piss off a reader that much.

The cover had come free but needed work before I'd feel comfortable taking it into combat. I sat on the edge of the bed and surveyed the possibilities. The front and back covers, still connected by the sinewy spine, would need to be separated. That was more difficult than you'd think. It reminded me of old-time carnival strongmen ripping phone books in half. Google it, kids.

Once I had the front cover by itself, I folded it lengthwise so the top right point was isolated, forming a sort of diamond shape. But that still wouldn't be good enough. So I walked into the bathroom, where the tile floor would provide some friction. Kneeling, I scraped the sides, gradually wearing down the binder's board and doing my best to maintain the corner's integrity. The idea was to create a semblance of a sharp point, at least sharp enough to break skin. It didn't need to be a stiletto; it just had to provide a solid poke.

After about 15 minutes I was sweaty but somewhat satisfied. As a whole it felt firm in my grip, and it was small enough to conceal in one of my pockets.

It also qualified as the strangest weapon I'd ever fashioned. Now I needed to see if Beadle would accommodate my wish by sending two men instead of three. Either way I would have to act, but a boy can dream.

I shoved the Ludlum shiv into my right front pocket and stretched out on the bed, waiting.

THE LOCK RATTLED in the door. I assumed the most innocent look I could muster, with my feet crossed at the ankles and my hands laced behind my head. I was the picture of nonchalance.

When they entered, I fought the urge to immediately count the bodies. Instead I lay still, staring at the ceiling over the bed.

"Hey," one of the guards called. After a moment I looked over.

Unless one lingered out of sight in the hall, there were only two of them. Thank you, Beadle.

"Come on," the guard said. "Let's go."

I swung my legs over the side of the bed, gave a nice, leisurely stretch, then got to my feet. It would help my cause if I engaged them in conversation. That would distract them just enough to give me a second's edge. You never expected an attack from someone in the middle of a conversation.

The next question for me was whether to take them here in the room, or wait until we got into the hallway. Much of that depended on how they aligned for the walk; would they both stay behind me, or would one lead with me in the middle. That's what I hoped for.

"So, it's moving day, I hear," I said, approaching them with a wry smile. "Are you guys coming with?"

"Shut up," the second one said.

"Okay. Is there anything I need to take, like from the bathroom?"

"No. Shut up and get moving." Now it was the first one again, and he looked pained and impatient, which was good. He clearly just wanted all of this over with.

It was about to be.

I stuffed both hands into my pockets, mostly to emphasize my lackadaisical attitude toward it all. My right hand found the right grip on the make-shift handle of my cheap-ass weapon. I grasped it in a way that it could be used with a powerful back-handed slash. When the time came, it would need to be the perfect combination of speed, power, and accuracy. The accuracy was most critical. The point had to enter the man's throat; if I missed and hit him in the jaw or the shoulder, I was dead. It would be one shot.

And even with a pinpoint jab, the next move would need to take place instantly. I couldn't afford to inspect any damage, because the other guy would react pretty quickly. The whole thing would have to go like this:

Pull out the weapon while spinning.

Slam the point into his neck.

Kick away the weapon of Shithead #2.

Use every bit of training to put him down before he could counter-attack.

If things went as planned, it should all happen in less than five seconds. Then I could double-check that Shithead #1 was either dead from the neck wound or on the way there. After that . . .

After that it was all ad-libbed. I didn't know where Devya was being kept, and I had no idea where the rest of the goon squad would be stationed.

I also had no clue where to find my real prey.

Just as I'd hoped, the second guy turned for the door. He'd lead me out. I subtly adjusted my pace to stay within range of him. The first guy, with his gun leveled at my back, fell in step behind me. The spacing was ideal, and the first real blunder these guys had made. Everyone was likely bored with their babysitting duties and anxious to get to the new base of operations. I'm sure they were also eager to get away from the new madman in charge. No doubt word had spread of the execution in the library, which would distract them from their duties. Again, thank you, Beadle.

The time was now. To occupy their eyes and minds, I said, "Careful of the dead rat by the door."

There's nobody on the planet who wouldn't look down.

Pulling out the crude knife, I spun, quickly determined the proper angle, and plunged the heavy binder's board deep into the man's throat, right beside his Adam's apple. A spray of blood shot out and I had only a fraction of a second to see his eyes shoot wide open. Without hesitating I spun back and launched a hard kick just as the guy in front stopped to look back. My foot connected with the wrist of his gun hand, sending the weapon skittering across the floor.

Against the backdrop of choking sounds coming from my first victim, I put all of my rage and training into the man in front. My fist connected with the bridge of his nose, shattering it, and knocking him backwards. I attacked, sending two hard blows into his gut, followed by a chop with the back of my hand into his neck. He reeled backward again, into the door jamb. For a moment he tried to recover, but it was too late. I launched another kick into his mouth, heard the dull shatter of teeth, and saw his eyes curl upward. Grabbing his hair, I yanked down hard on his head while bringing up my left knee.

He slumped to the floor. Kneeling, I lifted his head, and, with a twist, snapped his neck.

His partner was vainly trying to staunch the gush of blood coming from his throat. He had seconds to live. If there'd been time I would've marveled over the effectiveness of the Ludlum knife, which he'd managed to extricate. It lay beside him in his growing pool of blood.

I didn't wait around to watch the end.

Confiscating his gun, I stuffed it into my back waistband. Then, picking up the other gun lying against the wall, I checked the ammo status, crept to the open door, and glanced around the corner.

I was free.

CHAPTER TWENTY-SEVEN

I hurried along the corridor toward the back staircase, the one we'd used when going to the dining room or library. What you hoped for in a situation like this was peace and quiet, allowing you an opportunity to navigate without interruption.

What you usually got was some asshole popping out of a doorway. Which is exactly what happened now. It was one of the men who'd often escorted me to the gym, and I'm sure the last thing he expected to see was me traipsing down the hallway with a gun in my hand. It took him a second to comprehend that this was very wrong, during which time I accelerated, aiming to crack him across the head with the butt of the gun. But at the last second his instincts kicked in and he raised a hand in defense.

The blow still knocked him off balance, so I followed with a left that connected. Normally that would be enough to gain the upper hand, but apparently Butler had selected some tough-ass hombres for his team. The guy may have been a boxer at one point, because he took the shot and stayed upright. He gripped the wrist of my gun hand, preventing me from getting off a shot.

Which I had no intention of doing anyway, unless absolutely necessary. The last thing I wanted was the blast of a gun alerting the entire compound that trouble was afoot.

With my momentum, I slammed him backwards into the wall. He managed to get his free hand up to my throat. I couldn't have that, so I brought my knee up into his groin, once, twice, which was enough to loosen his grip. With another left I broke his nose. Now my gun hand was free, and I smashed him in the forehead. I felt him begin to crumple, but I wasn't about to trust that he was out. Guys like that will summon all sorts of reserve energy when they're up against death. I belted him again, this time across the jaw, and that finally took the fight out of him. He began to slide down the wall, so I eased him by his shirt collar.

Once he was down, I put a knee into his chest, then leaned over him and shoved the gun into his open mouth. I've found that often results in cooperation.

"As you can see," I said, my voice lowered, "I'm a lousy houseguest. I didn't pay for any of the groceries and I didn't strip my bed. My next rude act might be to blow your brains all over this hideous wallpaper. Are you paying attention?"

His eyes, watering from the busted nose but displaying all manner of hatred, locked onto mine. He gave one nod.

"Good. All I need is one piece of information. Is the lady scientist on the main level or above it?"

I pulled the gun out for him to answer, but added: "Save me the time and you some of your teeth, which I'll happily knock right down your throat. It ain't worth heroics right now."

He spat a wad of bloody phlegm into my face and lurched.

But I was ready. I kept the pressure on his chest and applied another solid whack of the gun across his face, surely dislodging teeth. With my other hand I wiped the grossness off my face.

"That," I said, grimacing, "was disgusting. Should I give you another chance?"

He uttered a vulgarity I had to grudgingly admit scored style points. But I hated tough guys; they were so damned stubborn about not appearing weak, even in the face of cracked skulls and expensive dental work.

"Well, hell," I said, then lifted the gun up high before crashing it down onto his head with everything I had. He slumped over and I stood up. "Thanks. You were no help whatsoever."

To be honest, I hadn't expected help. The job was rarely easy, and many times all I got for my trouble was a loogie in the face. But it was worth a try.

There was no telling how many soldiers roamed the grounds, but three of them were now officially out of action. The odds were improving.

I reached the staircase and looked up through the railing toward the main level. I heard footsteps, receding. After pausing another few seconds, I crept up, staying against the wall. Just before I reached the top a door across from the stairs opened and one of the servants who'd served us dinner stepped out of a bathroom. She saw me, covered in blood and holding a gun, and froze.

"Back inside," I said, motioning with my weapon for her to retreat back into the room. She was too afraid to move until I got close. Then she backed up and I followed her into the small powder room, closing the door behind us.

"Well," I said, "I've had an exciting day. How about you?"

No answer. She kept glancing down at the gun and back to my face.

"Don't mind this," I said, waggling the Smith & Wesson. "I only use this on people who don't play nice. But *you'll* play nice, right?"

Now she nodded and tried to say *yes*. It came out as a gasp.

"Good. What's your name? No, look at me. There you go. Now, what's your name?"

She swallowed hard. "Tula."

"Tula. That's lovely. Listen, Tula, here's how you can help me. You remember the nice lady who had dinner with us a couple of times?"

She nodded again.

"Where is she right now?"

"In . . . in the room where she works."

"Excellent. How would I find the room where she works?"

She pointed to the left, which made me laugh. The poor thing was terrified.

"Okay, that way. But *where*? Take a deep breath, it'll be okay."

After closing her eyes and calming herself, she looked back at me and said, "It's at the far end of the hall, on the right. Just past the library."

"Got it. Next question. You've seen a few tough guys walking around here the last few days, right? Lots of muscles but no manners. Since you're hired to help out, how many are around right now?"

She looked confused by the question, or was just having a hard time concentrating on anything given the adrenaline surge.

"Tula, I need you to think. How many men are helping Mr. Butler?"

She looked like she might hyperventilate, so I placed a gentle hand on her shoulder and pushed her down onto the closed toilet lid. I knelt so I was eye-level with her and gave a warm smile. "How many?"

"Um," she swallowed hard. "There were seven . . . seven helping Mr. Butler. But I think two of them left with him."

"Did Byron go with him? The big guy with the doodles on his dome."

"No. He's still here. I think."

"Very good. Now listen to me, this is important. I want you to sit right there. Do not leave this room for the next hour. Do you hear me? Now, hand me your phone."

"It's in my purse. In the kitchen."

"Fine. Okay, remember what I said: Don't even think about walking out of this room for the next hour. If you even think about leaving, just remember one thing." I indicated the blood covering my shirt. "None of this is mine. It's all from people who didn't listen to me. Are we clear?"

She gave a vigorous nod. I returned a smile, then stood and put a finger to my lips requesting silence as I opened the door.

Again, I heard voices somewhere, but they weren't close. I winked at Tula, shut the door behind me, then turned left and tiptoed down the hall. At the door to the library I stopped, poked my head around the corner, and scanned an empty room. I was about to stroll past when something shiny on the desk caught my eye.

After glancing both ways down the hall, I hurried over and snatched the letter opener Butler had been using when I arrived. The metal blade wasn't very long, but had a nice, solid heft. Not bad. Kneeling, I slipped it into one of my socks, then rolled the pants leg back over it. Now I had two guns and a much more substantial blade than the one I'd crafted from a book. The firepower was comforting, but I knew better than to let it create an inflated sense of invincibility. I wasn't armored; all it would take was one bullet from one asshole to put out the lights.

The room provided to Devya as her makeshift lab was just next door. It was safe to assume she'd have company, but probably just one to keep an eye on her. The doctor was brilliant, but she certainly wasn't a physical threat. And so far the lifeless dickheads I'd left in my wake had yet to be found, which meant there was still time before everything went to hell.

Just getting God Maker out of the building wasn't a victory. No, I somehow needed to defeat the small unit charged with guarding us while sparing at least one person who knew where to find Butler. Finding Agent One had to be Job One. With the investment technology—even a rudimentary version of it—in his control, we had a nightmare on our hands.

I stood outside the closed door Tula had identified as Devya's work room. Putting an ear to the dark wood, I heard no sounds from within. Of course, that meant nothing. With a deep breath, I flexed my fingers on the handle of the gun, then opened the door and rushed in.

Devya stood behind a table, staring at me in stunned amazement. And she was alone.

I let out an audible sigh of relief and closed the door.

"The room service here is shitty and they don't have Netflix," I said to her. "I say we check out. Are you game?"

She eyed the gun, then took in the gore splattered across me. "Are you hurt?" she asked.

"Not yet, but the day is young. I can't believe they left you alone."

"He's coming right back. He went to get me some water."

"He? So just one?"

She nodded.

"Better and better." If Tula's observation had been accurate, that meant there was only one other meathead in the house besides Devya's chaperone. Probably Byron, probably shadowing Beadle.

"Sit down over there," I said, pointing toward a chair across the room by a window. "If anyone starts shooting, hit the floor behind the desk."

"But—"

"No buts. Now hurry. He'll probably be back any moment."

Clearly nervous as hell, she went to the chair while I planted myself against the wall so I'd be behind the door when it opened.

Which was only seconds later. A thick shadow fell across the floor, but before he could enter I heard Byron's urgent voice yelling to him from down the hall. All I caught for sure was, "Lock her in her room and help me find him."

Okay, so the jig was up. It could make things more challenging, but I'd already knocked out 60 percent of their forces. Another 20 percent was about to be tallied, if he'd get his sorry ass in the room.

Like I said, things were rarely easy. He wouldn't enter. Apparently with my antics discovered, Devya's glass of water was forgotten. Instead he called out to her from the doorway. "All right. Let's go."

Hidden as I was, I couldn't see her through the opened door, but she must've been sitting there, frozen.

"Did you hear me?" he barked. "Let's go."

This was a mess. I didn't want to have to deal with this big turd in the hallway, out in the open. I silently urged Devya to remain in her seat, to make him walk in. Was she a good enough actor to play her part? Did she have the nerve to hold up under the heat? Perhaps having her granddaughter's life at stake would tip the scales.

Bless her heart, she wasn't moving.

"Goddammit," the man said, and stepped toward her.

Seconds later he was unconscious and I quietly lowered him to the floor to avoid the sound of a crashing body. One of my guns, now with a bloody handle, held Devya's attention. She looked scared to death.

She said in a trembling voice, "Did you kill him? I don't know how you can do that."

"He's not dead," I said, hustling over and pulling her up by an arm. "But *we* will be if you don't do everything I say."

I gently took her by the chin and turned her face away from the man sprawled on the floor, blood dripping from the back of his head. "Devya, we're not out of this yet. And even when we get out of the house we need to find where Butler has Tisha. Do you know anything about where that might be?"

She shook her head. "No. He hasn't told me anything." Then her face brightened. "Wait. He did say something. Night before last, when I demanded to see Tisha, he said if I behaved and did as I was told, he'd row me over to see her."

"*Row*?" I asked. "You're sure that's the word he used?"

"Yes. At first I thought he was just being cruel, taunting me. But he laughed when he said it, like he was so clever, dropping a little hint."

"Or just trying to throw you off," I said.

Time was wasting. I didn't know about Beadle, but Byron was still somewhere on the grounds. It wouldn't be long before he showed up here, wondering what had happened to his soldier. I pulled God Maker over to the door and listened.

Nothing. Stepping into the hall, I went around the corner into the library and took Devya to a closet door.

"Get inside here, hunker down, and wait. Don't come out until I return and get you."

"And what if you don't come back?"

I grunted. "Well, Doc, then try to convince Butler to not erase my hard drive. I'd hate to think of *that* light going out."

She looked pained, but stepped inside the oversized closet. "What are you going to do?"

"We've got to track down that other location. I don't think Byron will be very cooperative, and I know Beadle won't. If I could grab Marta I might be able to figure it out from her phone, because I know she's been there. But I'm afraid she's probably gone with Butler."

"No," Devya said. "I'm almost positive I heard her a little while ago." She looked at me, pleading. "Please don't hurt her. She's a kind woman."

"Who's working for killers," I said.

"But *she's* not a killer," Devya said. "Promise me you won't hurt *her*."

Promises right now were out of the question, even vows to protect sweet ladies like Marta. Instead, I reminded her to stay inside and keep quiet, then closed the door.

I was about to scamper out of the room when I glanced over at the large desk where I'd picked up the letter opener. Was it too much to ask that Butler had left some scrap of information lying around, something that might pinpoint his new location?

Of course it was too much. I set the gun on the desktop, then wasted a valuable minute sorting through the random scraps littering the surface. I quietly pulled open each drawer, not sure what I was even looking for. There was nothing.

It would've been miraculous if the location had just been sitting around for me to find. But as frustrating as it was, I had to admit that, all things considered, the day was going much better than I had any right to expect.

Of course, the minute you think something like that, the law of averages is instructed to kick you right in the crotch.

The kick arrived in the form of a tingling sensation rather than anything concrete. I got the creepy feeling I was no longer alone. And, when I looked up from the bottom desk drawer, I saw three faces studying me.

One of them held a big, ugly gun, pointed right at me.

CHAPTER TWENTY-EIGHT

I t was Byron, of course, with the nasty weapon, and he seemed determined to finally put me out of his misery. All he needed was an okay from the man standing in the middle. Beadle, naturally.

The other figure belonged to Marta, wearing her usual mask of concern. If she'd uttered a "tsk, tsk," I wouldn't have been surprised at all. I wondered if I could somehow bank on her show of compassion to help save my life, if it came right down to it.

In my peripheral vision I saw my own gun on the edge of the desk. There was no way I could make a move for it without losing my head. Literally. Ah, but the bad boys in the doorway didn't know about the bonus piece I'd tucked nicely into my back waistband. I had a fleeting image of a bloody and battered Bruce Willis at the end of Die Hard, laughing because he's about to bust out that surprise gun taped to his back. Yippee ki-yay, and all that.

Beadle noticed the gun I'd stupidly left lying there in plain sight, nodded at it to Byron, who moved slowly forward. With only the desk between us, and without taking his eyes from me or his aim from my chest, he reached down and picked up my gun. But he didn't back up; he stayed right there, threatening me with both his nasty weapon and his angry eyes. Byron was just about the worst kind of killer I ever dealt with: He was a bore. At least the other killer B's, Butler and Beadle, were interesting.

"Where is the doctor?" Beadle asked. His voice carried no real inflection, and no concern. He could've been asking me the name of Saturn's largest moon.

"She had an appointment with her stylist," I said. "Cut and color, I believe. Although, since you live every day with shitty hair, you might not understand."

Beadle took one step toward me and emphasized the word. "Where?"

I jerked my head backwards, indicating the French doors opening onto a back patio area. "She's on her way down the beach to find an occupied home. Someone who can contact the police, or the FBI. Hell, I'd settle for a park ranger or a mall cop right now."

He seemed to consider the possibility, then angled his head slightly toward Marta while keeping his eyes on me. "Go check."

Without a word, she glided past Byron and me, pushed open the French doors, and walked out, leaving them ajar. A cool breeze blew against my back. I sat down in the fancy desk chair, partly to keep up the confident charade that I anticipated help arriving any moment, but mostly to conceal the gun sticking out of my belt.

"You're going after the wrong person," I said.

"And who is the right person?" Beadle asked in his usual uninterested voice.

I leaned on the desk. "Don't tell me you're so dense that you haven't figured this out for yourself. Once the doctor and I are safely together at his other compound, who do you think Butler's going to eliminate first?"

Beadle said nothing. I looked at Byron.

"And you think *you've* got some special pass through all this? You were standing right there in that cabin, after you killed the government agent, and you heard exactly what your boss said. He makes no promises, and he leaves no loose ends." I gave a mirthless laugh. "Well, my friend, they don't come much looser than reckless killers for hire. You've just about used up any worth you may have had to get him the things he wants."

Now I turned back to Beadle. "Butler has always been, and always *will* be, a lone wolf. He does not work and play well with others."

"Then what makes you think you're valuable enough to be kept alive?" Beadle asked. "Hmm?"

I shrugged. "I'm probably not. He's already let one of his muscle-headed goons try to kill me with his fists. I'm sure I'll wind up dead not long after your bodies are found floating in the bay."

By the look on his face he seemed to find this humorous, but I had to believe that at least a fraction of it gave him pause. After all, Beadle worked independently, too. His very nature was distrustful; all I could do was stoke the flames.

Time to mess with his mind a bit more. "Besides, the people he's most likely to dispose of are the ones who know a little too much. You two, obviously, know a shitload. Marta will likely have her throat cut, too. And me? Well, I know a little something about each of you."

I pointed at him. "You like to think you're some mysterious, behind-the-scenes player. But I know your name. You're Beadle. And you've been causing trouble for a long, long time."

The slightly-amused expression on his face vanished. Now his eyes, always cold and opaque, became slits. If he hated anything in this world, it was being identified. I was taking a huge chance that he'd either have Byron blow my head off, or do it himself. But my best defense at the moment was keeping both of them off-balance.

"You've killed a lot of people through the years," I said. "Which is bad enough. But several years ago you killed someone I cared about. So, honestly, Butler doesn't get to kill you. That will be *my* pleasure. It's a little something I promised myself a long time ago. And, unlike Butler, I keep mine."

Everything I said was the truth. The motive for blabbing it all, however, was tactical. I'd learned early in the spy game that hired gunmen—dweebs like Byron—weren't usually very good at keeping up with intense dialogue. Once I got into the weeds with Beadle, Byron was as lost as a child listening to adults talking around the dinner table. He was confused, but, more importantly, he grew restless. His gaze, once firmly locked onto my face, now flitted back and forth between me and Beadle. Without appearing to look at him, I noticed Byron's finger had pulled off the trigger. He gently flexed it. His tongue swept out along his upper lip. His mental capacity was on overload, and his trained hitman muscles had no simple commands to follow.

Perhaps Beadle realized it, too. After another momentary pause, he addressed the gunman. "It's time to go. Bring him."

"What about the doctor?" Byron asked. "You heard him. She's calling the police."

"She's not calling anyone," Beadle said. "She's still somewhere on the grounds."

I stood up and moved slowly around the desk. "You're going to just walk right into Butler's lair? You may be a shit-sucking killer, but you're not that stupid, are you?"

My right arm hung limply by my side. There was a chance I could maneuver it behind my back without drawing suspicion. I needed to distract Byron again. "And what about you?" I said to him. "Still think you're going to survive all this after everything you've learned?"

"Shut up," he said.

"I have to warn *you* about something, too," I said to him, raising my left hand and pointing a finger toward his face. That gave me the distraction I needed to slip my right hand behind me. "That woman you killed at the cabin? The government agent? You know who she was?"

He glared at me. "I don't give a shit who she was."

I stopped. The gun was in my hidden hand.

"She was my friend," I said, and at the same time brought the gun up and fired a shot into his neck. He lurched backward, tumbling over one of the chairs on the other side of the desk. His gun fell to the floor as both hands clutched at the gushing wound beneath his chin.

Startled, Beadle had jumped, but froze again when he saw my gun now pointed at his face. I walked the rest of the way around the desk, keeping him locked in my sights. Then, when I stood beside Byron I glanced down, straight into his eyes.

"She was a really *good* friend, you son of a bitch."

I know he heard me, but moments later his hands dropped

away and he fell still, his eyes glazed over, lifeless, staring straight up at me.

Looking back at Beadle, I said, "And now, the moment we've all been waiting for."

It was true. I'd waited so long for this moment. Standing there, with a gun aimed right at the head of the man I'd vowed to execute. Years of fantasizing about actually pulling the trigger, or perhaps tightening my hands around his throat, watching him die, observing in the most intimate way the life draining from him, the way I'd watched it drain out of Byron. It was right there.

The man who'd snuffed out my life more than once. The man who'd murdered my sister. The sociopathic monster who'd never thought twice about the people he'd killed, the families he'd ruined. He was standing right there. With one feather-light squeeze of the trigger I could finally put an end to the pain that had haunted me for so long.

Beadle. Right there.

Surprised that I'd finally reached this point, I found myself laughing. Maybe Beadle understood why, maybe he didn't. His face betrayed nothing. And the longer I looked at it, the longer I wanted the moment to stretch. After years of pursuit, I wanted to savor it right down to the ground, soak up every second, knowing I'd finally won. Killing him would be sweet; watching him wait for it to happen was somehow sweeter.

But it couldn't last forever. I opened my mouth to say something profound before pulling the trigger.

The next thing I knew my head snapped forward, and pain shot through me. I turned to see who'd hit me, knowing I had to get the club out of their hand.

It was Marta. And she held nothing. The blow had come

from her hand. Her posture showed she was preparing to strike again.

Somehow, and I'll never know how, I held onto the gun. I saw a flash of movement and just happened to catch the sight of Beadle dashing toward the door to the hallway. As Marta launched another attack, I had barely a second to raise the gun and shoot at the fleeing figure. The gun roared, and as Marta's fist made contact with my ribs, I heard Beadle cry out, and caught a glimpse of him staggering to one knee. I'd hit him in the right shoulder, and blood was splattered along the wall next to the open doorway.

After that I couldn't devote any more time to Beadle. Marta swung a hard roundhouse kick at me, which I just managed to deflect, but at the cost of losing my gun. It clattered to the hardwood floor and disappeared under one of the big chairs in front of the fireplace.

A fist connected near my mouth, and I fell back.

Marta, the sweet, kindly innkeeper, was kicking the living shit out of me.

Now a variety of emotions surged: Anger that I'd waited too long to shoot Beadle, surprise that the tiny woman with the 100-watt smile was a martial arts animal, and concern that she was within moments of finishing me off. But the combination of all three sent a tidal wave of adrenaline and endorphins surging through me. Just as another kick sliced in for my head, I reached up, grabbed her foot, and tossed her to the side.

It didn't slow her down a bit. She rebounded instantly, assuming an attack pose.

"Jesus," I said, back on my own feet, wobbling backwards a little, and dabbing at the stream of blood coming from my mouth. "What happened to the sweet little angel who served me breakfast every day?"

She didn't answer. Instead, with a snarl she let loose with a flurry of kicks and chops that reminded me of the worst abuse I'd taken from Quanta in our training sessions. It was a true Jekyll and Hyde transformation, and I was being treated to the darkest side.

My head throbbing and my vision slightly blurred, I continued to react defensively, avoiding the most dangerous blows while absorbing too many to be good for me. I realized that, even as I watched this ferocious attack unfurl in front of me, I couldn't shake the image of the gentle, angelic Marta who'd waited on me for the last couple of weeks. That image prevented me from launching a significant counterattack. I found that I didn't want to hurt her.

Even though she was unleashing hell upon me.

But, given enough punishment, all of us will eventually reach the point where we've had quite enough. After blocking one of her hard kicks, I spied an opening and leaned into a solid punch that knocked her backward. She fell across the desk, shaken, which gave me a chance. I danced in and raised my hand to chop down on her neck, when she ducked, whirled, and extended a kick into my solar plexus.

The air rushed out of me and I tripped over Byron's body lying prone on the floor. I went down hard, rolling up against the heavy, solid cabinet holding the oversized aquarium. For a moment I feared it might topple over on top of me. Within seconds Marta pounced, first treating my face to a couple of hard blows while her knees secured my upper arms. Then her wiry hands were on my throat. Out of air from the gut kick and stunned from the head shots, I weakly tried freeing one of my hands. But she applied a wrestler's knowledge of leverage, pinning me while I fought to breathe. I couldn't believe what was happening.

Now, leaning down until her face was inches from mine, she finally spoke. "You've gone easy with me. Did you really think I was a delicate little thing?" She grinned. "You should've tried harder. In fact, you should've killed me when you had a chance. Because I'm not going to show you the same courtesy, Mr. Swan."

She started to laugh, and tightened her hands even more. I went limp, hoping she'd relax some of the pressure on my arms. She did, leaning more heavily on my windpipe.

That allowed me to pull my right leg up in a bicycle movement, and, with my hand, remove the letter opener from my sock. Just as darkness started to close over me, I summoned my last bit of strength, tore my right arm free, and rammed the letter opener deep into her back.

She spasmed, lifting straight up, and my throat was free of her hands. I coughed, sucked in lungfuls of air, and shoved her to the side. She reached around, trying to get a hand on the blade, which I still held. So I yanked it out, pulled my arm around to the front of her, and placed the point just inside her left ear.

"Thanks for the advice," I said with a raspy voice.

And jammed the letter opener into her brain.

She tumbled onto the floor between Byron and me. The three of us, stretched out in our various pools of blood, must've made quite a sight. I continued to take in air, the only one of us to do it.

When I felt like I could stand it, I pushed up onto my elbows and noticed two things.

Beadle was nowhere to be seen. The blood smear on the wall was a testament to the damage I'd inflicted, but it wasn't enough to stop him from running out. By now he was likely long gone.

The other thing I saw was God Maker. She'd crept out of the closet and now stood above me, looking down at the carnage. She spent a long time looking at Marta and the handle of the letter opener sticking out of her ear.

"What have you done?" she asked with disgust.

CHAPTER TWENTY-NINE

B eadle was gone. A trail of blood led to the front door of the house and down to a circular drive in front. He'd apparently climbed into a vehicle and sped away. I stood on the front porch, holding my shirttail to my mouth.

"Goddammit," I muttered.

I went back inside, where I found Devya sitting at the kitchen island, her head in her hands. Although her invention helped root out the worst criminals in the country, it was obvious she'd never seen the end result of that rooting. It was often an ugly, bloody mess, and God Maker had finally witnessed it for herself.

"I need a first aid kit," I said to her, but she didn't move. "Hey," I said with more force.

She looked up.

"Please help me," I said. "Go down the hall to a bathroom on the left. You'll find a frightened young woman by the name of Tula cowering in there. Ask her to gather some first aid supplies. Please, hurry. We have to get moving."

While she was gone I placed a kitchen towel under the

faucet then applied the cold, wet cloth to my face. It stung. That was just one of numerous aches and pains. My head felt like it was going to explode, my ribs were sore, and my throat felt like I'd barely survived a hanging.

Tula walked in, stopped when she saw me, then timidly approached. She had a metal first aid kit in her hand.

"You're a life saver," I said, and sat down. "Would you mind helping to clean me up?"

She just stared at me, incredulous. Then, before she could move, Devya reached around from behind and took the kit from her.

"That's okay," Devya said. "I'll take care of it."

Tula could not have been more grateful. "Hey," I said to her. "You'd be doing me and the FBI a big favor if you kept quiet about this for the next 24 hours, okay? Just go home, climb into bed with pizza and a bottle of wine, and try to forget everything you've seen. Can you do that for me?"

She gave a quick nod and hurried out of the room. I had to hope she'd honor my request.

God Maker pulled up another chair and sat facing me. She examined the damage, which must've looked pretty horrific. With a soft sound of disapproval, she took the towel from me and dabbed a few places. I winced, pulled back for a second, then let her continue.

I caught her eye. "I didn't do that just for fun. You know she was going to kill me, right? Or did you miss that portion of the show?"

She didn't answer, and I gave up for the time being. This modern-day Dr. Frankenstein was very unhappy with her monster.

"It won't take long for Butler to realize something's gone wrong. He won't hear from anybody and he'll have to assume shit blew up around here. I want to get to his other hideout before he has time to make other plans."

She applied some sort of ointment to the cuts around my mouth. "And how will you find him? You didn't plan very well yourself, did you?"

"I'm going to get help from someone who's been there."

FIVE MINUTES later we looked down at the corpse of Marta.

"This is your source?" Devya said.

I knelt beside the body. "Yeah. It is." I looked at Marta's pants pockets. The one on the right held the telltale bulge I wanted.

Getting back to my feet, I held up her cell phone. "She's been to the other compound several times. You're a tech wiz. Think you can pull the data from this?"

God Maker looked from me to the phone and back. "Probably. But it's locked."

"I think she used facial recognition." I held the phone up to the dead woman's face. Nothing happened. "Shit."

"Fingerprint?" Devya asked.

That didn't work, either.

"I'm sure I saw her use it with facial recognition." I studied Marta for a moment. "Hold on."

I stood up and went over to the desk. Pulling open drawers, I found what I was looking for.

Devya watched me bend back over the body. "What's that?"

"Super glue."

"What? Why?"

When I stood back up, Marta's eyes were wide open. I

placed the phone in front of her face, and it immediately sprang to life.

God Maker gave me another disgusted look. "You glued her eyelids open?"

All I could do was shrug and hand her the phone. "Here. First, change the login so it uses a password. Just make it 1-2-3-4-5-6 for now. Second, let's pinpoint where the hell *we* are. Then find the other location. It's not far, and if Butler wasn't bullshitting you, it's just across the water. If I'm guessing, I'd say Long Island."

"Let me call Quanta first," Devya said.

"No."

The force of my answer made her jump. She gave me a hard look. "Why not?"

"Trust me on this. No calls yet. I don't want to take any chance of storm troopers moving in and getting your granddaughter killed."

This seemed to mollify her, but just barely. Devya Nayar's trust level for me rose and fell like the tides. I, of course, had other reasons for waiting, but the doctor didn't need to be troubled with our personal problems.

WE WERE INDEED IN CONNECTICUT, near Westport. My Long Island guess had been correct, too. Marta's phone showed a handful of trips to Huntington, and we zeroed in on a substantial waterfront estate. I'd checked her text messages, and found a thread from Butler. The last, only 20 minutes old, had asked about ETA. I scanned through some of Marta's earlier replies, learning her style and abbreviations. Then I texted back: *Leaving in 10 min.*

Going through the pockets of the other dead soldiers turned

up a variety of keys for the vehicles parked around the property. I chose the large, black SUV for no other reason than the feel of the mission. It screamed dark SUV.

After collecting all the weapons I could find—and appropriating some spending money from the dearly departed—we loaded into the vehicle. It was dusk. I didn't want to take Devya along, but I also couldn't afford to leave her at the Westport property alone in case more bad guys showed up. Plus, I couldn't exactly deposit her somewhere else; if I did that she'd call Quanta for sure.

"Ninety minutes," I said to her as we buckled up and pulled out of the sprawling property.

For the first ten minutes we drove in silence. I contemplated taking the phone and calling Christina, but decided against it. The mission was far from over, and if I was going to die before the night ended, I preferred to leave it with the last long talk we'd enjoyed, just before this adventure began. Those were the memories I'd want her to have, not some hurried *I'm okay* phone call in front of other people. Besides, I didn't know if things were going to be okay or not. Instead, I'd use Christina as my inspiration to survive the night and get back home.

Thinking about her made me think about the life she was cultivating, the remarkable gift she was giving to people she cared for. If it wasn't the ultimate act of kindness, it was damned close.

While I was on my way to end another life.

I forced the thought out of my mind and turned to look at Devya. She sat placidly, staring out the passenger window at the dark countryside shooting past. We were on our way to the final showdown between her first two experiments in the investment program, and the life of her granddaughter hung in the balance.

"You doing okay?" I asked. Which was a stupid question, but the same stupid question we all ask.

She turned to look at me, her face drawn. "Not really." Then she faced the window again.

I let about a mile roll past before following up. "Are you worried about what happened this afternoon, or thinking about what's going to happen tonight?"

"Both," she said. Then she turned in her seat so she could talk to me. "How many bodies did you leave behind in that house today?"

"Um . . ." I reviewed the activity in my head before answering. "Five. Almost six, but the real bastard got away, thanks to Marta."

"And she paid for that with *her* life."

"I suppose it would've been better if she'd finished choking me to death?"

"She only did that because you became the aggressor."

I shrugged. "I'm paid to be an aggressor. And I aggress quite well. Or whatever the word is."

She uttered a small scoff.

"Listen, Doctor," I said, "a couple things you should know before you wade too deeply into the pool of righteousness. First, the reason I'm around is to save the most ungrateful people in the world, of which it sounds like you're a member. You love to be-bop through each day believing that everyone else on the planet shares your spirit of goodness. Most do. But many do not. And when those who are driven by a spirit of evil start demolishing your fragile world, you hate the idea that someone like me has to be called in. You'd rather not acknowledge that I even exist.

"Which leads to point number two. You resent the fact that you ever created this technology in the first place. So you're mad at *me* for making the most of it."

Her eyes narrowed. "I'm not a fool, Mr. Swan. I know evil exists."

"Yeah," I said, "because sometimes you read about it. Or on the news you see the clean-up after some horrible act. But until today you'd never really understood how the shit goes down. You want the garbage taken out, you just don't ever want to *see* the garbagemen. Well, what you witnessed today is how it gets done, Doctor."

She was silent for a moment. Then she said, "As for your other point, I don't regret creating the investment technology. Not at all. I'm just sorry that this is the only application. And even that is in danger of being grossly misused by this . . . this Mr. Butler."

I passed two semi-trucks, then edged back to the right lane.

"What other application could there be right now?" I asked. "How could you possibly let the public know this is available? It would be anarchy. Dangle the word *immortality* in front of people and they'll lose their minds."

"I know," she said. "I didn't say I thought it *should* be widespread; I just said I'm sorry it can only be this way."

"Fair enough," I said. "You spend years of hard work, make what has to be the most incredible discovery in the history of our poor, misguided species, and it's only used for the one thing you detest the most. Violence. I guess I have to ask: If you knew the government was going to use it for this reason, why did you finish the work?"

Devya softened a bit. "I had to. I'm a scientist. I can't tiptoe up to a major discovery like that and then just leave it incomplete. Besides . . . ." She paused. "I guess I always hoped it wouldn't be twisted this way. Especially with what Butler wants to do with it."

"If it makes you feel any better," I said, "people twist and misuse every tool imaginable when their minds aren't right."

Now it was my turn to fall silent. Without meaning to, I'd walked us right up to the issue that tortured me on a daily basis. The thing Devya Nayar had volunteered at dinner.

I had to talk about it. This might be the only chance I ever got to confront the woman we called God Maker.

"Explain this: How could you tell the government, tell Q2, that the technology was ready to be used on people when it obviously wasn't?"

She looked down at her hands in her lap. "I . . . told them it wasn't perfected yet."

I whipped my head around to look at her, and opened my mouth to respond. But this was dangerous on a dark highway. I hit the brakes, and pulled the SUV off the road onto the shoulder, where I put it in park. Then I turned back to her.

"You did *what*? You told Quanta the investment technology was flawed? And she still went ahead with it?"

"No," Devya said. "I was forbidden to tell Quanta. But I did tell the people who originally put the program together. They . . . they opted to go ahead and work through the bugs. They forbade me to tell anyone, including Quanta."

I stared in disbelief. "They opted to *work through the bugs*?" I slammed my hand on the steering wheel. "This is my goddamned *brain* you're talking about."

She didn't answer. Just kept looking at her hands.

I pushed my door open, climbed out, and walked back down the road. Cars and trucks rushed by, kicking up dirt and dust. I didn't care. After I'd gone about a hundred feet I stopped and stared up at the few stars able to pierce the New England haze.

All of the hours I'd spent fearful of what was happening to my consciousness, all the times I'd opened up to Miller that something was wrong, that my mind was being altered, fragmented . . .

And the bastards behind Q2 knew it. They *knew* it. And they let me continue to reinvest, to continue the splintering of Eric Swan, loyal servant to the cause.

I don't know how long I stood there. At some point I heard Devya approach and stand beside me. For a while she said nothing. Then she placed a hand on my shoulder.

"Swan, it's not Quanta's fault. She didn't know when she took the job."

A truck honked as it flew by, angry that someone stood so close to the road. So close to death. Pretty much the way I lived my life.

My fractured life.

"It doesn't matter," I said. "She knew enough, and she's done enough as it is." I shook my head. "But it's on me, too. I knew something was wrong and I kept on."

Now I looked over my shoulder at her. "This is on you, too, Devya. And it's on the bastards who formed Q2, Quanta, all of us." I grunted. "It's on Butler."

For the first time since I'd met her, Devya Nayar looked upon me with compassion. "I know there's nothing I can say right now to make things right. But you have to believe me when I tell you it's not like it was before. I've spent years working on it."

I gave a laugh devoid of all humor. "Got the bugs worked out, did ya?"

Now she stiffened. "*All* the bugs? No. Is it better? Of course it is."

When I looked away with a sad shake of my head, she marched around until she stood facing me.

"What exactly do you want from me right now, Swan? Hmm? You signed up for the program, and when you did you assumed bigger risks than what we're talking about right now. And why would you throw a fit that later versions are better than prototypes? That's foolish. The phone you use today is light years beyond the first phones."

"I'm not a phone," I said.

"That's right. You're a flawed, damaged human being. Just like the rest of us. Yes, Butler was version 1.0. You're version 2.o. And the next person to assimilate with the program will jump to version 3. It's a natural progression."

She was mad now, her hands on her hips. "And I'll tell you something else. Even version 2 is pretty damned good, and deserves more appreciation than its current occupant seems prepared to give."

It must've been quite a sight for the people flashing by at 6o miles per hour. Two of us on the side of the road, face to face, clearly unhappy with each other. Both of us had completely tuned out the traffic noise.

"I'm thrilled that the next candidate will have it better than me," I said. "Maybe they'll drop to their knees and thank you for sparing their brain cells. Me? I'm not that keen right now on thanking anyone for experimenting on me."

She let out a huff. "You're like a child. A child whose sibling got a better toy than you, and you want your parents to feel guilty about it."

"That's bullshit, Devya. I don't need to have anything *better*." I tapped my forehead. "I'd just like to keep what I started with. And you can't deliver that. You shouldn't have downloaded anyone until it was better. Butler *or* me."

Devya seemed to calm a bit, and so did I. I felt terrible for yelling at her, but I couldn't get past the betrayal I felt. She wasn't entirely to blame; but, at the moment, she was the only one I could take it out on.

Now she gave a small, humorless laugh herself. "People today demand that *technology* make them better. And yet nobody seems interested in making *themselves* better."

She walked around me and headed back toward the SUV. I stood there, staring at the ground, stewing on her comment. A moment later I turned and followed her. We got back in, I took a few deep breaths, then put the vehicle in drive and merged onto the highway.

At least three or four miles rolled past before I spoke again.

"Here's what your's truly, the screwed up lab experiment, is going to do tonight. I'm going to get your granddaughter out of there, and I'll at least let Agent One know the truth. He deserves to know as much as I do."

Devya only nodded.

"And then," I said, "I'll probably have to kill him. You don't have to watch."

CHAPTER THIRTY

It was nine o'clock and the grounds of Butler's rented compound in Huntington were well-lit, showing off landscaping that alone must've cost more than twice the price of the average three-bedroom home in America. Trees and berms were installed to suppress any sounds that might come from the road, which was ridiculous; in this neighborhood there were few homes, and they weren't exactly the type to host frat parties. All was quiet and still. For now.

We parked a block away. When I told Devya to wait in the car, she declined, using language that showed she'd spent considerable time around me. The only comeback I had was, "Then do as I say in there or we'll both be killed."

I'd offered her a gun to carry, and she looked at me like I was crazy. "You may be sorry later," I said.

Unlike the Connecticut property, here I had no Tula to reveal troop numbers. My guess was that Butler wouldn't have that many people; all he needed was one or two people to keep an eye on the teenager, and maybe a couple more to babysit the investment gear. He might keep one around as a personal bodyguard, too, but overall I couldn't believe there'd be more than five or six gunmen total. It was possible there were fewer than that. Assuming I still had the element of surprise, there was a good chance I could get to him.

We crouched in the shadows as I observed the property. A fence circled it, from one side near the shore, around the front along the road, and back down again to the shore. It wasn't built to withstand an army; it was mostly for show.

"Do we go in here?" Devya asked, her voice low.

"No," I said, pointing through the trees. "Most of this is probably wired for movement. Same with the property in the back, along the water. I'm sure most idiots would think that's the best way to storm a place like this. By boat. The dock area is probably rigged like the White House."

"So what do we do?"

"We walk down the front path to the door. With a guard going back and forth from the house to the gate, they can't allow the path to set off alarms."

She considered this. "So we just walk in?"

"Sounds easy enough, right? I've found it's often the best plan." I nodded at a spot near the gate. "All I have to do is convince that gentleman to let us pass."

After a moment of peering through the gloom, Devya caught sight of the guard, one of the jerks who had escorted me to the ring to get my ass kicked by Butler. She looked up at me and nodded.

"Wait here," I said and crept along the fence toward the main gate. Two minutes later I whistled for Devya to join me. When she got there she glanced at the unconscious man I'd tucked into the shadows, then quickly looked away.

"One down," I said to her under my breath. "Walk up the path with me, don't try to run. Stay right behind me. If you hear shots, get as flat to the ground as you can. Sure you don't want a weapon?"

"I'm sure. Just get me to Tisha."

"Doing my best."

The walkway cut between a large number of trees, which helped to shield us somewhat. But the final sixty feet was wide open, and illuminated by the landscape lights. I had to trust no one sat in front of security monitors, vigilant as they scrutinized the various camera shots from around the perimeter. We reached the large, ornate front door without hearing an alarm or shouts.

"Okay," I said to Devya. "Once we get in, there's a chance things happen really fast. Be prepared to move. Don't freeze on me."

"I'm scared."

"I know. But breathe. Us monsters do this shit all the time."

If the door was locked I'd have to find another way in, probably a window somewhere. If it was unlocked it meant one of two things: Either the guard came in and out frequently, so it was just a matter of convenience. Or Butler was expecting us.

It was unlocked.

I took a quick peek inside, then pulled the door back again and said to Devya, "Once inside we're going immediately to the right. Stay close."

This was one reason I preferred to not work with a partner. The constant communication necessary for even the simplest thing, like an incursion, slowed everything. On my own I would've been inside five minutes ago. But it complicates things having to watch your ass *and* somebody else's.

I pushed the door open, slid inside, and shut it behind us.

There was a formal living room to the right, what my mother always called 'the wasted room' because it never got used. She was right; nobody ever used a formal living room yet filled it with expensive furniture nobody ever sat on.

A hallway split off beyond this room, all of which was dark. In a flash we were down the hall and into a guest bedroom. Devya looked like she was about to hyperventilate.

"Please, let me leave you in here for now," I said. "I'll find Tisha and bring her to you."

She started to argue again, but the offer ultimately was too good to pass up. "Okay," she said.

"Great," I said. "Get over there, on the other side of the bed, and scrunch down out of sight. I'll be back as soon as I can."

Without waiting for another response, I slipped out of the room and closed the door behind me. For a moment I stood still, listening for sounds of activity. All was dark and silent. After making another quick check of my weapons, I investigated the rest of the rooms in this corner of the massive house. A second guest room, empty, but one that looked as if it had been recently lived in; a powder room; a guest laundry room; and what amounted to a craft room.

Back in the formal living room, I snooped around a corner and found a sprawling family room with vaulted ceilings stretching upward a good 25 feet. Contemporary furniture was arranged to look out the floor-to-ceiling windows showcasing the grounds out back, beautifully manicured and running down to an impressive dock area.

Just off the family room was a spacious kitchen, well lit. And occupied.

A man's back was to me as he hunched over, studying the contents of the giant fridge. He was a big dude, and when he turned to place something on one of the kitchen's two islands, I nodded. Yep, my old friend, Mr. Bolt, had made the trip. He grabbed a fork from a silverware drawer and began poking around inside the tupperware container he'd pulled out. From where he stood, facing this direction, I had no chance of leaving my spot. He'd see any movement I made unless he turned back around.

All I could do was wait patiently.

After wolfing down a few bites, he got thirsty, and soon had his head back inside the refrigerator. I saw the glint of a gun sticking out of his waistband. Using this brief opportunity, I hurried, on the toes of my shoes, across the large, Polynesian rug of the family room, and grabbed a knife from the heavy, wooden knife block on the counter.

Bolt heard this and turned. The look on his face was priceless as he summoned as many scrambled brain cells as possible to identify the face that must've been familiar to him.

"Hey," I said, but not very loudly. "Yeah, remember me? I'm the guy who kicked your ass in the ring the other day."

It sank in. He took a step toward me, but even his limited intelligence warned him that his hands were occupied by a fork and a Gatorade bottle, while I, eight feet away, countered with a butcher knife and a gun.

"Stay quiet for me, okay, Edwin? Nobody needs to get hurt. Well, not *very* hurt, anyway."

The moment was too big for him, and he lost control of his senses. Dropping the fork in his right hand, he reached toward his waistband to extract the gun. Which left me two choices: shoot him, or use the knife.

I held onto hope I could remain stealthy a bit longer, so a gunshot was not choice A.

Drawing back my hand, I threw the knife straight and true,

just as I'd been taught in special ops. It must be like riding a bike; the blade embedded in Bolt's left eye, up to the hilt. I covered the distance between us before he could hit the ground. But, damn, Edwin was a large man, and I nearly strained my back catching him and quietly lowering him the rest of the way.

I left the poor slob lying there, still clutching the Gatorade in his left hand.

Two down.

A minute later it was three. This one had the bad luck to run into me as he walked inside from the back patio, drinking something from a red Solo cup. I grabbed the cup as he dropped, unconscious, to the tile. Sniffing the contents, perhaps hoping for an adult beverage, I grimaced when I discovered he hadn't been drinking. It was his tobacco spit cup.

"Dude, disgusting," I said, setting the cup on the counter and dragging his body away from the door.

Looking around, I now saw a wide, carpeted staircase winding down into a basement, and that intrigued me. Butler had stolen the investment equipment and storage devices from the Q2 basement; would he find it poetic to set up shop in a similar location? That felt right, for some reason. Plus, it kept everything out of sight.

There was another hallway that I had to believe went to a master bedroom. That didn't strike me as a very strategic location for the stolen gear.

But would Agent One deem that a good spot to keep his hostage? He might.

I went to the edge of the hallway and peeked around a corner, down its dim length. At just that moment I heard a toilet flush, and seconds later a door opened. Yet another goon emerged. I didn't recognize this one, so he must've been at this location the whole time. He turned and went toward the far end of the corridor, to what had to be the master.

He opened the door, went inside, and closed it again.

How to play this? Well, sometimes you just have to completely bullshit your way through a situation. And I felt very confident about my bullshitting skills.

Hurrying back to Mr. Red Cup, I found his cell phone and went back to the hallway. Remember, act like you know what you're doing.

I strode confidently down the hall, holding the phone to my ear and pretending to carry on a conversation. This guy had no idea who I was, and would have to imagine I was just another of Butler's boys.

"Yeah," I said, loud enough that he could hear half a conversation through the closed door. "We just got here."

I turned the knob and walked in, praying there wouldn't be three assholes in there.

It was just the one. Along with a young girl, who sat in sweat pants and a T-shirt in an oversized chair, reading a book. I recognized her from the photos in Rhode Island.

Tisha.

"No," I said into the phone. "Butler doesn't want you to do anything right now. Just sit tight. You can do that, right?"

I walked up to the puzzled guard.

"Yeah," I said. "Look, I gotta go. There's a guy here who just used the bathroom and there's no way he washed his hands. Wasn't nearly enough time. And you know I can't stand that."

I dropped the phone, and at the same time raised my gun and stuck it under the guy's chin.

"Hi," I said, pleasantly. "Be honest. You *didn't* wash, did you?"

He was too stunned to answer with anything. But his eyes, now opened wide, darted between the gun barrel and my face.

"No, you didn't," I said. "And I'm afraid our organization is putting a premium on proper hygiene these days. So I'm going to need you to come this way." I nodded toward the master bedroom closet. Over my shoulder I said to the startled young girl, "Hi, Tisha. I'll be back in just a second. Don't go anywhere."

Using the gun, I pushed the man backwards until we got into the closet. Then I put him to sleep with two solid blows.

When I got back to Tisha, she'd set the book on the floor and was huddled back into the chair, trying to get as far away from me as possible.

I knelt down beside her. "Tisha, don't be afraid. My name is Eric. I'm here with your grandmother."

Her face lit up and she started to squeal something. I quickly put a finger up to her lips.

"Sshh. I'm going to get you out of here. But I need you to stay very quiet. Okay?"

She gave an eager nod, but was beaming.

"All right," I said, standing and helping her up. "Now, let's go get—"

The door opened. I spun around with my gun, only to see Devya Nayar stick her head through the opening.

"Nani!" cried Tisha, scrambling out of her chair.

I lowered the gun. "Jesus, Devya, I told you to—"

She walked into the room, and that's when I saw the gun that was pressed to the back of her head.

Holding the gun, brandishing his usual happy smile, was Butler.

CHAPTER THIRTY-ONE

I grabbed Tisha by the arm and held on. Devya, tears streaming down her face, shook her head. She mouthed *I'm sorry* at me.

"Well, I think you can set that ferocious looking weapon on the floor, right?" Butler said. "Wouldn't want me to get a nervous twitch right about now."

"You won't shoot her," I said. "She's everything to you right now."

He kept smiling. "Yes, that's true. But . . ."

The gun was now pointed directly at Tisha. Butler continued, "But this young lady is now serving exactly the role I intended. And remember, I can shoot her *and* you before you're able to even raise your arm." His smile faded. "Put the weapon on the floor."

Devya couldn't hold back her sobs as I set down the gun.

"Knowing you and your penchant for over-achieving," Butler said, "I'm sure you have more. Please dispose of them, too."

I chuckled. Then, with my left hand I reached into my back

waistband and pulled out the other gun. I set it next to the other.

"Hands up high," he said. "Good. Now turn around, slowly. I want to see for myself."

I did the spin.

"Excellent. You know, I expected you to arrive in restraints, with an escort, not alone and wandering the grounds like a ninja. Can't say I'm *totally* surprised, though."

He stepped into the room to give us space to get out the door. "But now that you're here, I have something to show you. Swan, you and God Maker first. I'll be right behind you with this sweet child."

As I passed him, I stopped to say something suitably rude. "Ah, ah," he said, holding up a finger. "Save your questions and comments until after the tour."

He pointed to the hallway with his gun. Devya, still choking back tears, walked ahead. I was right behind. Butler brought up the rear, keeping his gun trained on Tisha's back.

"Down the stairs," he called ahead to Devya. "You'll love what I've done with the basement."

We descended the wide, spiral staircase to a large entertainment space. An overly-ornate bar, complete with eight padded stools, sat to the left. To the right was a game area, with a pool table and poker table. Straight ahead was a living area with couches and oversized chairs. At the end of the room I saw a doorway into a plush home theater.

"Ladies, if you'd be so kind to have a seat there," Butler said, indicating the couches in the center of the room. "I'm going to have a quick cocktail with my partner."

Once they were seated, he waved me to the bar with the gun. I sat in one of the stools at the far end, while he went behind the bar and began making drinks. He set down the gun, but it was much too far away from me to even contemplate making a move.

"Well, a happy reunion," Butler said, filling two glasses with ice. "I expected you to show up in a boat with my friends, and instead you're on your own? Imagine my surprise to come walking upstairs to find God Maker sneaking around the house." He looked up at me. "I assume my *compadres* in Connecticut are in the same condition as Mr. Bolt, who I found on the kitchen floor?"

"Pretty much," I said.

He made a show of examining my face. "But not without a fight. Did Byron do that to you? He's a very tempestuous young man, isn't he?"

"Marta."

Butler threw back his head and laughed. "Oh, that Marta. I'd like to steal her away from Beadle. Or is she suddenly unavailable?"

"She's served her last omelet, if that's what you mean."

"Oh, now that's a shame. God, you're an animal, Swan. And Beadle? You didn't rob me of my fun, did you?"

"He took one in the shoulder and drove off."

Butler looked genuinely thrilled. "That's great to hear. Gives me something to hunt. Hunters need prey, you know, and I can't think of a better way to get our team off to a good start than tracking down the illustrious Beadle. Agreed?"

"*Our* team?"

He put a whiskey-diet a few feet away from me, keeping his distance. "Of course. I know damned well you already had misgivings about Quanta when I picked you up. Now that you've had time to chat with the lovely Dr. Nayar, I have no doubt you feel even less love for Q2." He sipped his drink. "Am I right?"

I reached over and picked up the glass. "I want to talk to you about that."

He raised one eyebrow. "Well, doesn't that sound somber. Good. We have a *lot* to talk about. But let me give you the tour first. Bring your drink."

Picking up the gun, he walked around the bar. "Ladies, please don't wander off. I've got my eye on you."

He went over to a door I'd assumed led to a storage room. But when he opened it I almost whistled.

It looked nearly identical to the basement lab at Q2 headquarters. Tables, gurneys, stacks of computers and other equipment. But somehow it looked more impressive here.

"It's the lighting and the decor," he said, reading my thoughts. "Not so stuffy. Until I walked through your lab, taking the gear, I'd forgotten how utterly grim that place is. I wanted my lab to be . . . oh, what's the right word? Joyful, I guess. If you're reinvesting life, for God's sake, it should reek of joy."

"Do you even hear how crazy you sound?" I asked, taking another sip of my drink. "Like a B-movie bad guy. I thought you were better than that."

"And right now you sound like a company man made of cardboard. You're a liar, Swan, if you say you don't agree with almost everything I've said these last few weeks."

I nodded. "You're right. I do agree with almost everything. But not *everything*. And the places in your manifesto where I part ways with you are too big, Butler. Way too big. Kinda pisses me off."

He laughed. "What?"

"Because you remind me of me in so many ways that I *want* to agree with everything. I know you used to be a great agent. I know you went off the rails. Now, after the last two weeks, I know we share a lot of the same ideas. Hell, we could almost be the same guy. But for the last few years I've worried myself sick that I was turning into Agent One. The insane agent. The one who lost his marbles and shot at his boss."

"You know," he said with a grin. "You say it in the most derogatory manner possible, but I must admit I love the sound of that." He moved his hand as if writing the words in the air: "*Agent. One.*"

I crossed my arms. "You already know that the investment technology was far from perfect when you were first uploaded. The changes in your mental state aren't your fault. You know that, too, right?"

"My mental state is not nearly as fragile as you and your boss have made it out to be. Just because my method of doing the same job is different than hers? That doesn't make me crazy, Swan. It makes me creative."

"Often the same thing."

He gave a rueful nod. "Well, this is true. I'll grant you that a lot of geniuses in history have been loons. But I'm not claiming to be a genius. Just a visionary."

"And you know the technology has improved," I said. "Or at least Devya claims it has. Now it's just a matter of finding out if the earlier damage can be repaired. Would you be willing to stop all this and try to get your mind right again? What if you could go back to the way you were, before all of this happened?"

"That," he said, his voice taking on an ethereal quality, "would be like glimpsing the promised land and turning away."

I grunted a laugh. "Well, that clears up one thing. I thought you had delusions of being Christ-like. But actually you think you're Moses."

He laughed with me, and gave a small, sarcastic bow.

I walked around the room until I found myself staring at a large stack of hard drives. My blood went cold.

Butler was standing only a few feet behind me. His voice was suddenly very low, very threatening. "Ah, you know what these are. One of these contains the soul and spirit of the great Eric Swan. All I need to do is remove one panel and smash the insides. And what happens to you? No more chances to find all your answers, eh?"

I turned and stared at him. "Answers?"

His voice was still heavy and low. "You said it yourself, Swan. We could almost be the same guy. You think I don't know what you're after? The same damned thing I'm after." He stepped closer, but raised the gun between us. "Don't be an idiot, Eric. And don't make me kill you. Live for something bigger."

I looked back at the hard drives. There was something about seeing the blinking light on the front panel. Something about knowing what lay inside that black box. It made everything crystalize. What I had often seen as cold and artificial now flashed in front of me, a small red light that pulsed like a heartbeat. My heartbeat.

My head felt light. I had to brace myself with one hand against the heavy metal rack holding the electronics. At first my gut instincts made me wonder if Butler had laced my drink with something.

But it wasn't that. It was a collision of every dark, scary thought I'd brooded over for years; every doubt about the integrity of my mind and my thoughts; every conversation with Quanta, Miller, Christina, each of them telling me I wasn't going mad, I wasn't turning into Butler.

And they were right. I wasn't turning into him—because *I was him*. He was me. The only two of a species, trapped in an ageless journey, fighting not only the battles assigned to us, but the ones we assigned to ourselves. Unable to ever truly communicate with anyone else because we were alone in our need to know what comes next. To know what my mother, my father, my sister, all experienced—and, for Butler, what his wife experienced—but without making the ultimate sacrifice. We wanted to cheat death, but in a way to cheat life, too. Take it all. Keep it all.

I let out a groan. And, without thinking, I turned and hurled the glass at Butler's head. He got a hand up, but not before the glass shattered against his head. I lunged, pushing myself off from the rack.

I was on him before he recovered, and I knocked the gun out of his hand. We grappled, each trying to establish leverage, he with blood oozing into his eyes from the broken glass, me with an ache in my ribs, hampering my movement.

But this was the fight. *The* fight, the one that I'd imagined for weeks. Everything rode on the outcome.

I got my right hand free and connected with a solid punch to his torso. He grunted and pushed me away. Rather than attack, we stood still for a moment, three feet apart, eyeing each other.

A slow smile spread across his face. Wiping the blood from his left eye, he said, "The student challenges the master. But the student can't win. You know that, right?"

"Unless the student held back during his training," I said.

"Never showed all your cards, is that it?"

Instead of answering, I feinted to the left, then spun with a kick that he barely blocked. By that point I was lunging, and connected a punch to the side of his head. Butler staggered, but fired a shot of his own that smashed into my cheek. It rocked me backward.

Neither of us would give in. For the next minute we boxed, kicked, and wrestled, using every martial arts move we knew.

It was clear only one of us would leave the room alive. For all of his pleading to have me join him, Butler had to know deep inside that his only possible solution was to kill me. But I wouldn't make it easy for him.

He bobbed in front of me. When I tried a swing kick, he sidestepped and, before I regained my balance, shoved me hard into the rack of hard drives. My head took most of the impact, and I felt woozy. A second later Butler rained blows onto me. My eye was belted, my lips bloodied, and another punch to my ribs buckled me. I let out a groan of pain from my knees.

Rather than move in and finish me off, Butler taunted me.

"Stupid son of a bitch," he yelled. "I gave you the greatest opportunity, and instead of taking it you fight. And you fight for an organization you don't even *believe in* anymore? What the hell is wrong with you?"

I struggled for air, my lungs heaving. "I guess there's plenty wrong with me," I said. "With both of us."

After all those rounds together in the ring, this was the main event. During those sparring sessions I'd wondered if it would ever come down to this, the two of us bruised, bloodied, and in pain, clawing at each other to win. Using every bit of training and drawing from every reserve. Each desperate to prove to the other he was the superior agent.

He didn't expect me to have anything left. So when I launched myself upward at him, he wasn't prepared, and my fist snapped his head back. He went down onto his ass, and I dove on top of him, getting in two more hard shots before he was able to retaliate and push me away.

Exhausted, I noticed the gun on the floor and reached for it. His foot hit the side of my head, and suddenly I was on my back.

When I pushed myself to a sitting position, Butler was pointing the gun at me.

"Stupid bastard," he said while gasping for air.

I got to my feet, barely. "Don't be an ass," I said. "You can't shoot me."

Butler fired.

I felt the burning hot metal enter my chest, slamming me backwards against the stacks of hard drives. For a moment I stayed on my feet, as if the round had pinned me to the metal at my back. Then, slowly, I slid down until I was in a heap on the floor. Blood poured from the open wound on the right side of my chest. I coughed, and tasted more blood in my mouth.

Butler was bent over, a hand on one knee, clutching the gun as he used his sleeve to wipe blood out of his eyes. It was enough to conceal most of the tattoo running along his face. "You fool," he said. Then he screamed at me. "Why are you making me do this? Why are you making me do it? I'm going to destroy you! You know what that means, right? *All* of you."

"Well," I said, the pain spreading throughout my body. "At least I'll no longer be a monster." A small laugh escaped my lips. "Or an angry young man, I guess."

I looked him in the eye. "And I'll have my answer."

He raised his gun to my head. "Swan, I hope it's everything you wanted."

The gun explosion was loud, echoing off the walls, making me jump.

But I felt nothing besides the pain already throbbing in my chest.

I looked up at Butler. A hole had bloomed in the middle of

his chest, and blood began to seep out. A second later another shot tore into his chest. His eyes rolled up into his head, and he collapsed on the ground beside me.

Through the pain I turned my head, feeling myself starting to black out. In the doorway, holding a smoking gun, was Quanta. She lowered it as we made eye contact.

I turned back to Butler. He was dead. With the strength I had left, I pushed myself over to his side, placed one arm over him, and tucked my face into his neck.

And cried until I passed out.

CHAPTER THIRTY-TWO

I was propped up on my couch with pillows, staring out the large picture window of my 7th floor condo in the Stadler Building. I'd been awake most of the night, unable to get comfortable in my bed, and had set up camp here to watch the sunrise paint the nearby park. It was warm for this time of year, the snow likely gone until late fall, and I saw several small figures dutifully logging their morning runs. It would be a while longer before I could join them.

Three weeks may not sound like much time until you spend it in a hospital. Then it becomes an eternity. The nurses and doctors of my wing could not have been more wonderful to me, and yet I'm sure they were as ready as I was for discharge day. Not because I was a grouch or anything; they'd just picked up on my restlessness. Take a person who's spent their entire adult life flitting from place to place every few days, tie them down in a hospital bed for close to a month, and see what happens.

As they rolled me in a wheelchair toward the elevator, the nursing crew had played Michael Jackson's "Beat It" for me.

My first night home had been bad, but good. Bad because sleep was difficult for a multitude of reasons, but good because I was at least in my own place.

With Christina.

For the first ten days she'd been at the hospital for most of each day, refusing to go to work. After I was officially moved from critical condition to serious she grew a little more relaxed. On the day they upgraded me to fair, she admitted something to me.

"I'm used to you walking in the door in a whole new body. Fixing up an old one is a real pain in the ass. Can't you just request a new model?"

I didn't want to laugh because that really hurt. But with a smile I told her, "I'm going to treat this one like a '68 Mustang and restore it."

When I got home she helped me into bed and brought me the most incredible food ever, naturally. I felt guilty because the pain meds had zapped my appetite. But I was a trooper and managed to eat a few bites.

Now, alone in my side of our dual condo arrangement, and alone with my thoughts, I tried not to think too much about the end of the mission. I'd had three weeks to stew over everything, working through every move I'd made, second-guessing every decision. There were several things I'd go back and do differently.

But I wondered if the ultimate outcome was somehow pre-ordained. I mean, Quanta firing the shots that killed Agent One? Was there ever a chance the script would *not* have that ending?

I hadn't seen Quanta since passing out in that Huntington estate basement. No visit to the hospital. No calls. No messages. And that was okay with me. I made no request to see her.

My company consisted of Christina and one very nice visit from Poole—who, bless her heart, had no idea what to say to me. At one point, while she sat fidgeting in the chair next to my bed, I couldn't resist messing with her. I told her I'd have to stay in the hospital longer because all of my blood was flowing the wrong direction and I couldn't leave until they got it reversed. The longer she sat and thought about that, the funnier it became to me, until a nurse had to rush in when my laughing spiked the heartbeat and blood pressure readings.

Poole was a good sport, but left the room convinced I was still the strangest person she'd ever known. After all this time I had quite a warm spot in my heart—or, hearts—for that woman.

The day before I was discharged I'd also received a surprise visit from an old friend. FBI agent Fife, the former Q2 employee I'd worked with on the case in the Caribbean, strolled into my hospital room and plopped a bottle of rye whiskey on the tray table.

"Screw the pain meds," he said. "This is what I prescribe."

I hadn't argued. We'd each enjoyed a quick sample in hospital paper cups while he teased me about how many times he'd seen me in the MASH unit.

"I leave it all on the field," I told him. "Unlike you FBI weasels."

"Sure," he said. "You're braver, we're smarter."

I told him the news about Parnell. He looked down at his feet, rolling the paper cup in his fingers. "I'm really sorry to hear that, Swan. I know she was something special. A good agent." He looked up, his face sympathetic. "I'm sorry, man."

We changed the subject to the cases he was working. "I

don't know if this is going to go anywhere, but I'm starting to look into some rumor about a group of people screwing around with crops. I have a meeting about it tomorrow."

"Crops?" I asked. "As in corn, wheat?"

He nodded. "Yeah. Why don't you get out of this lame-ass bed and back to work. You could help me."

I chuckled, which caused another stab of pain. "Uh, don't count on it. You'll have to take care of Old McDonald by yourself."

"Just as well," he said, finishing his whiskey. "You'd probably end up in the hospital again. Clumsy bastard."

That was the extent of my visitors in the hospital. When Christina wasn't there I did some reading and caught up on all the sports news I'd missed for months.

That is, when I could corral my brain and keep it from running out of control. Which wasn't often.

NOW THE SUN was reflecting off another building, sending a shaft of light through my condo window, right into my face. I held my hand up to ward it off.

"Want me to close the blinds?"

It was Christina. I'd been so caught up in my thoughts I hadn't heard the panel between our condos opening.

"Hi babe," I said. "No, it'll only last a moment. Thanks."

She perched on the coffee table beside me. "Didn't sleep so well?"

I shook my head. "No, but it's no big deal. I'm sure tonight I'll be comatose." I took her hand and nodded toward her belly. "What about you? How are things percolating in there?"

"It's all good. Doctor says weight-wise things are perfect, heartbeat is strong. Starting to have my first food cravings, but that might just come from the menu I put together each night. How many other pregnant women crave parmesan risotto with grilled shrimp?"

"So not something I could rush out and get for you at 1 a.m."

"I don't think you're rushing anywhere for a couple of weeks."

I did a face-palm. "Dammit, I promised to bring you a couple of bags of Reese's. I'm a horrible husband."

"Well, I wasn't going to say anything. Hold on, I'll get us some tea."

By the time she returned with two steaming mugs I'd found myself contemplating those upcoming weeks. This was the first time in my career I'd looked forward to extended down time. In the past I'd grow antsy after four or five days. But heading back to Q2 operations didn't appeal to me at the moment. I said something about that to Christina.

"Of course it doesn't sound good right now," she said. "They just patched up a hole in your lung. I hope you don't want to do anything for a while."

"Well, I said I'd help you during this surrogacy. So use me for that."

She smiled and squeezed my hand. "That's sweet." Then her face took on a pained expression. There was something I could tell she didn't want to talk about.

"Listen," she said. "Speaking of Q2. I, uh, I got a call from Quanta."

The mug was halfway to my lips. I lowered it without taking a drink.

"She's coming by today. I hope that's okay. When you got home yesterday afternoon it seemed like you were well enough to have a visitor. I didn't know you weren't going to sleep."

"Hmm," I said, and finally took a sip of tea.

"Are you upset?" she asked. "I can call her back and cancel."

"No. Just surprised. It's okay." I shrugged. "We have to talk eventually. Better get it over with."

Christina studied my face for a bit, then leaned forward and gave me a kiss.

QUANTA SHOWED up at 11 o'clock. Christina let her in, and I heard them making small talk by the door. They'd never met face-to-face, so I'm sure it was awkward, especially since Q2 rules stated I wasn't even supposed to be in a relationship, let alone married.

Screw their rules, I thought.

I'd put away the pillows and blanket, I'd showered, shaved, and gotten myself dressed, and now sat in one of my comfy chairs in the living room. I didn't want to look like an invalid.

She walked into the room and stood before me, her hands clasped.

"Swan," she said.

"Quanta. Have a seat."

She sat on the couch as Christina gave a small wave and disappeared through the panel into her own condo.

"I'm glad you're out of the hospital and feeling better," Quanta said. "For a moment there on Long Island I thought we'd lost you."

I gave a curt nod. "Yeah. I suppose the proper thing to do here would be to thank you for saving my life."

"I've never heard anyone sound so regretful that their life *had* been saved."

"Yeah, well," I said, but didn't finish the thought.

"Besides," she said, "you should thank Devya. If she hadn't texted me you'd be dead. Said she had a bad feeling with you going up alone against Butler and his team."

"I told her not to contact you."

"She saved your life with that text, Swan. We assumed you were still in the New England area, so I was with a team at Devya's house, waiting for news to come in. We barely got to you in time. So, really, you saved each other on this mission."

She shifted on the couch. "I thought you might like a quick recap of everything. Our usual debriefing after a case."

"All right," I said.

She never took her eyes off me. "Devya Nayar and her granddaughter were rescued, and all of the investment equipment safely recovered and returned to Washington. Your mission was successful on every count. You have the gratitude of everyone involved.

"Dr. Nayar especially wants to extend her thanks. She has asked when it would be appropriate to contact you. I told her I'd enquire."

"Tell her no thanks are necessary. Just doing my job. The job she created."

Quanta kept silent for a moment, gauging my mood. It couldn't have seemed good. To her credit, she moved on.

"I was surprised to learn that you'd killed Marta Jelani."

I stared at her. "Wait. Marta was . . . *That* was Marta Jelani?"

"So you've heard the name."

"Not for years. Holy shit. I never put it all together. I thought she was . . ." I shook my head.

Now I remembered the deference shown to the small, smiling woman by the other guards at the compound. Nobody would ever cross Jelani, and I'd failed to make the connection. Her size had fooled me. I naively thought she was just a sweet, smiling helper.

And to think while I planned my escape I'd considered using Marta as a shield, as if she was a tiny, helpless thing.

Quanta said, "One of the top assassins ever to come out of Africa. She disappeared a couple of years ago. Some wondered if she might've been killed somewhere."

"She was working with Beadle," I said.

"I see. Well, you can either consider yourself lucky, or feel immense pride. Marta's responsible for the deaths of several top agents around the world over the years. Before I joined Q2 I came across her during one of my cases in Europe."

After a short pause, she said, "I'd like to talk to you about Butler."

"I'd rather not."

"Can you tell me why?"

I glanced out the large window. "Quanta, if we start talking about Agent One we could spend hours. The only thing I'll say is that he was—"

"Misunderstood?" she said.

I looked back at her, a touch of anger simmering below the surface. "Yeah. Yeah, he was. You can laugh, you can write that off as bullshit. But for all the warped, crazy thoughts he tried to make sense of in his damaged brain—damaged by Q2, I should add—he was a field agent. And a helluva field agent, judging by what I saw in a short time. And the thing is, he wasn't too different from me. Maybe not that different from how you *used* to be. Before you took the desk job."

She raised an eyebrow. "Insult noted. Go ahead."

"I—" Then I stopped. "Oh, really Quanta, what's the use? He's dead. The world has been saved. Mission accomplished.

We all go back to our perfect lives and scrape his name from the records so he doesn't tarnish that bastion of decency, Q2."

There was silence between us for a long moment. Then she changed the subject. "I have no new information on the location of Beadle."

"And you never will," I said. "I take responsibility for that. I had the chance to kill him. Standing right there, as close to me as you are right now, my barrel lined up between his eyes. And I didn't pull the trigger."

This was something I'd brooded over the entire time I lay in the hospital bed. My chance to finish off the son of a bitch. A frightening thought had occurred to me at one point during my recovery, and I'd tamped it down. But it came back more than once.

It was what Butler had said to me when I'd told him that Beadle had escaped. His gleeful response was: *Gives me something to hunt. Hunters need prey, you know.*

That couldn't possibly be why I'd hesitated to pull the trigger, was it? What I wanted to believe was that I'd simply been savoring the moment, drinking in the satisfaction of ending a personal vendetta that had lasted for years.

But since Butler and I were alike in so many ways, was it possible I *needed* to have Beadle in my life? The thought repulsed me.

Quanta brought me back to the present. "I'll leave you and Christina alone, but there are two other things I want to share with you before I go. One involves Parnell."

My eyes narrowed and my face twisted into a snarl. Quanta had to know what a sensitive spot this was for me. I was ready to throw her out.

She held up a hand. "Hear me out. You need to know that at the time this mission started there were things about Parnell we didn't feel you needed to know. *She* didn't want you to know everything. She must've had her reasons for keeping you in the dark. I didn't ask. But I agreed."

"What are you talking about? She's dead, too, like Butler, so what difference does any of that make now?"

Quanta shook her head. "She *was* dead."

It took a moment for the words to sink in. Then, I sat forward in my chair, causing another stab of pain.

"She *uploaded*?" I asked. "But you said—"

"I said she hadn't. She had. Two days before Butler's raid on the lab."

Now I sat back, my head spinning. So much began to make sense. All the questions Parnell had asked me in our short time together. She didn't ask about uploading; her questions were about the download, reinvesting into a new body. That's what she feared the most.

When she'd looked at me on the floor of that cabin, moments before she was killed, was she trying to let me know it would be okay?

I looked at Quanta. "So she'll be reinvested?"

She nodded. "Once everything is put back in place and tested. She has chosen to continue with the program and become a full-time field agent."

"Oh my God," I whispered. I closed my eyes and took a deep breath.

"And the system *will* be tested," Quanta said. "Thoroughly. But Devya is convinced that almost all of the problems have been worked out. Any issues we may have had with the technology have been addressed."

"*Almost* all of the problems," I said. "Which, of course, is good enough for Q2."

I'd pushed and pushed. Quanta didn't have to sit there and

continue to take my insubordinate abuse. Her sympathy for my injured condition would only grant me so much of a free pass, and that pass had run out. Her face took on a scowl.

"The program is a success, Swan. It is, regardless of your low opinion of it. It's helped the nation, and the world, many times over. You are understandably concerned, and no one begrudges you that. But what I'll eventually need to know is if and when you're ready to get back to work."

I glared at her. "Those are my only two options, right? Go back into the fire, or walk away and deal with the nightmares for the rest of my life."

After a pause she said, "That's the other thing I wanted to share with you. A third option. One that eliminates the night-mares. But if that's what you choose, you'll find it has serious side effects of its own. The biggest of which is time displacement."

"I can't wait to hear this."

She took her own deep breath. "When you first joined Q2 and made your very first upload—like the one Parnell did a few weeks ago—we set aside that first upload. We consider it your baseline. That particular upload survives on its own, in a controlled location."

"What does that mean?"

"It means that every time you've downloaded into a new body, it's been from your most recent upload. But this initial baseline was held back. It contains all of your thoughts, feel-ings, and memories up until the time of the first upload, years ago. And it's available to invest in a new body."

Now I sat forward again, but felt no pain. I don't think I would've felt it if a nail had been driven through my foot.

"But that means—" I said.

"It means these last years of your life, from the moment

you joined us, would not exist. It means you'd wake up with no memory, no recall whatsoever, of anything that has happened since then. Your life could go back to the way it was, with no memories. And no nightmares."

"But . . ." I looked over her shoulder at the sliding panel in the wall.

"That's right," Quanta said. "It would mean you'd have no memory of Christina at all. These years of your life wouldn't exist."

"For her they would," I said.

"Yes. And if she chose to, she could start from scratch with you. I don't know if that's something you'd be willing to do. Or if she would."

I couldn't respond for a long time. My mind was in chaos. But then something leapt into focus.

"Wait a minute. If you kept a baseline of my mind, have you done the same thing with all of the agents?"

She only stared at me.

"Quanta," I said. "Did you store a baseline for Butler?"

She stood up. "I have to go."

Then she extended her hand toward me. "Let me know what you decide to do. If it means you leave Q2, there will be no hard feelings."

After a moment's hesitation, I reached out and shook her hand.

"I'll let you know."

WHAT'S NEXT FOR ERIC SWAN?

Will Q2's super-spy hang it up for good? Has he had enough?

Or has Quanta had enough of Eric Swan?

Here's all we know for sure: The next book in the Eric Swan thriller series is called *Field Agent*.

And it's coming soon. Turn the page to find out how you can join the Swaniverse and never miss an adventure.

JOIN THE SWANIVERSE - GET FREE STUFF!

Eric Swan is
The Spy Who Can Never Die

With each new tale you'll learn a little more about Q2's super spy, Eric Swan.

To learn of each new adventure *before* they're published, just let me know where to find you.

As a thank you for joining the Swaniverse, I'll send you a free copy of **Origin**, the Eric Swan short story detailing his very first assignment for Quanta and Q2.

It's simple: Just visit *EricSwan.com.*

Thanks, and happy reading.
   Dom Testa

REVIEWS MATTER - THEY REALLY DO.

Reviews are critical for independent authors like me.

We don't have mega-publishers in New York or London pumping millions of dollars into promoting our work.

What we have . . . is you. And you're very important to us.

One honest review from you can do so much to help an indie author. People *do* read them, and they *do* make decisions based on them.

So please, log on to your favorite online retailer and, no matter how brief it is, let other thriller fans know what you thought of Eric Swan.

It's VERY appreciated.

Dom Testa

Made in the USA
Monee, IL
24 September 2020